Where There Is
HOPE

A SEVEN VIRTUES RANCH ROMANCE BOOK 2

BECKY DOUGHTY

BraveHearts

Press

HOPE

"Where there is hope, there's life."

Ann Frank

CHAPTER ONE

SHE WAS TOO LATE. THEY HAD WAITED TOO LONG to call her, and by the time she arrived on the scene, there was little she could do except to pull the dead baby from the birth canal. The first-calf heifer was on her feet and actively pushing with the contractions, but it had been a good six hours or longer since the onset of labor, and the poor girl only shuffled her hind legs half-heartedly when Hope slid a well-lubricated arm inside her.

The first order of business was to get the calf's head through the pelvic opening. The front feet were protruding enough for Hope to get the OB chains around them, but unless she got that head dislodged, the baby wasn't going anywhere. With one last effort, she slid her arm into the birth canal all the way to her shoulder, until her cheek was practically pressed against the trembling, filthy flank of the cow. This would all be worth it if we were pulling a live calf, she silently bemoaned.

There! With a forceful downward push on the calf's nose, the head shifted and engaged. "I think that did it," she said to Doug Hayward over her shoulder. "Let's get the jack on her."

The farmer was ready with the calf puller, and while Doug set the steel yoke into place against the cow's hips, Hope notched the pull chains onto the gears. Then Doug cranked the ratchet with each contraction, while Hope continued to manipulate the calf's position until finally, it was expelled onto the hay-strewn stall floor.

She peeled off the shoulder-length glove and assessed the baby for any signs of life. She already knew it was futile. There was no pulse, no response to any stimuli, and the opaque cloud over the eyes indicated the little female had succumbed to oxygen deprivation a couple hours ago.

"Will she be all right, Dr. Hope?" Mona, Doug's wife, stood on the other side of the stall wall, a tiny baby in an infant carrier strapped to her chest. She'd stayed there throughout the ordeal, speaking low and soothing words to the distressed mama cow.

She wasn't asking about the calf, Hope knew. Doug and Mona, a young couple with a tiny homestead, two young school-age children, and the new baby, had spent their savings on Lola. She'd come to them already bred, and they'd had high hopes of getting a family milk cow, as well as a calf to sell, to recoup some of their investment. There'd been nothing left to pay for vet services, and they'd done everything they could on their own before finally conceding that they were in trouble. They'd called Hope already knowing that the best thing they could do now was to save Lola.

"She should be fine, Mona. This was tough, but it's pretty common for first-time mamas to need help. We'll treat her for any potential infections, and you'll need to monitor her for the next couple of days, but I have high hopes for her to have a full recovery." Hope stood and dragged the calf around to Lola's head, then released the cow from where she'd been tied to the stall gate so she could have some time to examine her baby.

"Will she be able to be bred again?" Doug asked as he dissembled the calf puller, careful not to watch as Lola nudged and licked the lifeless form on the ground in front of her. He was likely already trying to figure out ways to come up with the money for Hope's visit.

Hope understood their financial dilemma and didn't condemn them for it. As picturesque as Plumwood Hollow looked on the surface, there was some real need in the community. A lot of folks lived paycheck to paycheck just to keep the utilities on, and having healthy livestock providing basics, like milk and meat, was essential for survival. She could see it in the worry lines on Doug and Mona's faces, and it broke her heart to know that the couple, already in such a tight financial situation, would now have another bill to pay. Hope would do jobs like this for next to nothing, but most folks in the hollow weren't keen on that kind of charity. They understood the value of hard work, of earning what they called their own, and they had a sincere appreciation for the services Dr. Hope provided. Sometimes payment came in the form of eggs, meat, and garden produce, other times, it might be a quilt, or homemade soaps and salves. She'd even received some home-distilled moonshine—apple pie once, and another time, peach cobbler—but her clients always paid, one way or another.

"She will," Hope assured him, circling the cow to do a final examination. "Everything seems intact, and she's alert and doing what a new mama should." She glanced over at Mona. The young woman was watching the tragic scene with tears tracking slowly down her cheeks, her arms wrapped tenderly around the child in the sling. Hope had to look away lest she succumb to the emotions she worked hard to keep at bay in circumstances like these. This family's grief was for so much more than just a lost calf.

"I will be upfront with you, Doug. Sometimes, for whatever reason, cows that have had a difficult delivery will sometimes have a harder time getting pregnant again. But Lola here seems quite healthy to me; she's been well cared for." She ran a hand down the knobby ridges of the cow's back. "You'll need to give her a little time to recover, but I don't see any reason for her not to go on and produce many fine young animals for you."

"I'll talk to my foreman about taking on some extra hours at the plant." Doug faced her with his chin high, then picked up Hope's bulky medical bag from where she'd dropped it in the corner of the stall. "You'll bill me?"

Hope eyed him speculatively. He was a sturdy country boy, probably about her age, and he'd been easy to work with, quick to respond to anything she'd asked of him, and he'd paid close attention to her instructions throughout the ordeal. "I'll bill you, Doug; that's my standard protocol. But if you're looking for extra hours, I could use your help, if you're open to it."

Mona sniffed softly and wiped at her eyes as she turned her attention on them. Doug frowned, already suspicious. "What do you have in mind?"

There was no running water in the small barn, so Hope popped the lid off a gallon jug she'd brought in, and poured generous amounts of the cold water over her hands. She'd wash again more thoroughly when she had access to hot water and soap. She dried off using one of the clean towels she kept in her kit, giving herself a few more moments to make sure she was handling things right with Doug. She hadn't really thought this through, and she didn't want to make an offer she'd regret, but it did seem like providential timing.

She opted for honesty with these good folk, no matter how hard it was. "You may already know this, but, um, my husband—soon to be ex-husband—is no longer living in Plumwood Hollow." Her cheeks burned with a sudden wash of humiliation and a sense of inadequacy that seemed to catch her by surprise far too often since Chet's departure. She glanced first at Mona, then Doug. Their stoic faces showed no surprise at her revelation. Good old small town gossip.

Chet worked from home as a consultant who specialized in

creating business plans and financial statements and doing market research for small startup companies. He liked animals well enough, which was a good thing in light of the fact that Hope spent so much time with them. Because the majority of his business was conducted online, his work hours were flexible, making him available around Hope's crazy schedule so they could spend time together. It had seemed like a match made in heaven. At first, anyway.

Mona's baby, a tiny girl no more than a month old, made a sweet, cooing gurgle that melted Hope's heart. One day she might end up with a baby of her own. She was already accustomed to functioning on too little sleep and trying to care for creatures that couldn't tell her what was wrong. She'd probably be good at being a mother. She supposed having a father in the picture might be nice, too. Her oldest sister had already pulled the single mother routine, and Hope had seen firsthand how difficult it could be, even with a huge family around to help her out, and a child who was so delightful, she had to be part angel.

Start with a man who wants to stick around, then we'll go from there, she reminded herself.

"You needing someone to explain things to him?" Doug's question sounded so innocuous, it took Hope a moment to figure out what he was asking. Then her eyes widened as his meaning donned on her.

"Oh!" Yep. They'd definitely heard about Cheating Chet. Doug was a good ol' country boy, for sure, the kind who had certain ideas about how a real man should behave. "No, no. Thank you, but that's not what—I mean, no." She shot the man a sardonic grimace. "Tempting, to be sure, but that's not really the kind of help I need right now."

He nodded, but left it at that. Hope couldn't help wondering what it would be like to have a man like Doug looking out for her. A little scary, a little intense, yes, but maybe a little nice, too. As long as "explaining" things didn't involve tire irons or hunting rifles, or anything else that might wind him up in jail, she supposed, which would only leave her as alone as she was now.

She continued. "Anyway, I had started the process of recruiting a new vet right before—you know, before he left," she said, waving a hand in an impatient gesture. "We've been in need of another one—and another assistant or two, truth be told—for some time now, particularly to help during birthing season. Sometimes my dad is available to help out, but he can only do so much." Everyone in the hollow had rallied around the Goodacres several years ago when Jedediah's tractor accident nearly killed him. He'd survived, by the grace of God, but his right leg and hip were permanently damaged, and his back often caused him severe, debilitating pain, preventing him from doing many of the ranching activities he'd known all his life. Hope did her best not to let Jed do any heavy lifting, although she had to do so without embarrassing him. He knew his limitations, but he was also a proud ranching man accustomed to hard work. "But because of the divorce, I've had to put everything on hold until the air clears a little. In the meantime, I'm begging, borrowing, and bartering for any muscle power I can get."

Doug, with her medical bag and calf puller in hand, held the stall gate open for her, still not saying a word.

Mona had no such reservations. "Why do you need to wait until the divorce is final? You need help now." She came around to stand next to Doug. "Birthing season is already well underway."

Hope grimaced as she stepped out of the pen. "I know. Unfortunately, my husband—soon to be ex-husband—is trying to convince the courts that I should sell my practice and give him half the proceeds. So it's been suggested that I put the brakes on any hiring for now."

"Dr. Hope!" Mona gasped. "That's terrible. Does he have any idea how much our community depends on you? Please tell me you're not considering it."

The good thing about being forthright is that it took Mona's attention away from the sad scene still unfolding inside the stall between the cow and her stillborn calf.

"No. I am not. I am fighting this tooth and nail. And I did not tell you this to bad mouth my husband. Soon to be ex-husband."

"Why don't you just call him by his name?" Doug suggested in his hill country twang. "Seeing as how you don't really have a hankering to claim him anymore." He looked like he might have a hankering to 'explain' things to Chet whether she wanted him to or not.

"Good idea," Hope said with a nod. "Anyway, think about it. Clearly, I'm not really built to manhandle anything much bigger than a miniature goat," she said with a self-deprecating grin. That wasn't quite true; she might hit five-foot-three on a good day, and only first thing in the morning before the weight of the world compressed her spine and made her shoulders droop, but Hope knew her way around large farm animals, and they were her favorite to work with. "Sometimes dealing with trouble in the bigger horses and cattle can be a bit of a task for me when I'm on my own. During the day, if I get desperate, I can have Sarah help me, although that leaves the clinic with only Patty Lynn manning the desk and taking phone calls. I do have a part-time tech, Rodney—have you met him?—but he's only there three mornings a week." Rodney also preferred working with dogs and cats and other domesticated pets, and the few times she'd taken him on farm calls with her, she'd been as worried about him as she'd been about the patient. He was great around the clinic, but out in the field, not so much. "We simply need more help. And with Cord Overman working to get the rodeo set up on his property?" She shrugged, feeling overwhelmed just thinking about the influx of new patients to come out of that.

But because of Chet's selfish demands on something he had no share in....

Thinking of the man who had promised to love and cherish her for the rest of his life, but who seemed to love and cherish her business, instead—or the money he thought he could get out of it—always made her a little worked up.

"Anyway," she said, drawing the word out in an effort to curtail her thoughts. "I know you work full time, Doug, and you have a family." She smiled at Mona who absentmindedly stroked the top of her baby's head. "Those need to remain your priorities if you're going to help me, so I'd only call on you if it were somewhere close by, and I really needed you. Most of the time, I can handle things with the help of whatever rancher or farmer is on hand. But sometimes, I end up at a place where I'm kind of on my own, and it would be helpful to have an extra body with a little bit of muscle on the scene. It would just be after hours, like being on call." She was blabbering. She did that when she got nervous or upset, and thinking about Chet always upset her. "Maybe once or twice a week for two or three weeks—that would more than cover my bill."

Doug nodded once, then exchanged a meaningful look with his wife.

"So if the only reason you're considering taking on extra hours at the factory is so you can pay this bill, maybe instead, you'd consider helping me out now and then until I can hire some more help." She sounded like she was trying to sell him something. She should just be quiet and let him think. Chet had said that to her once or twice or a hundred times…

"I'll do it." The man held out a large, work-roughened hand to shake on the deal.

"We haven't even discussed how much your bill is or how much your time is worth." It didn't matter; Hope already knew she'd be shaking hands with the man regardless of the details. He'd clearly already made up his mind.

"I trust you'll do right by me, Dr. Hope. I'll do the same by you. I'm a good listener, you can ask my wife."

"He is," Mona said, beaming up at her husband.

Doug brushed the backs of his fingers against Mona's forearm. "And I ain't afraid of hard work, ugly situations, or a little bit of bone and gore, I can assure you."

Hope laughed. "I think you and I will do just fine." Then she turned and smiled at Mona, but when the young mother stepped close to hug her, Hope held up both hands. "You don't want to hug me. I'm pretty sure there are at least five different kinds of bovine bodily fluids on me."

Mona hugged her anyway, and from the corner of her eye, Hope saw Doug smile for the first time since she'd arrived. He watched his wife and child with something that made Hope's heart ache to see.

Had Chet ever looked at her that way?

Enough! She silently berated herself. She turned one last look on the stall behind her. The cow had lost interest in the calf and was in a different corner with her nose in a trough of fresh hay.

Stillbirths always hit her hard. They were one of the hardest aspects of her job.

Hope's day didn't get any better. Sally Fields—not that Sally Fields. However, this Sally Fields liked to point out that she and that Sally Fields did share some similar features, like brown eyes and brown hair—brought in her old Bassett Hound, Burt Reynolds. Not that Burt Reynolds, either, although some in the hollow liked to point out that this Burt Reynolds and that Burt Reynolds did share some similar features, like their brown eyes and thick coats of brown fur. Apparently, Burt Reynolds discovered Sally Fields' stash of chocolate kisses in the bottom drawer of her bedside stand. "Somehow he managed to get it open just enough to pull the bag out," Sally explained in between sobs. Unfortunately, the dog had also managed to eat the nearly full bag of the dark chocolate treats, and Sally hadn't realized the cause of his horrific symptoms until she'd gone to her room to grab a pair of shoes so she could drive the dog to see Hope.

By the time they arrived, Burt Reynolds was having seizures, and because the dog was ancient and already suffered from congenital heart disease, all Hope was able to do at that point was to make him comfortable before putting him down.

Right after lunch, she was called out to check on one of the reindeer at Klaus's Christmas Tree Farm. The animal was only about nine months old. He'd been born on the farm last summer and had charmed tree shoppers with his playful antics during the holiday season. But now, having made it through the worst of the winter months, he was flagging noticeably, and for the life of her, Hope couldn't figure out why. She took some blood and fecal samples, and gave the animal a vitamin boost, but left Peter Klaus no less concerned than when she'd arrived. The man had four reindeer, and he took care of them like they were his family, so Hope didn't think it was due to mistreatment or inadequate care. She hoped the lab work would clear things up quickly.

She got back with just enough time to treat a fat hamster with a respiratory infection, followed by a cockatiel who'd been roughed up by the family cat, before she headed out on another call to Ben Crawley's sheep farm. A ewe had been discovered in great distress after having delivered a stillborn lamb, which was sad enough on its own merit. The concern, however, wasn't the lamb, but the fact that the sheep was on the ground with a prolapsed uterus hanging outside of her body, and Ben had no clue how long she'd been down. Hope found some significant discoloring of the uterine tissue, indicating it had been a while. She'd done what she could to repair the damage, but the ewe seemed to have given up already. It was common with sheep; the animals reminded her of Eeyore from Hundred Acre Wood, in that when they ran into trouble, they simply decided they were doomed and quit trying to survive. She left Ben doing what he could to coax and encourage the animal to stay on her feet. Hope wasn't sure which of the two would give up first, but she had a feeling Ben would be the only one left to tell of it come morning.

Around four o'clock, she headed across town to assess a goat buck who had gotten his horns stuck in a section of hog wire. Seeing easy pickings for the taking, a stray dog had dug under the fence to get to it and had managed to tear a pretty big chunk of flesh from the big goat's side before the farmer intervened. "I couldn't help but think of that scene in Jurassic Park," the owner said, so matter-of-fact that Hope couldn't tell if he was trying to be funny or not. She glanced up from examining the animal as he continued. "You know the part. It's where they tied that goat to a stake for the T-Rex's lunch."

The goat would survive, but the stray dog had met its maker, according to the farmer. Hope didn't ask for details.

She returned to the clinic only minutes ahead of a man and his two young children bringing their family dog in. The yellow lab had been hit by a car, and Hope could tell just by looking at him that the animal was shutting down. Watching the kids grieve was hard enough, but when their big, strong daddy broke down and wept behind his hands, and the kids moved in to hug and comfort him, Hope had to leave the room lest she hurtle herself into the middle of the melee and fall apart, too.

By the time she closed up and started next door to her little cottage, all she wanted to do was take a shower, eat a whole pizza pie by herself, and fall into bed. She was already exhausted, and there was no telling what the night would bring. Being only one of two animal hospitals in the county, hers was always bustling with activity, but because Hope specialized in large animals and particularly stock animals, she was in high demand around the clock, especially during birthing season. As much as she didn't want to attribute anything good to her soon to be ex-husband, having Chet around had eased her load a little. On days like today, when she was worn out, he'd field her calls so she could sleep. And he'd kept her fed when she was too tired to even remember to eat. Granted, he didn't do any cooking, so the meals were typically take-out, and his efforts were motivated more by his own hunger than by hers, but food was food, and she was grateful for it. Besides, she wasn't much of a cook herself, so she wasn't about to pick on Chet for something so mundane.

No, it was the big things she wanted to pick on him about. Or rather, the one big thing named Shelby Whitaker. And truth be told, she wanted to do a whole lot more than pick on Cheating Chet. If she had her way with him, why she'd—she'd....

"You're hopeless," she muttered. "Pitiful and hopeless." Because, truth be told, she wasn't the type to rip his heart out or throw a vase at him. No, she'd probably get all weepy and ask him why.

Which would be futile, because she already knew why. Chet had quickly grown to hate her unpredictable, round-the-clock hours. He'd come to loathe the late night calls that pulled her out of their warm cocoon of a bed, leaving him alone with his arms empty of anything except her cold pillow. He hated how she smelled when she got home at the end of the day, and the way her scrubs and Crocs—not to mention the Carhartt coveralls she pulled on over top of everything for messy or cold jobs—made her look so frumpy. He hated that she was too tired to go out on the weekends with him. He hated that she could be called away at any moment, no matter how inopportune. Most of all, he hated that she would interrupt whatever it was they were doing and go.

It didn't matter that he knew what he was signing up for when he married her. It didn't matter that he was the one who'd changed, not her.

Because eventually, he came to hate her, which he believed gave him license to find someone to take her place.

CHAPTER TWO

HE WAS TOO LATE. HE HAD WAITED TOO LONG, and now she was leaving for the day. Levi sat in his SUV and watched Hope pull the door of her clinic closed after her. She'd made it halfway down the sidewalk before she turned around and went back to check it, only to find it unlocked. She looked exhausted, like she could barely hold her head up, and Levi tightened his grip on the steering wheel.

He imagined, just for a second, that he held Chet Willis' scrawny neck in his hands, and he squeezed just a little harder. The fact that the man had abandoned Hope Goodacre last summer was bad enough. That he'd left her for the bit of arm candy Levi had seen him with several months ago over in Muldoon was even worse. From what Levi could surmise, the girl plastered against Chet's side was little more than cotton candy on legs. He didn't think it was possible for anyone to be that air-headed, or that sugary sweet, not in real life. Either that, or she was as much of a chameleon as Chet Willis was, using whatever worked to get what she wanted. If so, they both deserved each other.

Hope Goodacre, on the other hand—he still had a hard time thinking of her as Hope Willis—deserved a heck of a lot better than Chet Willis. Sure, the guy was inarguably a golden boy with his slick charm, fancy suits, and ridiculous curly blond hair. But Levi had a feeling Mr. Willis was the kind of man who was accustomed to getting what he wanted, to having things his way. According to Faith, Hope's older sister, Chet's gripe about how much time Hope spent with other people's animals wasn't because he worried about her welfare, but because it meant she wasn't spending time with him.

In Levi's not so unbiased opinion, Chet Willis was still nothing but a spoiled little boy.

None of that changed the fact that Hope was clearly suffering over the man's actions and decisions. Levi hoped it had more to do with the embarrassment and inconvenience he'd caused her, rather than a broken heart. On the other hand, he understood how devastating it could be to have someone you love not love you enough to stay.

He would never forget the day he came home from work to find his wife of four years, Veronica, sitting on the top step of the front porch, her packed suitcase waiting beside her. Their baby girl, Yvette, not quite six months old, was asleep in her crib in their bedroom. Ironically, Veronica hadn't slept in their bedroom since before the baby was born, but Levi had believed her when she said it was due to her hormones being completely out of whack, that she just needed time. The midwife assured them that the postpartum blues Veronica was experiencing were common, and encouraged her to get help if she felt like she couldn't handle it. Levi paid close attention to how his wife behaved with Yvette, and although she remained distant and reserved toward him, he was confident that she was a good mother to their daughter. Yvette was remarkably sweet and content, and when Veronica put their tiny infant to her breast, there was nothing more beautiful to Levi than his two girls connecting so intimately and naturally.

As he approached the porch that day, he could tell Veronica had been crying for some time. Her nose was pink, and her pretty brown eyes were puffy and red-rimmed, although she'd taken extra care with her makeup to camouflage it. But the look on her face told him everything he needed to know. She was leaving, and there would be no talking her out of it.

"I need you to take me to the airport, please. I just fed the baby, so she will probably sleep the whole way there." Veronica's accent was always noticeably richer when she was emotionally charged, but that day, her words came out flat and dry. "I'll feed her again when we get there so you won't have to worry about her being hungry on the way home."

Levi had felt a strange combination of relief and horror as what she was saying sunk in. She wasn't just leaving him, she was leaving their child, too. "How long do you plan to stay away?" he asked, trying to keep his own voice steady and calm.

"I won't be back, Levi." She'd stood, picked up her bag, and moved down the porch steps, heading for the truck. When he reached for her suitcase, she jerked away as though she thought he might try to force her to stay. Her reaction hurt almost as bad as her words.

"Let me at least carry your bag for you," he'd said in as soothing a tone as he could muster. He didn't want Veronica to see how gutted he felt in that moment. She needed him to be strong, even though she was the one tearing his insides out. It had always been that way.

Her eyes filled with tears again, but they didn't spill over. "I'll wait in the car while you get the baby," she'd said.

"Her name is Yvette, remember?" He hated hearing her refer to their daughter as a nameless infant, but when she climbed into the passenger side of the vehicle without saying another word, Levi had suddenly recognized what she was doing; Veronica was distancing herself from Yvette just as she'd done with him over the last six months or more.

It had been the longest, yet shortest drive he'd ever had to endure.

Just like Veronica had predicted, Yvette slept peacefully the whole way there.

Levi, on the other hand, wept silently as he drove, unable to staunch the tears that ran in slow rivulets from the corners of his eyes.

Veronica sat stiff and still in the passenger seat, her focus trained on the road ahead of them.

He'd finally worked up the courage to ask her where she was going, and she hadn't hesitated to tell him. She was heading to Florida where she had a job and a place to stay already waiting for her. One of her best friends from high school—a girl who'd been a bridesmaid in their wedding—lived in Tampa, and Veronica would sleep on her couch until she could get a place of her own.

When they arrived at the airport, she asked Levi to hand her the baby, and she nursed Yvette without even looking at her. Unable to stay and witness the irreparably broken scene, Levi had taken a walk to try to process through some of the immense grief that threatened to consume him. Somehow, he'd failed his beautiful wife, and in so doing, he'd failed their precious baby girl. For the life of him, he couldn't figure out what he'd done to make Veronica prefer leaving to staying.

He returned to the truck to find her standing beside the open passenger door, her suitcase by her side, its handle extended. She'd already buckled Yvette back into her car seat, and the tiny girl waved a chubby hand in front of her, fascinated by the sounds of the wrist rattle she wore.

"I will text you when I arrive to let you know that I'm safe," Veronica had said without preamble. Then she'd lifted her eyes to meet his, the only time she'd looked directly at him since he'd gotten off work, and said, "I will be changing my phone service when I get there. I will send the baby a birthday card each year so you will have my address, and you will know how to reach me in case—in case of emergency only. Please do not come after me. Please do not try to convince me to come back. If Yvette wants to look me up when she is an adult, she can." Then she'd handed him a large white envelope. "These are our divorce papers. You'll see when you go over them that I've asked for nothing from you but the things I have with me today. Please sign where I've marked them and put them in the mail as soon as possible. There is already a postage paid envelope in there."

She'd turned on her heels and walked away without even saying goodbye.

The sound of suitcase wheels on asphalt still made him queasy, even after all these years.

Veronica hadn't left him high and dry. In the freezer back home, he'd discovered several weeks' supply of meals for him, and a bin of disposable bottle inserts filled with pumped breast milk for Yvette, enough to last a couple months or longer. Each one was dated according to when she'd expressed it and the date it had to be used by, and it broke his heart all over again to see that some of them went back almost four months. On the counter beside the cordless phone was a list of sitters, emergency numbers, all of Yvette's medical information, and a printed out instructional on weaning an infant. The document suggested waiting until the baby was at least six months old to begin. The refrigerator was stocked with fresh groceries, and a whole shelf in the pantry held jars and jars of baby food for several different stages of development. The house was spotless, and every piece of clothing he and Yvette owned were freshly laundered and put away. Veronica's side of the closet and the drawers she used in the dresser they shared were empty.

It was more than evident that his wife had thought through her decision thoroughly.

How had he not known?

Levi had sold his truck two weeks later, and replaced it with a gently-used Dodge Durango. Not only did the silver SUV rank well for being safe and family-friendly, but it came with four wheel drive and a decent amount of horsepower, which helped Levi salvage at least a tiny shred of his manhood. An added bonus was that the Durango didn't hold any memories of Veronica.

A month after his wife moved out, his mother moved in. Naomi "Nona" Valiente took over caring for the house and Yvette while Levi worked, and life had settled into a new normal for all of them.

When Yvette was one, Nona began pushing Levi to start dating again. He'd resisted at first, but somehow, word got around that he was open to the idea, and when he didn't ask anyone out, the invitations came to him. He had a good business in their small community, he was young and healthy, broad-shouldered and strong—he had to be in his line of work—and he had a tiny daughter he was head over heels in love with, which only made him that much more endearing of a catch. According to the women he dated, he was tall, dark, and handsome with his *cafe con leche* skin and black hair, and it all came together to make him one of Plumwood Hollow's most eligible bachelors.

For about a year, he'd gone a little crazy over the female attention—Levi hadn't realized how much he'd missed it until he started accepting it again. He went out almost every weekend, sometimes with a date, and other times by himself, knowing he wouldn't stay that way long. He built quite a reputation for himself as a guy out for a good time, and he never had any trouble finding someone who wanted to have a good time with him.

But Levi wasn't a player by nature, and he soon realized that he preferred his simple routine to the complexities of dating games. He liked coming home in the evenings to a hot meal and the two ladies he loved most in all the world. It was his favorite time of day to spend with his horse, too, that magic hour between light and dark, when the fire of sunset burned down to charcoal, leaving behind stars like embers glowing against the dark of night. He'd much rather stay in and munch on Nona's homemade churros while watching silly movies with his daughter on the weekends, instead of dressing up fancy and trying to act like he was having the time of his life at the bars and clubs. No, having tasted it, he knew without a doubt that he just wasn't cut out for that lifestyle.

Oh, he'd made some good friends along the way; Faith Goodacre—now Faith Overman—for one. It was Jed Goodacre, a regular customer of Levi's, in fact, who suggested he ask his eldest daughter out, seeing as they had so much in common. She was several years younger than Levi, and not long out of high school, but they were both raising little girls as single parents, and according to Jed, Faith would one day take over Seven Virtues Ranch. "She has a good business head on her shoulders. You two could benefit from getting to know each other, even if you don't fall in love," the rancher had said, a wry smile on his face. Levi had appreciated the man's candor, and because he knew and trusted Jed, he asked Faith out the following weekend. She accepted, but to his surprise, she invited him, Nona, and Yvette to join her whole family—except for Hope, who was away at her first year of college—for their family night. They had dinner around the massive kitchen table, followed by popcorn and brownies in the living room while they watched a couple episodes of Planet Earth. It had been an evening filled with laughter and camaraderie, and he'd enjoyed himself so much, he'd asked her out again.

The second date, he'd taken Faith out to dinner where they'd shared a little about their pasts, about the struggles and triumphs of single parenthood, and about their love for their work. Faith was in the process of incorporating new and still somewhat controversial grazing methods on her daddy's ranch, and although Jed was resistant to the changes, she was excited about the success of her projects so far. She listened attentively as he talked about how he got into butchering, and some of the plans he had for the future. He'd been actively looking for ways to reduce waste from his business while increasing the quality of his meat, and they spent a good deal of time brainstorming about how they could help each other in that capacity. In so many ways, they'd seemed perfect for each other.

By the end of the night, however, after a rather awkward attempt at a goodnight kiss, they'd laughingly agreed that they'd be better off as friends, a decision that laid the groundwork for their daughters to become best of friends as well.

Yvette was ten years old now, Levi was still a single parent, and his favorite place to pull up a stool—other than his own little spread—was at the counter of his butcher shop, keeping his customers happy by providing them with the best meat he could get his hands on. Not only was it comfortable in its familiarity, but the plate glass window happened to look out on the street that took folks to and from Plumwood Hollow's Animal Hospital...including the good doctor, herself. He got a pleasant jolt every time he noticed her Jeep pass by, and with her idiot husband out of the picture, he allowed himself the freedom to entertain thoughts of the woman.

All he had to do now was figure out a way to get Dr. Hope to notice him.

Levi remembered the first time he'd felt that jolt. Hope was home for the summer after her second year in her doctorate program at Purdue, and Faith had invited Levi, Yvette, and Nona over for dinner after church. He'd noticed Hope tucked between Jed and Jasmine in the church pew with the rest of the family, but when he'd first arrived at the ranch house, she'd been in her room making a phone call. It wasn't until she slipped into the seat across from him at the table, and their eyes met, that he'd suddenly lost his ability to form a coherent thought. He was pretty sure he'd heard choirs of angels singing in the background, maybe even a Mariachi band or two.

She drew him in like never before, and yet, he couldn't put a finger on anything that had really changed about her. She still wore her long hair pulled back in its usual ponytail, she still wore jeans that were more comfortable than fashionable, and she still spoke in that soothing, modulated voice of hers. Oh, he'd always appreciated her down-to-earth personality, her kind, and gentle spirit, and she was really quite lovely with those marine gray eyes and full lips that should have been kissed often and well, in his opinion. But because of his relationship—platonic, though it was—with Faith, he'd maintained a respectful reserve with all the Goodacre women over the years, and on the rare occasion that Hope was home between semesters and Levi happened to be at Seven Virtues, he treated her as he might a younger sister.

Until that summer. Suddenly, he wasn't sitting across from a kid sister anymore, but from a woman, and one he was undeniably attracted to.

In retrospect, it was he who had changed, not her. He'd become comfortable with who he was and where he was in life, and although there were things he still wanted, including a wife to love and a mother for Yvette, he no longer minded waiting for the right woman to come along.

Those two months flew by for him in a blur of roller coaster emotions. He warred with the fact that Hope still had a couple years of school left; was it fair to initiate a relationship in which they would be separated more often than not? He didn't want to distract her from her studies—she was taking an extra load so she could graduate early—and he knew long-distance affairs rarely worked out in the end. He didn't want to jeopardize anything by jumping the gun. Could he hold out? Would she? What if she met someone and chose to stay away? Impossible. Hope had too many ties in Plumwood Hollow. Not only was it her family home, but she'd worked at the animal hospital all through high school, and Doc Harper had hand-picked her as his successor at the hospital.

No, Hope would finish her degree, come home to the hollow, and take over the practice, just as planned. Two more years. Only two.

Levi could wait another two years.

He would remain reserved when she was in town between semesters and over the holidays. He would treat her no differently than he treated Faith. And he would hold his heart under lock and key until she was free to love him back.

Two years later, Hope graduated and returned to the hollow, and dove headlong into taking over from Doc Harper as he geared up to retire. She'd been home about a week when she came into the butcher shop with Jed and Faith, and for a moment, Levi had been struck speechless all over again. How he'd missed her, longed for her, and anticipated her return with every fiber of his being, and the knowledge that nothing left stood in their way—not time, or distance, or anyone else—had him almost desperate with the need to tell her how he felt. Yet there she stood before him, and he could think of nothing to say. He'd had to pry his eyes off her, and it took all his willpower to focus on the order Faith had brought in. He'd only dared glance at Hope a few times during the visit, lest he lose all capacity to think, and when the trio took their leave, he'd still said nothing, only waved like a mute schoolboy.

That day when Hope walked into his shop, Levi was pretty sure his wait was over.

Except that it wasn't.

For a while, Hope all but ignored him after that visit, often to the point that it seemed she avoided him. Sure, she was busy. Sure, she was taking over a business and making it her own. She was donning the full mantle of independent adulthood, including moving out of the ranch house at Seven Virtues and into her own place; the hospital came with the tiny cottage next door to the property. Doc Harper had used it mainly as storage, but also as a place to sleep on the nights he needed to stay on site to monitor a patient. By that fall, Hope had cleared his things out and moved her things in.

So Levi thought perhaps it was too soon to make a move after all; maybe she needed to focus on getting established as the new resident chief before she could indulge in anything personal. He understood that. He knew how hard it was to launch a business amidst the distractions of life. So he gave her space. Just a little longer, he told himself. Then she'll be ready.

But the following spring, Chet Willis showed up. Apparently, Hope had dated him during her last few months at Purdue, and when the guy realized she meant what she'd said, that she wasn't going to change her mind and stay in Indiana after graduating, he'd moved to Plumwood Hollow to be near her. Within a few months, they were married by a pastor friend of Chet's in front of a small gathering of family at a hotel in Bowling Green. Of course, Levi hadn't been invited to that, but he'd known about it because Jed had stopped by, and the rancher had alluded to his concern for his second daughter's happiness.

"He's not one of us, Levi," Jed had said with a shake of his head. "I shouldn't be voicing this to anyone, not this late in the game, but I can't quite wrap my head around what I'm feeling. I suppose it could be simply that I'm her father and no man is good enough for any of my girls." He'd complimented Levi on an especially fine pork tenderloin roast in the glass cooler, then added, "But Hope seems to care for the fellow, so I'm praying the good Lord changes my heart toward him."

Even if he had been invited, Levi would have come up with an excuse to get out of attending the event anyway. There was no way on earth he would subject himself to the misery of watching Hope celebrate her union with another man.

Besides, Levi wasn't nearly as righteous as Jedediah Goodacre. His own prayers had leaned more toward the good Lord changing Hope's heart toward—or rather, away from—Chet Willis.

Once married, Hope had softened toward Levi. They often ran into each other in the course of their days. They were both on a few town committees, they had similar political leanings, and because they both worked with animals—although she dealt with the living and he dealt with the dead—they'd grown to respect and admire each other, and had become friends.

That said, in the last couple of years, Levi's prayers hadn't changed a whole lot, and although he felt guilty as sin for it now, he couldn't help being more than a little pleased that the Goodacre-Willis marriage was unraveling. He hated seeing Hope hurt, but all along, he'd agreed wholeheartedly with her daddy. Chet Willis wasn't half the man he claimed to be and didn't even register on the scale for being good enough for a woman like Hope Goodacre.

Levi wanted to believe that he, on the other hand, might be exactly the kind of man a woman like Hope Goodacre needed.

He'd take it slow; he knew it took time to recover and heal from the pain of a broken marriage. But he wasn't going to stand by while she went through it alone. Levi understood the road she was on, perhaps better than most, and he wanted her to know that she could lean on him when she didn't think she could hold herself upright anymore.

Sure, he admitted he had ulterior motives. When Hope finally lifted her head and looked around again, he wanted to be the first person she saw, and it was his hope—pun intended—that she would want him to continue being the first—and last—face she saw every day for the rest of her life. Hope Goodacre was the right woman for him, he had no doubt about it, and when she finally figured that out, he'd make sure she knew that he was the right man for her.

That had been the motivation behind his plan for this afternoon's visit. Yesterday after school, Yvette had found a kitten behind the butcher shop, and although Levi wasn't a cat person, he could understand why she'd gone a little goo-goo-eyed over the cute little fur ball curled up in the box in his front seat. He'd promised Yvette she could take the cat home after Dr. Hope gave it a clean bill of health. He'd intended to catch Hope at the end of her day once the last of her other patients had gone home. Then during the exam, Levi would invite her over to share in their Friday evening family festivities, just as Faith had once done for him. He thought Hope could use a little rest and relaxation, a little time away from her own house and the memories that surely haunted every room. In his home, she'd find a safe place where she didn't have to put on airs or pretend like she was okay when it was clear that she wasn't.

He should have come a little earlier. She was finished for the day, and by the looks of it, entirely done in. He wasn't about to burden her with a request to check the kitten now.

He could wait another day.

He was good at waiting, yes, indeed.

CHAPTER THREE

THE HAIR ON THE BACK OF HOPE'S NECK ROSE, and she straightened her shoulders before turning around. The first time she'd come out of the clinic, she hadn't paid attention to anything except the ground beneath her next step. But it suddenly registered that there was a vehicle still in the patient parking lot, and from her peripheral vision, she could see someone sitting in the driver's seat.

"Oh geez!" Hope lifted a hand to her chest to quiet her pounding heart. It was Levi Valiente, Plumwood Hollow's favorite cowboy butcher. She waved at him, double-checked the clinic door to make sure it was locked this time, then started down the steps. Levi was already out of his SUV and across the parking lot before she hit the asphalt.

"You scared me!" she said as he approached. "I thought you were some creepy stalker guy." Wow. There were worse things than being stalked by someone as gorgeous as Levi Valiente.

"Hey there, Hope." He removed his hat and held it to his chest. "I'm so sorry. I should have thought that through a little better." Levi had one of those voices that made you think of sunsets and cold drinks, the kind with skewered fruit and tiny paper umbrellas. The rhythm of his words was like waves on the sand, the ebb and flow of them making her want to close her eyes and sway a little.

Or close her eyes and fall asleep on her feet. Dang, she knew she was tired, but getting all swoony like that over Levi? Over any guy right now? No. "What can you do for me?" she asked.

Levi's brows lifted, then he slowly returned his hat to his head, keeping it tipped forward just enough to hide his eyes from her.

Hope felt the heat shoot from her belly all the way to the top of her head. She was certain her cheeks were the color of hothouse roses. Then she snorted, unable to bite back the slightly hysterical response. She covered her face with her hands and shook her head. "Go ahead and laugh at me. I'm too tired to care."

Levi did chuckle, and Hope's stomach muscles tightened in response. What a lovely, lovely, lovely sound. She didn't dare look at him; God forbid he should read her thoughts.

"Let me try that again," she murmured, crossing her arms, keeping her gaze fixed just past his left shoulder. "What can I do for you?"

Levi slid a step to the left, putting himself in her line of vision. "I'm not laughing at what you said, Hope. I was merely appreciating your intuition, because I'm here for that very reason, for what I can do for you. Would you like to have dinner with us tonight? Nona is making her famous fish tacos, and Yvette has your niece over to spend the night. Other than the antics of a couple of silly girls, it is sorting out to be a pretty low-key evening at the Valiente home. We'd love to have you join us if you're up for a night of good food, decent company, rest, and relaxation." He smiled, making the ends of his thick mustache curve upward. It was rather remarkable the way that subtle motion changed his whole expression. "Unless, of course, you have some wild Friday night plans already in the works."

Hope realized she was staring at his mouth and quickly looked away. Had he noticed? "I don't know what kind of company I'd be tonight, Levi," she said with a shake of her head. "It's been a brutal week and an even tougher day. I think I'm probably better off going home to indulge in some emotional eating and binge-watching Justified." She drew the lapels of her jacket together and crossed her arms in a self-conscious move that she knew looked defensive. But truth be told, it bothered her how much she longed to say yes to Levi's invitation. Not five minutes ago, she'd wanted nothing more than to crawl into her big comfortable bed and relish in the fact that she had the whole house to herself. Now, however, sharing a meal at the Valiente home seemed exactly what she needed to restore her spirits.

Apparently, Levi could tell she was waffling. He took a step closer and dipped his head so he could look her in the eye. "Nona just called and said the tacos will be ready in less than an hour. You look hungry, Hope. Let me feed you." In a soothing tone that came out almost as a caress, he added, "You look tired, too. Come home with me, and you can put your feet up on my coffee table. Let me serve you; you won't have to lift a finger."

For a moment, Hope wasn't quite sure how to respond. He'd essentially told her she looked awful, but in the next breath, he said he wanted to take care of her, to serve her. If it weren't for the tone of voice he used, she would've believed Levi felt sorry for her, but that smile, the way his eyes held hers? Hope thought that maybe, just maybe he was feeling something else altogether for her.

Or was she just reading into things? These days, she didn't trust her judgment. As far as she knew, she was the only one who'd been surprised by Chet's abandonment.

Besides, she'd always had such mixed emotions about Levi, primarily because he was Faith's friend, and Hope had once believed the two of them were on their way to becoming an item. Over the years, she'd thought she'd sensed a spark between Levi and herself—she'd felt it like a jolt of electricity when their eyes met, or when they sat beside each other and their knees bumped. She'd catch him staring at her with a look on his face that she'd only seen in movies, and every time she did, her fingertips tingled, and her pulse raced. So when she returned from school for good, she'd been excited to see him, especially since Faith had made it clear that she and Levi were only friends. So she'd tagged along with Faith and Daddy when they'd stopped by Levi's shop.

To her utter disappointment, Levi had hardly noticed her. But she certainly noticed him, and the way he looked at Faith. There was no denying that his expression said he was head over heels about her big sister. Faith may have insisted they were just friends, but it was obvious Levi wanted so much more, and if anyone deserved a man like him, it was Faith. So Hope made every effort to stay out of the way of things, at least during the day.

At night, however, she was plagued with dreams about the mustached man with his coffee eyes and mocha skin, the tan cowboy hat he wore tipped forward just the tiniest bit, the muscles in his arms bulging with every move he made. And in her dreams, he made some moves that woke her up in such a state that she was almost afraid to go back to sleep.

So when Chet showed up at her front door just after the new year, claiming that if he had to move to Plumwood Hollow to be with her, then so be it? Well, she leaped at the distraction he offered. Within a few weeks, Chet was talking about marriage, and because she had so enthusiastically welcomed him into her life, Hope didn't have the heart to ask him to suddenly slow down. Three months after he moved to the hollow, Chet publicly proposed to her on the stage of the Smokehouse Grill, and amidst the catcalls and shouts of congratulations, especially when he announced that if she said yes, the next round would be on him, she let him slide his ring on her finger.

The thing was, Hope did love Chet. Or at least she had fallen in love with him, which was a good place to start, wasn't it? She knew marriages were built on commitment as much, if not even more, than on love alone. When she said yes to him, she had reservations, but not because she wasn't sure if she could commit to him. No, it was because she wasn't sure if he was ready to commit to her. Hope was a small town girl, and all she'd ever wanted was to work with animals, large and small, right here in the place she'd grown up. Chet had never fully understood that, and although he seemed so supportive of her—he'd uprooted and moved from West Lafayette to tiny Plumwood Hollow to be with her, after all—she couldn't help wondering if he would eventually get tired of the country life. Of her.

She should have trusted her instincts.

"What do you say?" Levi asked, breaking her out of her reverie. "You push yourself too hard, Hope. I think you need a dose of Nona's home cooking and an evening spent with a couple giggling girls. I assure you, it does a body good."

Why was he trying so hard to convince her? Did she really look so awful?

Who was she kidding? Of course, she did. And the longer she thought about it, the more appealing his offer sounded. "You know what? Nona's tacos sound great. Thank you." She looked up at him and attempted a smile. It was probably more of a grimace, but when he grinned back and nodded, she was suddenly infinitely glad she'd acquiesced. "But I do need to shower and change first, so you go on ahead, and I'll come as soon as I'm ready. I promise I won't be long."

She started to turn away, but he put a hand on her arm. "I'll drive," he said. "I don't want you falling asleep at the wheel, especially at the end of the night."

Hope shook her head. "I'll be fine, I promise. A shower will do me wonders in more ways than one. I'll make myself a cup of coffee, too."

But Levi was having none of it. "How about this? I will go get us some coffee while you get ready. Then I'll come back to pick you up, and you can drink it in the car on the way."

Hope wavered for a moment, wondering if she should invite him in now and make coffee for both of them, but she wasn't sure how she'd feel knowing he was hanging out in her house while she was in the shower. She did, however, like the idea of being whisked away for a quiet evening of family and friendship, then delivered back to her door at the end of the night. Especially with Levi Valiente as her escort. It sounded like the ultimate getaway after the week she'd had.

"You can take as much time as you need," Levi assured her. "I'll wait for you."

"All right." She gave him her coffee order, then told him, "If I'm not ready to go when you get back, just come on in and make yourself comfortable. I'll leave the back door unlocked for you."

Twenty minutes later, she stepped out of her bedroom and into the little hallway that led toward the living room. She could hear Levi talking softly, presumably to his daughter on the phone. His tone was sweet and cajoling, the way a parent would speak to a child. Hope made her way into the living room quietly, not wanting to disrupt his call, only to find him sitting on the floor with a cardboard box beside him. Propped high against his chest was a tiny little kitten, and although it playfully batted at one of Levi's fingers, Hope could tell the baby animal was content right where it was.

"What have you got there?" she asked, liking the sweet vignette a little too much for her own good.

Levi looked up with a tender smile that sent a rush of warmth through her. "I hope you don't mind me bringing her in. I wasn't sure how long you would be, and I didn't want to leave her in the car." In spite of his tiny burden, Levi pushed to his feet in one fluid motion, his presence filling the room in a way that made her step back. He shot her a questioning look, but all he said was, "You look nice. Feel any better?"

Hope nodded, her cheeks warming with embarrassment. Levi was a big guy, there were no two ways about it. He wasn't barrel-chested like the stereotypical butchers in movies, but he was easily over six feet tall, with ridiculously broad shoulders and a slim waist. His sleeves were rolled up to reveal thick muscular forearms, and he held the little fur ball in the palm of one large hand before returning it to the box. Compared to Hope's petite frame, Levi Valiente seemed Herculean, especially in the confines of her diminutive cottage. She momentarily wondered at the wisdom of inviting him into her home, but then mentally berated herself for even having the thought. Faith trusted the man with her precious daughter; there was no reason for anyone or anything to be afraid of him, ever.

Unless, of course, you were an animal scheduled for slaughter. But even then, Hope knew Levi went about his business professionally, humanely, and frighteningly efficient. The man could butcher a whole cow in less than thirty minutes; she'd seen him in action on more than one occasion, and his skill with his knives was an art form.

"What's the story on the kitty?" she asked, steering her attention away from Levi. She bent over the box and touched the tiny pink nose. It was cool to the touch, and the kitten blinked up at her with bright hazel eyes.

"Yvette found her behind the shop yesterday." He shot her an apologetic look. "I agreed she could have it if you gave it a clean bill of health."

Hope chuckled. "Ah, so you're bribing me with dinner so I'll take a look at your new pet." She knelt down in front of the box and ran her hands over the kitten's body, palpating the spine from skull to tail, manipulating the joints of each limb, then pressing her fingertips into the plump abdomen.

"If it works, then, yes." Levi crouched down beside her, and she caught a whiff of him. A working man's fragrance, she thought. Clean, pleasant, like mild soap, with a hint of the bleach solution he used to hose down his workspaces. He leaned over the box, too, his head close to hers, and she couldn't help it. She breathed in a subtle sniff. Oh. Oh, yes. Aftershave, or his pomade, or maybe just Levi, but something about the way he smelled was a bit intoxicating.

She picked up the kitten and sat back on her haunches just to clear her head. "There's a little flashlight in the coffee table drawer. Can you grab it for me?" Could he hear the breathlessness in her voice?

A few minutes later, she returned the animal to the box and stood. "From what I can tell, she looks really healthy. She's already about a month old, so she's fine to be weaned. No sign of a mama or siblings?"

Levi shook his head and picked up the box. "I've been watching out for any signs of one all day, but so far, no."

"I think you've got yourself a new pet, then, Mr. Valiente. But bring her into the clinic next week sometime, and we can do some blood work and talk about options for vaccinations and spaying."

CHAPTER FOUR

LEVI WAITED UNTIL HOPE WAS SETTLED in the passenger side with her seatbelt on before handing her a still piping hot coffee. Then he gently closed the door.

Hope Goodacre, the woman of his dreams, was in his car. He circled to the driver's side and climbed in, took a quick look at the kitten in the box on the fold-up console seat between them, then started up the engine. "You ready?" he asked.

"I'm ready." She held up the coffee cup. "Thank you for this. It's perfect. Just the way I like it."

He'd have to remember that. Strong coffee with half-and-half and a sprinkle of cinnamon and nutmeg stirred in, no sugar.

The drive wasn't long, and they rode a good while in silence. Levi didn't mind the quiet, and from what he could tell, Hope seemed to relax a little more with each passing minute. Finally, as he turned the vehicle off the main road, a few blocks from his street, Hope said, "Have you been out to Seven Virtues recently?"

Levi nodded. "I'm out there often, but not in the capacity of a butcher. It's the girls; Jasmine and Yvette would spend every waking moment together if we let them. Between Jed, Faith, and now Cord, and me, we're constantly carting the girls from one place to another, including Whispering Hills, now, too."

Hope smiled. "What do you think of Cord?" Something in her voice had Levi glancing over at her. She sounded reserved, perhaps even wary, which seemed strange coming from Hope. But the look on her face told him she was concerned. Presumably for her sister. Having a marriage end the way her own did would put anyone on alert, he supposed. He smiled, hoping to set her mind at ease.

"I like the man. I'm glad he's back, for Faith and Jasmine's sake, for sure, but also because of what he's doing at his ranch. Already so many changes for the better; that place needed new blood, and a little bit of money pumped into it." He really did like Cordell Overman, especially because he made Faith so happy. Jasmine had taken a little longer to warm up to the man who was also her father, but because she hadn't even known of his existence until last May, she'd had to make some major adjustments. "He's good to your sister," he added. "I've seen the way he looks at her, the way he treats her. And as a father, myself, believe me, I've also watched him with Jasmine, I'm not ashamed to say. He's got it bad for both his girls. He's the real deal, don't you worry." Which is more than Levi could ever say about Hope's idiot husband.

"That's what I think, too," Hope said, a note of relief in her voice. She shifted in her seat and tucked one leg up underneath her. "I'm just not the most trustworthy when it comes to reading people, you know? Give me a horse or a dog? I can see into their souls. But men?" She chuckled dryly and took another sip of coffee.

"Hey," Levi began. "Be nice to yourself."

"Everyone can see it with them, how much in love they are," Hope said, ignoring his admonishment. "He can't stop touching her, you know? If he isn't holding her hand, he's got his arm around her waist, or he's touching her hair or her face. It feels so intimate to witness, even though he's not doing anything inappropriate. Just makes you feel like you should look away to give them their privacy." Then she added in a near whisper, "Makes you wonder what the rest of us are missing out on."

A thousand thoughts raced through Levi's head. He wanted to hurt Chet. Badly. He wanted to comfort Hope. Badly. He wanted to be the one to show Hope precisely what she'd been missing. Instead, he reached inside the box between them and ran a gentle hand down the kitten's back, wishing he could do the same to the woman in his passenger seat. The little fur ball arched into his palm and started purring.

Levi glanced over at Hope to find her watching him. She smiled sweetly, but then turned away to look out her window.

She was so tiny, sitting there in the large passenger seat of the SUV, practically curled up in a ball like the kitten, both hands wrapped tightly around the coffee cup she held. He imagined scooping her up and cradling her against his chest the way he'd held the kitten earlier. Would Hope purr, too? Arch her back into his touch? The thought made his blood run hot, and he reached up to adjust his hat in a self-conscious gesture.

"I think Jasmine is about as much in love with him as her mama is," Hope began again. "They're practically attached at the hips these days. All three of them."

"Except when Jasmine is over at our place with my daughter," Levi said with a chuckle.

"Exactly. And I'm sure Faith looks forward to those precious moments alone with her man." She glanced over at him, a pretty blush coloring her cheeks. "So on behalf of my sister, thank you."

"That's me," Levi said, tipping his hat at her. "Champion of True Love."

Hope lifted her cup to toast him. "Here's to you. Levi Valiente, Cowboy Butcher of Plumwood Hollow. Champion of True Love,

Father of the Year, Defender of Lost Baby Animals, and Rescuer of Hungry, Weary Vets. You're pretty much a saint in my book."

Levi laughed out loud. "I'm no saint, Hope Goodacre." Her name hung suspended in the air between them.

"It's still Willis," Hope finally said in a subdued voice.

Levi felt like a heel. He needed to check himself; this was not a date, and Hope was not a free woman. He needed to remember that. "Sorry. I've always thought of you as just one of the Goodacre girls." Well, that didn't come out the way he wanted it to, either. He certainly did not think of her as 'just one of' anything, other than the woman of his dreams. "I mean, it's hard for me to think of you as married." He grimaced. He was just making it worse.

The look Hope sent his way wasn't very encouraging.

So what did he do? For good measure, he added, "At least not to him."

"Really?" The word had a jagged edge to it.

He couldn't tell if she was mocking him or if she was offended, but even to his own ears, he sounded like a little kid. Which was ironic, as that's exactly what he thought of Chet Willis.

She straightened her shoulders and narrowed her eyes at him. "So does that mean you see me married, but to someone else? Who on earth do you have in mind, might I ask?"

Me! Marry me! "I'm sorry, Hope. That was out of line." He brought his hand up to scratch his jaw. "As you can see, I'm definitely not a saint."

"It's all right." She reached inside the box and stroked the kitten, too. With her head bowed, she said, "I can hardly see myself married to him, either, truth be told. And yet I was, wasn't I? But you know, it actually sounds kinda nice to hear you say my name like that. I'm going back to it anyway, as soon as the divorce is final." They idled a few moments at a stop sign, and she did look at him then. Her eyes were shadowed with misery and resignation. "I wanted it to work, my marriage. I really did. I was willing to do whatever it took to make it work."

"Hope," Levi began. "You don't have to —"

She raised a hand to stop him. "Actually, I feel like I do. I think if I don't talk about this to someone right now, I'll implode on myself. I probably should have stayed home and let this pass, but you wouldn't let me, so now you're stuck with my need to unload." Her voice had risen with the intensity of her emotions, but it faded a little now. "But I need to trust that you won't criticize me for being a bad judge of character and for making stupid mistakes in my life and for not knowing what I want or need. And I really don't want what I have to say to change things between us, because—well, I feel like I kind of need a friend like you right now, and I don't want what I'm saying to scare you away." She closed her eyes and brought her hand up to pinch the bridge of her nose. "I'm sorry, Levi, I'm rambling. I'm so tired, maybe I need to just close my mouth."

Levi reached over the box and laid a gentle hand on Hope's shoulder. "You can trust me. I'm the last person to judge anyone, and I don't scare easy. I promise." He wasn't sure he wanted to hear what she had to say, especially if she wanted a shoulder to cry on so she could unload about the husband, but if that's what she needed right now, then that's what he would be.

She lowered her hands and nodded, then he pulled into the intersection, but not before he saw the glisten of tears in her eyes. "I kinda had a thing for another guy," she began.

What? That was the last thing he'd expected to hear from her. Levi gripped the steering wheel a little tighter, but said nothing. When? Before the marriage? During the marriage? Did Chet have a valid reason for leaving her, after all?

It wasn't possible; Hope wasn't that kind of person. Levi would bet his life on that.

As though she'd read his thoughts, she said, "It was before I was married. There was this guy..." She took a deep breath and started again. "Well, when I first met him, I was really young, not yet out of high school, and I thought maybe my attraction to him was just a juvenile crush, you know? He was a little older than I was, and from my teenager perspective, very much a man." She was leaning over the box again, petting the kitten with single-minded focus. "Besides, I was sure he had a thing for my—for someone else."

She paused for a few moments, and Levi glanced over at her. They had just turned onto his street, but he was pretty sure she had more she needed to say. Without asking, he continued past his driveway to take another turn around the block. Hope didn't even notice.

"I went away to school thinking I'd get over him. Grow up, move on, as I was sure he would, too." She set her now empty cup in the cup holder on her door, scooped the kitten out of the box, and held it up to her cheek, nuzzling it gently before tucking it into the crook of her neck. "But I didn't. Not really. I tried. When I met Chet up north, he did kind of sweep me off my feet, but it didn't feel permanent, so I didn't really invest much of myself into the relationship at the time." She shrugged gently, as though not wanting to disturb the kitten who was purring so loudly, it sounded like a little engine. "After I graduated, he asked me to stay in West Lafayette where he lived. That wasn't an option, even if I had been in love with him, because of the hospital. I don't know if you know this, but Doc Harper helped me out with my tuition. I don't think I could've gone to Purdue, otherwise."

"I didn't know that. He's a good guy, Doc Harper." Everyone liked the old vet, and it was no secret that he had a special place in his heart for Hope Goodacre. Hope Goodacre Willis, Levi reminded himself silently.

"I think I learned more from him than I did in all my years of schooling," Hope said with a chuckle. "He's kind of old-school, and a lot of his methods might seem dated and grassroots, but my patients understand his ways a lot better than they do some of the contemporary, high tech methods used in clinics and hospitals today. Especially when we do farm calls."

They were rounding the bend back toward the house, and Levi drove slow, wanting to give her as much time as she needed. "We're almost home," he began. "And there's no rush on my part. I'm going to drive around the block a few times, okay?"

Hope looked out the window, then turned back to him, a hesitant look on her face. "I don't know, Levi. I thought I was ready to spill my guts, but now that I've started, I'm not so sure." She sighed deeply, clearly still unsettled. "Maybe this is God giving me a chance to shut up before I stick my foot in things."

Levi made the decision for her. "I'm going to keep driving. You can talk if you want. Or not. I like having you in my car, Hope."

She didn't argue, and he thought he saw a hint of a blush, but she didn't start talking right away, either. He was just beginning to wonder if she was going to keep her thoughts to herself after all, when she said, "The fact that it wasn't a difficult decision, choosing the hollow over Chet, should have been a red flag. The first of many that I seemed to have missed."

"One thing I learned from my own marriage, is that red flags, they are hard to see when you're stumbling around in the dark." That's what it felt like, back in those days with Veronica, when he couldn't see anything beyond his next step. "Ironically, it seems like everyone else can see them just fine."

"No kidding," Hope said, the words bittersweet. "Both Faith and Charity asked me—must've been a thousand times if it was once—what it was I saw in him, and Daddy actually warned me to slow down, but I was pretty determined to go through with things at that point."

She fell silent again, so Levi prompted her. "Why?"

After another pause, she said, "That man I had a thing for?" She wouldn't look at him. "I'd heard he was still single, and I naively believed that maybe, just maybe, I had a chance with him. Silly, I know, but I thought my life was just beginning to take off, and that my happily ever after was sitting here waiting for me. I was coming home, I was ready to take over Doc Harper's practice, and I was convinced I'd get the man, too." She shrugged again.

The light was beginning to fade outside the window. The days were getting longer, but it was still pretty frigid after the sun went down.

"What happened?" Levi asked, his stomach twisting with the revelation that Hope had been pining for someone else all this time. He kept his focus on the road ahead, but shifted slightly so he could see her from the corner of his eye.

What if she meant him? Was it possible? Surely, she'd felt some of the same sparks he had over the years. What if she'd been pining for him the way he'd been for her?

But she'd been so standoffish after coming home. At least with Levi. "Are you telling me there's another idiot man in this town who didn't know how to love a woman like you?" He tried for a light tone, but he sounded a little gruffer than he'd intended.

Hope let out a sound that might have been a laugh if the conversation wasn't such a serious one. "I don't think it was a case of him not knowing how to love me," she said, her tone resigned. "It had more to do with the fact that he was clearly in love with someone else."

It was someone else, then. I'm such a fool, he railed silently. A dreamer. Hoping where there is no hope.

She finally turned to face him. "The tragedy of this story, Levi, is that neither one of us got the happy ending we wanted. The woman he loved eventually found someone else, and me? You know what happened to me. When I knew he wasn't available after all, and then Chet showed up in hot pursuit, I settled." She reached up and covered her face with her free hand, dipping her chin to rest it against the curve of the kitten's spine. "Just saying that out loud makes me sick to my stomach. I settled. Who does that? Stupid people, that's who."

"Hey," he said again, this time a little more firmly. "You are not stupid."

"Maybe not stupid, but I must be naive, or something like it. I'm lousy when it comes to reading men, that's all there is to it." She was beginning to get a little agitated, and the kitten seemed to sense it, lifting its head and mewling softly.

Levi reached over and touched her shoulder again. "Stop beating yourself up, Hope. We've all made mistakes, especially when it comes to love."

"Yes, but as much as I want to blame Chet for being a cheating—" she broke off with a grimace. "Do you know how badly I want to call him every terrible name in the book? It would feel so good right now. But then I'd feel guilty as sin, and I'd have to put a few hundred dollars in Daddy's cuss jar when I go over for Sunday Dinner." She made a self-deprecating snort. "You know he still does that?"

Levi chuckled. "Yes, I've seen it. From what your niece tells me, that Cuss Jar fund has paid for a lot of different projects around Seven Virtues. Your daddy is a smart man."

Hope nodded. "Yes, he is, and I should have listened to him when he warned me about Chet." She snuggled the kitten close again, and it settled back in. "But as I was saying, I can't really blame him for what he did."

Levi cocked his head and frowned at her. "What do you mean? Yes, you can. There is no excuse for being unfaithful." On this point, he would be adamant. It didn't matter if it was Hope, Veronica, or anyone else. Marriage vows were promises that should never be broken, at least not while two people remained a couple. "Chet could have left at any time. He didn't have to wait until he had someone else on the side."

"But don't you think that what I did—marrying him knowing I was still hung up on someone else—don't you think that was essentially the same as being unfaithful, at least in my heart?" Her voice was so small, so filled with doubt, Levi could hardly bear it.

They had turned onto Shadowbrook Lane, and instead of driving past his house again, he pulled in to the driveway and parked. He turned off the engine and turned so he could face her. "Let me ask you a question."

"Okay," she said, her eyes downcast.

"If that man, the one you say you were hung up on, if he approached you after you were married, and he wanted to—" Levi broke off, feeling a little uncomfortable having this discussion with Hope, partly because he'd thought of doing the very thing he was suggesting on many occasions. Of course, he would never have acted on it, and when the thought did come to him—and it seemed to on a daily basis —he did his best to reject it, to not allow himself to entertain it. He cleared his throat and began again. "If that man you were hung up on asked you to leave your husband for him, would you have?"

Hope stayed silent for so long, Levi began to wonder if perhaps he didn't know her as well as he thought he did. He'd been absolutely certain of her answer, and to find that she wasn't so certain of it herself, made Levi want to take the question back.

"You don't have to answer that, at least not—"

"No," she said, cutting him off. Her brows were drawn, her gaze locked on the figure eight pattern she was tracing with her finger on her thigh, around and around again. "It's a legitimate question. Because the thing is, I want to believe I would turn him down, that I would do the right thing. But the truth is..." She swallowed hard and started again. "The truth, Levi, is that there was a dozen—no, a hundred, maybe even a thousand—times when I dreamed, imagined, even hoped he would." Her voice cracked, and in a husky tone, she asked, "Doesn't that make me a terrible person? You see why Chet did what he did, don't you? He must've known I wasn't completely his. How could he not have known?" She let out a snort of disgust. "Then again, how could I not have known? About... you know."

Levi was way too familiar with that question. The surprise. The shock. The hurt. The sudden stripping away of the blinders he'd subconsciously worn.

He moved the cardboard box into the back seat and reached over to take her hand. To his surprise, she let him curl his fingers around hers. "Let me help set your mind at ease," he began. "No, that does not make you a terrible person. No, I do not see why Chet did what he did; at least not the way he did it. Like I said, he could have left at any time. It still would've hurt, because failed marriages hurt, no matter what, but adultery is never the answer. It is never justifiable. Chet should have left first. And as far as knowing? Him or you?" He squeezed her hand, but she kept her eyes lowered. "It's those darn red flags in the dark. We miss them when it's too dark to see them."

She said nothing, so he added, "And if it makes you feel any better, I already know your answer to my question, Hope. You would have said no to that other man. You would have done the right thing. I have no doubt, and neither should you."

Hope shook her head. "That doesn't change the fact that I wanted to say yes. I may have been committed to my marriage, but the truth is that my heart was divided. I can't pretend otherwise."

Levi thought for a moment, then took the conversation in a different direction. "People get married for a lot of reasons. Most of the time, at least in this country, it's for love, right? But love alone is just a feeling. You know, my mother compares love to air. Sometimes it's still and quiet, gentle and peaceful. Other times it moves like a storm, sweeping you off your feet. Sometimes it's so badly polluted you have to wear a mask just to survive it, and other times, it's raining so hard, there doesn't seem to be any air left to breathe. And yet, you still need air if you want to breathe, so you do whatever it takes to make it work in whatever condition it's in." He frowned, frustrated that he couldn't say it exactly right.

Hope nodded. "Wise woman."

"But it's not the air that keeps us alive, Hope. It's our commitment to breathing. That's the way love should be in marriage. In all its different states, we still have to commit to breathing it in. And the moment we choose to stop breathing, we die. It's not the air that kills us, it's that we stop breathing. And the moment we choose to stop being committed to our marriages, that's when they die." He chuckled softly. "Nona explains it a lot better than I just did, but I guess I'm trying to say that we can be committed to a marriage even when love looks better somewhere else. When love is a storm, we need to learn how to plant our feet and lean into it. When it's soft and gentle, we need to learn to stop and appreciate the peace it offers. When it's toxic, then it's time to put on the oxygen mask and fight our way through it so we can come out the other side still breathing together." He tugged on her hand until she finally lifted her gaze to his. "If it's raining, the best place to breathe is under a shared umbrella, right?"

When she didn't answer, he said, "Chet should have shared his umbrella with you. Not with another woman."

"You make marriage sound like something worth fighting for," she murmured.

Before he could stop himself, the words were out. "I'd fight for you if you were my wife." He dipped his head, so his hat hid his face, not wanting her to see how much he meant those words. Then he lifted his chin, cleared his throat, and said, "He should have fought for you, Hope."

Hope pulled her hand from his, reached into the back seat for the box, then gently returned the kitten to it. The baby shook its head, pawed at the soft towel a few times, then curled up and went back to sleep. "Thank you, Levi." It wasn't much more than a whisper.

Levi wondered if perhaps he should be the one worried about scaring her off, rather than the other way around. It was time to break the tension in the air. He'd invited her over to help her relax, to give her a night off from her stress. Not to make her burden even heavier. "Are you hungry?" he asked.

Her stomach growled at that exact moment. "Starving." She shot him a sheepish look.

"Then come on. I promised you a hot meal, giggling girls, and a coffee table to put your feet on." He climbed out and moved around the hood of the car quickly so he could open hers for her. "Your servant, madam." He grinned and held out his arms. "Or if you're too weak from hunger, would you like me to carry you?"

"I may be weak with hunger," she said with a laugh. "But I think I can manage to walk from here. Besides, you have another little lady to carry inside." She handed him the cat box, and then hopped out of the SUV and closed the door behind her.

"After you," Levi said, gesturing toward the front door. He was happy to see the smile on her face again, in spite of the fact that she was quite possibly still hung up on someone else. And according to her sad story, that someone else was still available. Once her divorce was final, would she consider that old flame as a new option?

But Levi had meant what he said. He'd fight for her. Even against an unknown opponent.

That was exactly what he was doing now.

CHAPTER FIVE

THE FISH TACOS WERE OUT OF THIS WORLD, just as Hope had known they'd be. Nona had a reputation for being an exceptional cook, and anyone who had tasted her authentic Southwestern dishes rarely set foot in any of the few Mexican restaurants in the area. "Nona, can I bribe you to be my grandma, too?" she asked the elderly woman.

Nona let loose a deep throaty chuckle. A smoker's laugh, Faith called it. Hope loved the sound of it, not because of the damage caused by Nona's cigarette habit, but because it was genuine and kind. She was as authentic as her food, and Hope had a feeling the apple didn't fall far from the tree, at least not where Levi was concerned.

True to his word, the man had not allowed her to lift a finger all evening. They'd walked out to the barn together to check on the horses. Levi's mare was due to foal again in the summer, and Hope was happy to see her in such good health. She'd been monitoring her pregnancy all along, so she simply enjoyed watching the man and his horse interact. Levi spread a clean saddle pad on a hay bale and instructed Hope to just sit while he fed and watered the beautiful Mustang, then did the same for Yvette's sweet-natured Kentucky Mountain Saddle Horse, Charlie. When they headed back inside for supper, he held her chair for her.

He'd all but filled her plate for her, too, holding the serving dishes close enough that she didn't have to reach for anything. He kept her sweet tea topped off, and then cleared her dishes before she had the chance to ask if she could help clean up. In fact, he cleared everyone's dishes, taking them to the sink where he filled a plastic tub with hot, soapy water, and began to make quick work of washing up.

When she offered to help him, he shook his head. "This is my part of the evening meal. Nona and Yvette cook the food and set the table. I clean up the dishes."

"Well, what can I do to help, then?" she asked. "I'm not used to just sitting around while everyone else is busy."

"Nothing," Levi insisted, shaking a finger at her. "I told you that I was going to take care of you tonight. You sit and relax. I've got this under control."

Hope rolled her eyes and lifted her hands in surrender. "Okay. Then I'll sit here and visit with my two favorite girls."

"I'm glad you got to eat here with us tonight, Aunt Hope," Jasmine said, coming around the table to give her aunt a hug, Yvette right behind her. "But we want to go check on the kitty. We still have to come up with a name for her." They started to walk away, arms linked companionably, then Jasmine stopped and turned back. "Are you going to be okay if we leave you sitting here all by yourself?"

"We can wait with you if you want us to," Yvette offered amiably.

Hope waved them away. "You girls go. I'll be just fine." It made her as proud as a mother hen to see the two of them being so kind and sensitive, especially knowing that there was a baby kitten waiting for them in Yvette's bedroom.

Besides, she could use a few moments alone. "I'm going to go sit in the living room," she called out to Levi and Nona who quietly conversed in Spanish as they worked side by side in the kitchen.

"I'll bring you some coffee," Levi called back. "Just the way you like it, too."

"And fried ice cream," Nona added, her voice loud enough to be heard by the girls down the hall. Their squeals of excitement rang out, making Hope's heart light. Levi had been right. Giggling girls really could make a person feel better.

She propped her socked feet up on the edge of the coffee table, rested her head against the back of the couch, and closed her eyes, relishing in the sounds of happiness drifting around her.

When was the last time she had put her feet up and relaxed? When had she ever sat in her living room and listened contentedly while someone else did the dishes? It was usually the other way around, now that she thought of it. Early on in their marriage, she and Chet had spent a few evenings a week cooking together, eating together, cleaning up together, then snuggling together on the sofa while they watched television or a movie. But she liked shows that took her out of her own life, while making her think, like Sherlock, or Dr. Who. Justified, of course, or even the old Saving Grace series. She was also a sucker for a feel-good rom-com, while Chet, on the other hand, had a preference for anything that raised his adrenaline, and he tended toward shows with gratuitous content. After the first few months of compromise on both their parts, the benefit of snuggling on the couch no longer outweighed the cost of having to watch the other person's taste in entertainment, and they eventually gave up trying. They talked instead, until they realized they didn't have a lot in common to talk about—he wasn't interested in hearing about her latest breech birth, and she had a hard time paying attention while he practiced his sales pitches on her.

It wasn't that they didn't try, but it seemed like the more effort they put in, the more apparent their differences became.

"And yet," she murmured softly, shaking her head at how blind she'd been. "And yet, I was still surprised." Why was hindsight so brutally clear?

"I don't want to startle you," Levi said quietly from the doorway. "Nona is getting the girls. Coffee?"

She opened her eyes and turned to watch him enter the room, a loaded tray in his hands. She straightened up and sniffed the air when she saw the coffee, and the five bowls of golden crumb encrusted ice cream. "Do you guys eat like this every night?" she asked.

Levi chuckled and set the tray on the coffee table in front of her. "We eat desserts only on Friday night and Sunday dinner, but otherwise, I have to say yes. Nona can't help herself."

"How do you stay so fit?" As soon as the words were out, she felt the flush creep up her neck to stain her cheeks. But instead of letting embarrassment change the mood, she opted to run with it. "Seriously, Levi," she said as she took the cup of coffee he handed her. "I'd wear a couple hundred pounds if I lived in this house, but look at you." She gestured at him with her free hand, waving it up and down in front of him. "You look amazing."

Levi bent to pick up another cup, jostling it against the tray as he did. The coffee sloshed on his hand a little, and he muttered something under his breath in Spanish. He wouldn't look at her.

Had she actually rattled him with her compliment? The thought made her duck her head to hide her smile. She inhaled the aroma of the coffee in her hand. "Mm. This smells wonderful." Then she braved a sideways look at him.

One side of his mouth crooked up in a pleased smile, but he wouldn't meet her eyes. He settled on the other end of the sofa with his own cup. "I'm a couple hundred pounds," he said with a hint of humor in his voice.

Hope nudged his knee with her toe. "Yes, but you're more than a foot taller than I am." She took a careful sip of the hot coffee. Once again, it was perfect. "A couple hundred pounds on you looks really good. On me? Not so much." Goodness. Was she flirting with him?

How long had it been since she'd flirted with anyone? Was she even doing it right? And why was she doing it? She dropped her gaze to the tray of ice cream. "I think I'm gaining weight just looking at that."

"Aw, come on. You could use some fattening up. You should come to dinner more often."

Hope sat forward and set her coffee on a coaster. Then she turned on the couch so she was facing him, and crossed her legs in front of her. "You know, tonight you have said, in so many words, that I look tired, hungry, and scrawny. A girl could get a seriously big head around you, Levi Valiente."

Levi put his cup down beside Hope's, then slid toward her on the sofa, hitching one leg up so he could turn to face her. "Actually, Hope, what I said in so many words was that you needed me." Their knees bumped ever so lightly, and Hope's breath caught. Mercy, he was too close.

"Haha. Nice save." She shook her finger at him. "I know what I look like. I have a mirror, and I have eyes. I am kind of a mess, and I want you to know that in spite of your backhanded compliments — if you can call them that — I have had a very nice evening so far. I can think of only one thing that would make this better."

"And what is that?" His eyebrows rose slowly, and he leaned toward her just the tiniest bit, his knee now pressing against hers.

"That my phone stays silent so I can go home and get some sleep." Then she laughed and poked his leg with her finger. "I've probably just jinxed it. Watch, it'll start ringing any minute now."

But the phone didn't ring, and a few minutes later, Nona escorted Yvette and Jasmine from the back bedroom so they could all enjoy the fried ice cream together. They watched an episode of the girls' current favorite TV show about a mother and daughter who rescued horses, then Nona excused herself to go to bed. Jasmine and Yvette had their heads together talking quietly about something, the kitten sprawled out spread eagle on her back on a pillow between them.

"My mom gets up early to make me breakfast," Levi explained. "She doesn't have to, but like I said, she can't seem to help it."

"She sounds like Charity. That girl would cook every waking moment if she had someone to eat her food." Hope was slumped comfortably in the corner of the sofa, a fluffy throw pillow tucked behind her low back, her legs stretched out in front of her with her feet propped on the coffee table again. In the opposite corner of the couch, Levi lounged in a similar position, one foot on the ground, the other sharing the table with Hope. They'd playfully jockeyed for position, the closest thing Hope had ever come to playing footsie with anyone in her life, and she couldn't deny the little buzz of pleasure that shot through her at the silly antics. It was like high school all over again, and it was kinda nice. Kinda sweet.

"She's been working part-time for Cord, did you know that? He's got that full crew over there with all the major renovation on the property, and he's hired her to cook for everyone. It's only the noon meal, at least for now, but she said it might turn into something more in the future." She smiled as she thought about her sister whipping up huge trays of Texas Ranch Casserole and bottomless pots of chili to serve to a roomful of hungry men. It was the perfect job for Charity. "Are you providing her with meat?" she asked, turning to Levi.

"I am. In fact, I butcher Cord's own cows for her. I head over there about once a week to select which animals to process, then Cord or one of his guys brings them to the shop on their scheduled day," he explained. "I'm there most Saturday mornings before I open shop, so I get to see the progress weekly. The Maddox brothers really know their stuff, from what I can tell. It's pretty amazing.""

Faith and Cord had been married last fall out in the tiny clearing in the woods the Goodacres called Caroline's Secret Garden, named so after Caroline Goodacre, who'd passed away shortly after the birth of her youngest daughter. It was where the family spent every Mother's Day, and the intimate ceremony had been held in that place because Faith wanted to feel like her mother was there with them. Due to the restricted space, only family and a few close friends gathered to witness the event, including Levi, Yvette, and Nona, but the Overmans announced that once their new barn was finished, they'd host a barn dance in lieu of a wedding reception in the spring, and the whole community was invited to celebrate with them.

But spring was now upon them, and with calving season well underway, followed closely by planting season, folks were anxious for a reprieve in the middle of the busiest time of the year.

Cordell Overman had marched back into town last May after being gone for nearly ten years and had made it inarguably clear that he was there to win back the hand of his high school sweetheart, Faith, the eldest of the seven Goodacre sisters. When he discovered that Faith had a daughter who also happened to be his daughter, things got a little chaotic, especially when Jasmine learned of her paternity from a bully in school, and decided she wanted nothing to do with him. To complicate matters—but in truth, it rather simplified them—because of injuries, Cord had retired early from his football career and moved to the enormous, albeit rundown ranch right next door to Seven Virtues. He'd bought it from his cousin, Frank Flanner, Jr., a career military man, whose father, Frank "Judge" Flanner had passed away six months earlier. Relieved that the old place would remain in the family, Frank, Jr.—Frankie to his family and childhood friends—was thrilled at all that Cord was doing to restore the property to something of its former glory. Cord and Faith were indeed making a lot of changes, converting the ranch into more of a diversified business. They were incorporating a Quarter Horse breeding program in a section of the property where Judge had at one time held cattle auctions, and they were meeting with the rodeo organization to sponsor a regular stop on the circuit on some of the unused acreage of the ranch. The community was abuzz; the rodeo coming to Plumwood Hollow was the kind of news that got hearts racing and spirits flying. Tourists and their money, buying and selling local stock and farm produce, pageants and competitions, rodeo jobs, and the chance for cowboys and cowgirls alike to show their muster in the arena.

The barn dance the first week in May was also an open house so folks could get a look up close and personal at all that the Overmans had planned for the property. Besides, everyone loved a barn dance, and any excuse for one would do. Cord and Faith were doing it up right, that was for sure. Making up for lost time, everyone said. The lovebirds had spent the last decade pining for each other, a world of hurt and betrayal wedged between them. But it had taken them only a few short weeks to realize that with forgiveness and grace as their weapons, they were prepared to fight for the love they still had for each other.

Hope let out a happy sigh for her sister. Although part of her longed for the same joy in her own life, she didn't covet what her sister had. No, she celebrated with them. Faith deserved every moment of her happily ever after with Cord. She returned her thoughts to the man beside her. "Do you start pretty early in the mornings?"

"I do. I get the slaughtering part of my day done as early as possible—I schedule my first appointment at seven, and that's only because I have to wait for the inspector to be on site to begin. But I make sure the animals are ready and waiting the moment he shows up. I try to wrap that part of the day up in a few hours, and by noon at the latest, the new carcasses are hung in the cooler to age, the inspector is on his way, and I'm serving customers their meat orders. I don't make a lot of house calls anymore, although I do still have a few customers who pay extra to have me pick up their animals for them. But because Cord is culling his herd pretty heavily, he's not only having me butcher for him and his crew, but he's selling cows to me for a great price since he won't have to pay to send them out to a feedlot. Which means I'm getting grass-finished beef out of the deal. It's not organic or antibiotic-free—at least not yet, but Faith's working on getting him switched over in the next couple of years. Even so, it's a whole lot better than what you'll find in a grocery store."

Hope knew Levi took great pride in knowing exactly where his meat came from and how the animals were treated in life.

"Hey, Aunt Hope," Jasmine said, interrupting her thoughts. "Uncle Chet isn't coming to Daddy and Mama's barn dance, is he?" she asked. Her tone held a hint of censure, and both girls looked somewhat concerned over the possibility.

"Yeah, is he?" Yvette chimed in.

"Yvette," Levi said, sitting up taller in his seat. "That's not any of your business."

"It's okay," Hope said, sitting forward herself, and putting a hand on his knee. "It's a good question, Levi. I'm sure there are a lot of people out there discussing the same thing, but they just don't have the decency to come to me directly." She turned to her niece. "The answer is no, girls. He won't be welcome there, and if he sets foot on the property, I'm sure Cord will have words with him."

"I'll have words with him," Jasmine said, with a sassy bob of her head. "Me and my steel-toed boots. I might even wear my spurs to the party if Mama lets me. Just in case he doesn't understand the first go-around."

Levi chuckled quietly, and Hope shot him a long-suffering look. "Don't encourage her." To Jasmine, she said, "Thank you for your support, my sweet little vigilante niece. But I think you'll be too busy having a grand time to worry about old Uncle—" She broke off and shook her head. "You know what? Let's not call him that anymore, okay? Just Chet. Or Mr. Willis."

"How about Dumb Butt Turd Brain?" Jasmine suggested.

"Jasmine!" Hope's voice rose in pitch, but she had to bite back a snicker.

Levi, on the other hand, laughed outright and held out a hand for Jasmine to high five him.

"Stop it, you guys. We don't call people names." Although truth be told, she kind of liked the ring of it. She'd called Chet Willis something close to that on several occasions, at least in her mind.

"But who are you going to go to the party with, then?" Yvette asked from beside Jasmine. She held her kitten tucked up under her chin just the way Hope had earlier.

"Again, *mija*, not your business," Levi said, sobering slightly.

Hope felt her cheeks grow warm, but lifted her chin and said, "No one. I'm family, so I don't need a date."

"Of course you do, Aunt Hope," Jasmine scoffed. "It's a dance. Who are you going to dance with if you don't have a date?"

"Who are you going to dance wit, silly girl?" Hope shot back, doing her best not to look at Levi, even in her peripheral vision. It wasn't working. He was watching her; she could feel his eyes on her.

"Grampa, of course, silly lady," the girl said with another head bob. "He's my date because Mama and Daddy won't let me bring Lucas Pithey." She leaned in a little closer, and in a dramatic stage whisper, she said from the side of her mouth, "But Lucas is coming with his family, so it's kinda like his sister is his date, which means he's fair game for all us single ladies. Me and Vetty here are going to show him a good time."

"Jasmine!" Hope squawked at the same time Levi spluttered and choked on his laughter beside her. "You do not know what you are saying. You two are not going to show anyone a good time, ever. Got it? That means something completely different than what you think it does."

The girls exchanged innocent looks, then Jasmine's eyes grew wide with shock. "Does that mean, like, you know, sexy time?"

"Like, you know, yes!" Hope gasped out before bursting into laughter, too.

Levi, holding his stomach, stood and headed for the kitchen, but his shoulders were shaking so hard he ran into the door jam and grunted in pain, making Hope laugh even harder.

Finally catching her breath, Hope leaned forward over the coffee table and asked, "Sweetie, where on earth did you hear that?"

"I was listening to Mama and Daddy talking about the barn dance." Jasmine's voice came out a little less sassy, but Hope didn't pick up on any real contrition over the misused phrase or the eavesdropping. She wondered if she should warn her sister. "And she told him she was going to show him a really good time that night." The girl rolled her eyes and crossed her arms over her skinny chest. "I thought they were talking about the party, but I should have known it was sexy time stuff. They're so gross when they don't think anyone is looking. All that kissing and holding hands and—and...sniffing each other."

"Sniffing?" Hope asked, her eyebrows raised nearly to her hairline. Her voice cracked as she tried not to laugh again, but in the kitchen, Levi let out a guffaw that annihilated her restraint. She stood and circled the coffee table to wrap her arms around her niece. "Oh baby, I'm so sorry I'm laughing," she said, not wanting Jasmine to be embarrassed.

"I don't care," the girl said, much to Hope's relief. "I'm glad they have the hots for each other. Abby says that way, I won't have long to wait for a baby brother or sister."

Abby was the youngest of the seven Goodacre sisters, a senior in high school, and a teenager through and through. "Is nothing sacred in our home?" Hope muttered as she covered her face with her hands. "And do they really sniff each other?" she asked, then wished she could suck the words back in. She suddenly recalled how she had, in fact, sniffed Levi Valiente back at her house. "Never mind. I'm afraid of what your answer might be."

She had every reason to be afraid.

"They do," Jasmine declared with another roll of her eyes. "They're like monkeys. Or dogs. Except they don't sniff each other's bu—"

"Jasmine!" Hope screeched, covering her niece's mouth with her hand. "Have a little class, child."

"Sorry," the girl said, but her eyes were twinkling with mischief, reminding Hope a little too much of Abby at that moment.

"If you're not going to the dance with anyone, then why don't you go with my papa?" Yvette asked, tugging on Hope's sleeve. "He doesn't have a date, either. Except for that gross lady at church who shows her tetas too much," Yvette added in a loud whisper, glancing surreptitiously over her shoulder toward the kitchen where her father lingered, still trying to compose himself.

"Yvette," Hope chided softly. "That's not a nice word to use." Hope's mind raced through a myriad of women who typically had ample cleavage showing in church. She was drawing a blank, but then, cleavage wasn't something she paid a whole lot of attention to.

Yvette hung her head and sighed dramatically. "I know. But I didn't know what else to call them." She lifted pleading eyes to her. "Please, Dr. Hope. Please. She keeps asking him, but I don't want her to go with him, so you have to." Then she raised her voice and hollered, "Papa! Why don't you ask Dr. Hope to go to the dance with you? She's a nice lady."

"Pepita!" Levi called out from the kitchen, his voice still tight with laughter. "You're my date." He came back in the room doing his best not to smile, but the moment his eyes met Hope's, he cracked up again.

"Papa!" Yvette said, drawing out the word into about five syllables, and rolling her eyes just like Jasmine had done. "I'm not your date, I'm your daughter. Besides, I'm going to be hanging out with

Jasmine, not you, so you'll be lonely. You and Dr. Hope should go together. Then you won't be lonely by yourselves."

"Wow," Hope chortled, amused by how pitiful Yvette made them both out to be. "That sounds like a whole lot of fun to me, don't you think, Mr. Valiente?"

She'd meant it to sound sarcastic, but it came out like an invitation.

CHAPTER SIX

LEVI STOPPED MID-STRIDE AND MET HOPE'S EYES AGAIN. This time, he didn't crack up. Was her question asked in jest or was she serious? Did she really want to go to her sister's barn dance as his date?

"Come on. Ask her, Papa."

"Go, Mr. Mostacho," Hope's niece interjected with that ridiculous wobble of her head. The girl was fascinated by his mustache and loved finding opportunities to call him that. "Show us how it's done, Mr. Mostacho! Woot-woot!" Then both girls were on their feet, fists raised in the air as they danced around the room, chanting "Mr. Mostacho! Woot-woot! Mr. Mostacho! Woot-woot!"

"Shh. You're going to wake Nona," Hope reprimanded, reaching for Jasmine's arm.

Levi crossed the room to intercept his daughter, his own expression growing serious. "Hope is right; Nona is in bed, and we need to keep it down out here."

"The girls are right, too, *mijo*. You should ask her." It was Nona this time, shuffling down the hall toward them, an empty glass in her hand. She paused before turning into the kitchen. "You should take the pretty doctor to the party. She shouldn't go alone; you would bring shame on yourself if you let her." Then she shuffled off, leaving the room in poised silence behind her.

"Well," Hope finally said, apparently at a loss for words. Her voice came out a little breathy, and she didn't look at him.

"Well," Levi echoed, but he didn't stop there. He was not going to let this opportunity slip through his fingers. The girls wanted him to show them how it was done? He spun on his heel and ducked back into the kitchen. On the windowsill above the sink was an assortment of orchids his mother grew. Several of them were blooming, and because Nona knew what she was doing, each plant had multiple flower spikes on them. He would just have to risk his mother's wrath because he wasn't going in empty-handed.

Nona, who was filling her glass at the tap, raised a questioning brow at him. "Well?" she asked.

Levi grinned at her, snatched a pair of kitchen shears from the knife block, reached over his mother's head, and snipped off one of the loaded stems. "*Lo siento*, Mama," he apologized, then bent to place a quick kiss on her cheek before hurrying back to the living room.

Hope, a bemused expression on her face, was gathering up dirty dishes, and the girls both shot him dirty looks as he approached. Apparently, they all thought him less than a gentleman. He held up the stem of white, pale pink, and burgundy petaled flowers, a little like holding up the white flag, then tucked it behind his back as he circled the coffee table to stand in front of Hope. She looked up, a faint blush coloring her cheeks. Without saying a word, Levi took the dishes from her and set them back on the coffee table `, one at a time. When her hands were empty, he stepped back and brought the orchid flowers from behind him.

"These are for you," he said, dipping his head so he could look her in the eyes. He waited until she took the flowers, and smiled when she brought them to her nose. He knew what she'd smell; Nona only grew orchids that had fragrances like vanilla or chocolate, coconut, and even raspberry, or plum.

"Oh, my," Hope exclaimed softly. "These smell as lovely as they look." She brushed a fingertip over the surface of a petal. "They feel like velvet. Thank you."

Levi nodded, and then took her free hand and brought it to his lips to kiss her knuckles.

Jasmine and Yvette giggled like the schoolgirls they were.

"Hope Goodacre—" Levi began, then broke off, refusing to add Willis to her name. He knew it was childish, but he didn't care. He simply wouldn't give the man any more of her than he'd already taken. "Hope, will you be my date for Faith and Cordell Overman's barn dance next month?"

Hope's cheeks turned a soft shade of pink that matched the petals of the flower she held. She glanced over at the girls, and he immediately realized that he'd put her on the spot, in a position where she probably felt obligated to say yes, even if she didn't want to. "I—" she stammered, pulling her fingers from his grasp. "Um..."

"Say yes, Aunt Hope," Jasmine demanded. "You can't go alone. It's a dance. It's totally bad form to go to a barn dance without a date. You need him!" she added dramatically.

Yvette threw in her own impassioned declaration. "And he needs you." She cupped her hands out in front of her chest, shimmied her shoulders suggestively, then rolled her eyes. "Please, Dr. Hope," she begged.

"What are you doing?" Levi asked, appalled at his daughter's gestures.

"She's being Miss Tetas from church," Jasmine explained to him when Yvette pressed her lips together. "You can't go with her, Mr. Levi. She's gross."

"Miss What?" Levi asked just as Hope started to reprimand

Jasmine. Then it hit him. "Oh." He squeezed his eyes for a moment and with great effort, bit back another chuckle. He knew exactly who the girls were referring to. Jenny Stuben was between fiancés again, and she'd recently set her sights on Levi. Again. "You have nothing to worry about, Yvette. I will not be going anywhere with Miss Stuben. Please do not call her that, girls. It is rude."

"I second that," Hope said, giving Jasmine the stink eye. "You know the rules about name-calling, girlie."

"Yeah, but if she doesn't want people to know her for her bosoms, then she shouldn't show them off so much." Jasmine shook her head and shot a disgusted look at Yvette for support. "And in church, no less."

"You may have a point there," Hope conceded. "Still, we don't call people names."

"Except for Mr. Mostacho," Levi interjected. "I kinda like that name. Makes me sound super macho, yes?" He winked at Hope when she shot him a glare, then he turned and struck an Atlas bodybuilding pose for the girls.

He thought he heard Hope whisper "Wow" under her breath, and the tiny sound filled him with immeasurable pleasure. He dropped his arms, hitched his thumbs in his front pockets, and turned back to her. He felt a little like he was back in high school, flexing nonchalantly for the pretty girls, grinning like a young stallion when they noticed.

Hope put her hands on her hips and glared at him, but he could see she was trying not to smile. "It's your fault they're like this," she said, reaching out to tap his chest with her finger. "Why do you encourage them?"

Levi laughed and grabbed her wrist before she could pull away again, then slid his hand up, so he was pressing her palm flat against his chest. He wondered if she could feel the way his heart pounded beneath her fingers, but he decided he didn't care. "Please," he said, his eyes locked with hers. "I would be honored to be your date for your sister's celebration." He lifted her hand and kissed her knuckles once more. "If you'll have me."

Both girls clasped their hands in a prayer-like posture, and Yvette even dropped to her knees, barely missing the kitten who had awakened and was rubbing against her legs, hoping for more attention from her new mama.

Hope sighed dramatically. "How can I possibly say no to all of you?"

"Is that... a yes..., then?" Levi asked, dragging the sentence out slowly. When she started to look away, he dipped his head a little further, making sure he stayed in her line of sight. "You'll let me take you to the Whispering Hills Barn Dance?"

"Yes, Levi. I'll let you take me to the Whispering Hills Barn Dance."

Yvette and Jasmine linked hands and waltzed around the room, repeating their chant, but slightly quieter this time. "Mr. Mostacho! Woot-Woot!"

"Watch out for the kitten," Levi said, raising his voice to be heard above their noise. He didn't try to quell them; if he weren't a little afraid of scaring Hope off, he'd have joined them. Besides, Nona stood in the doorway from the kitchen, a satisfied smirk on her face.

And he was still holding Hope's hand.

"I think I need to call it a night," she said, stepping back until he let go of her. She peered around him at Nona, then crossed the room to hug her. "Thank you, again. Your food was exactly what I needed tonight. I couldn't have asked for a better meal or better company."

Levi felt his heart skip at least one full beat. Probably better that her hand wasn't still on his chest for that.

Nona smoothed Hope's hair back from her face with gnarled, gentle hands. "You come to eat my food any time, Dr. Hope. Next time, you tell Levi what you like, and I will make it for you."

Levi ducked his head to hide his smile. His mama didn't make that kind of offer to just anyone. "I'm going to take our guest home now," he said, lifting his head to catch Nona planting a motherly kiss on Hope's forehead. "I'm leaving the girls here, okay?"

"We'll be fine, Papa," Yvette promised.

Nona turned to head back into the kitchen. "I'm going to make my special bedtime hot chocolate," she said over her shoulder. "I wonder if there are any pretty girls who might want to help me."

"Me! Me!" The delighted squeals reverberated around the room, startling the cat so it leaped to its feet and darted around the room in a frantic circle. Then it disappeared under the sofa, making the girls collapse on the floor in fits of giggles.

Several minutes later, after a few more affectionate goodbyes between Hope and the girls, Levi once again held the door open while she climbed into his SUV. Nona had wrapped the stem of the orchid in a wet paper towel and stuck it inside a little bag. She told Hope if she cut a half an inch off the bottom of the stem, and put it in water with "a pinch of sugar, a squeeze of lemon juice, and one or two drops of bleach" as soon as she got home, that the flowers would last for weeks. She still looked tired, but she was beautiful to him, sitting there in his car, the exotic flower held close to her face; she kept bringing it to her nose to breathe in the fragrance.

He leaned against the open door and asked, "Did you have a nice time tonight?"

"I did," she said, smiling at him as she buckled her seatbelt. "In fact, I think this has been the best Friday evening I've spent in a long time."

Just then, both girls burst out of the house, each of them holding a travel mug in their hands. "This is from Nona," Yvette explained as they held out their offerings. "Her special hot chocolate for the road. She said it will help you sleep, Dr. Hope."

Levi reached around Hope and lowered the console in the middle seat so they'd have a place to put their mugs, bringing him so close to her that he was sure she could hear his racing pulse. Cord and Faith weren't the only ones who appreciated their olfactory senses; he was close enough to smell the fragrance Hope used, and he thought the whole sniffing thing wasn't such a bad idea.

They thanked the girls, and he shooed them back inside, reminding them to lock the door after themselves.

Hope took a sip of the chocolate and closed her eyes. "Oh my goodness. This is so good." She shot him a tender sideways glance, then murmured, "It tastes like Christmas and—and happiness. You have the best family, Levi. Thank you for sharing them with me."

Levi said nothing. He just smiled, closed her door gently, and rounded the front of the car to his side. They rode in silence at first, just like they had on the drive over, but it was Levi who initiated the conversation this time. "Are you all right, Hope? I shouldn't have put you on the spot that way. If you're having second thoughts about the dance, just tell me."

She pressed her lips together, her brow furrowed, then made a small huffing sound, like she was trying to make up her mind about something. Pulling the collar of her jacket a little higher around her ears, she hunched her shoulders, making her neck all but disappear. He wanted to smile and tell her how cute she looked, but he cleared his throat and focused on the road ahead. Having a daughter had taught him some pretty important things, one being that there was a time and a place to acknowledge how cute a girl was... and it was only when she was trying to be cute. Otherwise, it was an absolute deal breaker.

"I know I'm going to sound like a prude," she suddenly began. "But I just need to say this, okay? Get it out there. I'm—I'm still married." The statement came out in a whoosh of air, something between a sigh and a groan. But she regathered quickly and continued. "And unless a miracle occurs, Levi, I'll still be married by the barn dance, so maybe we can call it something besides a date, okay?" She crossed her arms, careful not to damage the orchid, and frowned before adding, "I'm sorry. I'm just kind of old-fashioned that way."

Levi straightened in his seat and nodded. "I know. I know, Hope. You don't have to explain or apologize." At the next intersection, he let the car idle until she lifted her face to look at him.

He didn't like it. In fact, he wished there'd never been a marriage at all between Hope and Chet Willis. On the other hand, if she hadn't rebounded with Chet, then she might have married the other man she'd told him about, the one she was really in love with. He couldn't help wondering who it was; he had to live in Plumwood Hollow since she'd said that she'd returned home to find him. But part of him simply didn't want to know. He was the one who would have Hope Goodacre on his arm at the dance. Not the faceless guy from her past. Not Chet Dumb Butt Turd Brain Willis. He, Levi Valiente, mustached cowboy butcher—and undoubtedly far more mature than anyone else on the list, he thought with a subtle roll of his eyes—would be escorting her that night, and if he had his way, he'd be the only one dancing with her, too.

"It's one of the many things I appreciate about you—your unwavering sense of right and wrong," he said. "I promise you this; you can trust me to respect you in every way. You deserve to be treated right."

"That might be the nicest thing anyone has ever said to me," Hope murmured around the fabric of her collar.

Levi could think of a lot of nice things he wanted to say to her. But he would take his time, and he would speak gently, appropriately, at the right time and place, so she would know that his weren't words of flattery, but genuine sentiments.

He turned to look at her briefly, noticing the glimmer of moisture in her eyes. He would start now. "I know you are capable, and you're strong and brave. But what you're going through? It's not easy, and I hope you know you're not alone."

For several moments, Hope didn't respond, and when he glanced at her again, he saw a tear slip from the corner of her eye to trail down her cheek. She wiped it away with the back of her hand, not bothering to try and hide it. Finally, she said, "Honestly, Levi, sometimes I think I'm doing just fine. Most of the time, I know Chet leaving me is the best thing that could ever happen." She wiped away another tear. "And good riddance, you know?"

Levi clamped his jaws together tightly to keep from declaring "Amen." He reached over to pop open the glove compartment and dug out some of the fast food napkins he always kept stashed there.

"Thank you," she murmured, taking the one he handed her and dabbing her cheeks with it. "But other times, I just want to hide my head in the sand like an ostrich, and pretend like none of this is happening. Pretend that the next time I come up for air, everything will be back to the way it was. No Shelby Whitaker, no divorce, no ugly fight over who gets what."

He didn't like the sound of that. Did she mean she'd actually consider taking the man back?

For a panicked moment, he thought he must have asked the question out loud when she spoke again. "Don't get me wrong," she said with a swift shake of her head. "I'd never take him back. Now that he's out of the picture, I can see so clearly how broken things were from the very beginning—even before the beginning—and I hate the way that makes me feel. I'm so embarrassed when I stop and think about how stupid and blind I've been. I believed him when he said he loved me. I believed him when he said he was fully devoted to me—I mean, the guy gave up his life in the big city to be with me, right? But now I know he didn't marry me because he loved me and wanted a future with me. He married me because he thought he could make bank on me." She made a fist and pounded the console, jostling the cups in the holders. "You know, I thought I was naive, but he actually thought a country vet would be rolling in the dough! I remember telling him about the hospital and the cottage and how Doc Harper was handing it over to me. I clearly remember how excited Chet was for me. For me. Ha! All he heard was the bit about it being handed to me, and he ran with it, as though it was some kind of inheritance or something. He played me like a finely tuned fiddle, Levi, waiting until the place was in my name and then showing up on my doorstep telling me he couldn't live without me."

Levi let his mind wander to what he might do with the strings of a finely-tuned fiddle. Stop it, man. She needs you to listen, to pay attention to what she's saying about her heart, not what she's saying about her man. From what she was saying, she had no desire for Chet Willis to be her man ever again, and that made him relax his grip on the steering wheel a little.

"But the joke was on him, wasn't it? When he filed for divorce, demanding half the proceeds, he's the one who got served. I haven't even begun to pay on the principal of this place. If I sold now, we'd both take a loss. But he doesn't believe me. What an idiot."

Levi agreed wholeheartedly, but only nodded. She was on a tear, and he was kind of enjoying being a witness to this feisty side of her.

"You know what's the worst part about all of this?" She thumped the console again. "The part that makes me want to curl up in a ball in a closet and never come out again?"

She fell silent for so long, he thought she wasn't going to tell him. He reached over and wrapped his hand around her clenched fist, marveling at how small and fragile it felt curled against his palm. And yet, so capable. Those delicate fingers stitched bits and pieces of animal flesh back together, salvaging and repairing and restoring life, while his over-sized paws tore that same flesh apart. The irony of it almost made him pull away....

But then she opened her hand and laced her fingers with his.

"When I'm at my lowest, I am ashamed that I wasn't enough to keep Chet happy," she whispered. "I wonder if I wasn't pretty enough, or if I should have dressed more ladylike or got my hair done. Silly stuff, you know? And then I'm consumed with guilt for ruining his life, for embarrassing my family, and even worse, for jeopardizing Doc Harper's legacy. I feel like the worst judge of character, the most untrustworthy person on earth. I don't even trust myself these days."

Levi squeezed her hand gently. Oh, how he knew and understood that dark place. "I know," he said softly. "I've been there."

She lifted tear-filled eyes to him. "But the worst part is—even worse than my self-loathing—is that I think I actually hate him. I mean, hate him. As in, there's a part of me that wishes he were dead. And that makes me sick to the very marrow of my bones, because I have never hated anyone in my life. It scares me how intense these feelings are."

She squeezed his hand, her grip fervent. "And I know I need to release it. I know it stems from my unwillingness to forgive, from my deep bitterness and resentment toward him, and I know that those are all things that will eventually break me—not him—if I don't let go of them." She laid the orchid on the dashboard in front of her, then wiped at her face with the napkin again. "I don't want to hate him, Levi. I don't mind hating what he's done, but I don't want to feel like this anymore, and sometimes, I actually consider giving in and selling the hospital just to get him out of my life for good."

"No," Levi said, pulling her hand toward him. "No. Don't go there. What you're feeling is part of the process. You already have a much healthier understanding of it than so many people who walk through the valley you're walking in. Don't give in to his demands—you'll regret that decision the rest of your life—and don't give in to that dark place that wants you to hate him, either. You call me. You call Pastor Treadwell. You call one of your sisters, or Sarah, or even Nona. We'll walk with you through it. Pray you through it. You're not alone, Hope. You're not alone." He squeezed her hand back, then offered up a quick prayer right then and there. "God, please help Hope to know that she's not alone."

After a couple moments of silence, Hope nodded. "Thank you, Levi. You're so good to me. I don't know what I did to deserve your friendship, but thank you."

"I'm here for you," he said, not knowing what else to say. He was there for her in any way she wanted, and if his friendship was what she needed right then, that was fine.

"I hate crying over him," she murmured, sweeping the napkin across her cheeks again. She took a deep breath and blew it out. "He hasn't earned a single one of my tears, Levi. Not one. So I'm done."

He smiled at her sass. "Tell me about your work," he said, glad when she kept her hand in his. "You said you'd had a rough week. What happened?"

He already knew that Chet was demanding half the proceeds from the practice, but when she explained how it was preventing her from being able to hire additional help, Levi had a compelling urge to sharpen his boning knife. He wasn't a violent man by nature, but something about Chet made him want to explore that untapped side of himself. Like Hope had said about her own feelings, it scared him a little, too, the depth of his ugly emotions toward the man.

"So I'm working all day, six, sometimes seven days a week because animals don't know that Sunday is supposed to be a day of rest, and I'm on call pretty much every night. Sarah is doing what she can, but she's got a family and a life outside the clinic." Hope lifted a shoulder in a resigned gesture. "I don't. The clinic is my whole life, especially now that Chet's out of the picture. Almost. So it makes sense that I'm the one on the other end of the phone, you know?"

"If you were a machine, maybe," he said, frustrated for her. "But you need to take care of yourself, Hope. If you get sick, or if something happens to you because you let your guard down with an injured animal and you get hurt? Where would everyone and their animals be then?"

She let out a long sigh. "I know. With my hands tied the way they are, I'm trying to think out of the box for now." She told him about asking for Doug's help in lieu of him paying for her services that morning.

"You know, I can help you anytime you need it, Hope," Levi said, his brow furrowed. Why hadn't he thought to offer his assistance before now? Her long hours hadn't started last year when Chet left. She'd been overworked for a long time, and everyone who knew her on a personal level was fully aware of it, including Levi. Granted, her own husband should have stepped up to help her more, but now that he was out of the picture, why hadn't Levi thought about offering? "Nona will help with Yvette, and I can come any time you need me, especially in the middle of the night when you are trying to do stuff by yourself. I don't mind getting up at three o'clock in the morning, Hope. I mean it. Let me help you until you can hire on more staff."

Hope squeezed his hand. "Thank you, Levi. You're a good friend. I'll think about it, okay? For now, I have Doug. He wants to work off his bill; I think it's easier for him to give up his time than it is to give up any money they can make. They need every penny they can scrape together," she added.

Levi had a notion that Doug might be upset at Hope for talking about their circumstances with him. The men in the hollow were proud folk in the best sense of the word. They worked hard for what they had, and they took pride in knowing that they'd earned what was theirs.

Except for Chet Willis. That man wanted half of what Hope had invested the last ten years of her life in. Jed had been right; Chet Willis was not one of them, and he never would be. Good riddance, indeed.

"I like the Haywards. They're good people, a good family. Doug has a natural way with animals, and he doesn't mind taking orders from a little lady, if you know what I mean," she explained. "He's like you that way. He respects me for who I am, not for what I am."

Levi nodded, tamping down the small surge of jealousy toward the guy. Doug would be the one to get her call in the middle of the night. Doug would be the one awakened by Hope's request for assistance, and Doug would be the man who raced off into the dark night to come to her aid.

Levi wanted to be that man. "I understand. But if Doug isn't available, will you promise to call me?"

After a brief hesitation, Hope nodded. "Sure. Okay. I'll call you if Doug can't make it."

He'd have to be okay with that.

CHAPTER SEVEN

HOPE SAT DIRECTLY ACROSS FROM FAITH AND CORD at Sunday dinner. She was pretty sure the two were holding hands under the table; she could have sworn Cord was right-handed, but he was doing a fine job of stabbing green beans with his left today. Their sticky-sweet mushiness was a little more than Hope could handle today. She frowned and looked down at what was left of the delicious meal on her own plate, feeling petty and mean over her unkind thoughts. She should be happy for them — she was happy for them. She was just sad for herself.

Yep, she was feeling sorry for herself.

She'd endured another long, stressful week laden with an inordinate amount of tragedies: a horse that suffered a heart attack and didn't make it through the night, a beloved family dog with advanced arthritis that had stopped eating and drinking, and a cat with inoperable cancer. There were stillborn calves and unhealthy mamas—it was common to have a 2-5% loss at calving season, but did it all have to happen in the same week? A litter of newborn pigs was attacked by their first-time mama, and Hope could only save three of the nine babies after the farmer separated them.

There were undoubtedly happy endings, too, and Hope did her best to focus on those, but every once in a while, the hard stuff really got to her.

She'd already had to call on Doug twice, apologizing profusely both times for waking him in the middle of the night. The first time she called him was in the early hours of a Wednesday morning for a breech calving. Often with breech births, there is more than one calf, and time is critical in saving both babies. The couple who owned the cow was elderly, and although Hope was confident Garrett Ford would be game to help her, she needed strength, stamina, and speed. Doug had arrived looking like he'd quite literally rolled out of bed, pulled on his overalls, and ducked out the door. His hair stood on end, and his eyes were puffy with sleep. When he greeted her with little more than a grunt, she was pretty sure it was the first word — if you could call it that — he'd spoken since she called. They'd somehow managed to keep both calves alive, and Judy and Garrett Ford couldn't stop beaming at each other, in spite of the ungodly hour. It was one of the happy endings that week, and Hope had made a point to follow up with the Fords on Saturday; both babies and the mama were doing well.

She'd needed Doug again just two days later. It was a Friday evening, and a bull had gone down with a lame leg after an especially competitive fight with one of his buddies. The bull's owner, Teddy Truman, had waited, hoping it wasn't anything serious, but after a couple hours, he'd called Hope to come take a look. By then, the animal was angry and in pain.

"He's a mean one," Teddy had warned her when he'd called. "You might want to bring help. I'll do what I can, but it's only me, and I've got a persnickety back."

Doug had arrived looking exhausted, as though his week was going about the way Hope's was. It wasn't quite eight o'clock, and when she questioned him, he'd waved her concern away and explained that their baby was colicky, so no one in their house had gotten much sleep in the last two days. Needless to say, Hope felt awful keeping him from his family. She'd tried to send him home, but he'd chuckled softly and told her that she needed him.

"You certainly aren't going to get any help out of Teddy," he'd said with a discreet nod toward the farmer. The tubby man had bit of a reputation in the hollow for having good stock, but more by the grace of God than by any effort the farmer, himself, expended.

Hope shot Doug an amused grin. "Persnickety back," she said. "So I've been told."

Between the two of them, they'd managed just fine without Teddy's assistance, and she had Doug back in his truck within the hour.

That farm call was a timely distraction for her. Like walking around with a tiny pebble in her shoe, she'd suffered all week from a bout of irritation over the fact that Levi hadn't been in to see her, and by the end of the day on Friday, it bothered her way too much that he hadn't invited her over for dinner again, either. When he hadn't made an appearance by closing yesterday, Hope went home surprisingly disappointed. She stuck a frozen pizza in the oven while she showered, then crawled into bed with the steaming hot pie and half a bag of Charity's chocolate chip oatmeal cookies. She watched an hour of Timothy Olyphant strutting around in his cowboy boots and Stetson as Deputy U.S. Marshall Raylan Givens in Justified for good measure. It didn't really lift her spirits, but the boatload of carbs from the pizza and cookies made her crash early enough to get a good night's sleep for once. And no phone calls came in to yank her out of bed, so when her alarm clock went off in plenty of time for her to get up and go to church, she'd felt a little off her game all morning.

Hope lifted her head and glanced around the table at her family as the rise and fall of different conversations melded with the clinking of silverware and dishes. Sunday dinner was the one meal each week when tradition required the attendance of every family member. Exceptions were made if a person was out of the area, contagious, homebound by natural disasters, or dead. Daddy sat in his place at the head of the table, surrounded by his seven daughters and one granddaughter—the king and his princesses—but they always made room for friends and significant others, too. Levi and Yvette, and even Nona a few times, had joined the Goodacres for countless after-church meals over the years, usually coming as Faith and Jasmine's guests, but Faith now had Cord sitting with her, with Jasmine squeezed between her Mama and Daddy. The trio had a table of their own over at Whispering Hills Ranch in the pretty little two-story home Cord had built for his bride last year, a house that sat right up against the property line between the two ranches. It even had a skylight in each upstairs bedroom so they could sleep under the stars every night. Hope thought it a deliciously romantic sentiment.

Charity Goodacre Banner. It wasn't long ago that Charity had pulled her husband's chair away from the table for the last time. Theo Banner had been the victim of a suicide bomber in Afghanistan. He and three of his buddies had lost their lives; two others had come home with missing limbs. Charity moved back into Seven Virtues Ranch a little over a year ago, took over the kitchen, and before long, she was picking up catering jobs around the community. She'd recently taken on working part-time for Cord, feeding his work crews, and loving every minute of it. Charity had invited no other guest since Theo.

The twins, Courage and Justice, were as different as night and day, but they were two halves of a whole when it came to the twin-connection thing. They could share complete conversations without saying a word out loud, and because they seemed to communicate with horses the same way, they had turned to trick riding as a hobby, calling themselves The Twisted Sisters. Their reputation grew and spread quickly, and before long, the hobby had become a part-time job, and although neither of them had plans to continue the show indefinitely, it was certainly helping pay for their college tuitions. Between the two of them, they'd made their way through more boyfriends than the rest of the family could keep track of, but not one had lasted long enough to bring home to Sunday Dinner. Not yet, anyway. Hope had the feeling that might be changing soon; Justice seemed to be getting serious about the guy she was currently dating; Brian or Brandon, with a Native American last name, if Hope remembered right. She'd met him only once when her sisters had dragged her out dancing after Chet made his departure official.

Courage, on the other hand, just laughed when asked about anyone stealing her heart away.

Then there was Prudence. Dear, sweet Prudence. Folks in the hollow said she was part fairy, and some of them probably believed it, too. Lithe and graceful, she kind of drifted along instead of walking like everyone else. She always had some sort of organic thing tucked in her hair, sticking out of a pocket, or fashioned into some kind of jewelry. A spray of colorful leaves, a daisy chain, feathers hanging from her ears. And Lord, how she loved that black-haired horse of hers. The two were never far apart from each other, Prudence and Shadow Dancer, her rescued Andalusian, and all the sisters teased her about not having any room in her heart left for a man.

Abby—whose real name was, indeed, Abstinence, after the Seventh Heavenly Virtue—was the baby of the family. A senior in high school, she was a straight-A student, a gifted musician and composer, and her boss's favorite and most dependable employee down at Ripley's Auto Parts. But the girl regularly put a good portion of her paycheck in Daddy's Cuss Jar, she knew how to work the dance floor at The Smokehouse Grill on a Saturday night, and when she strapped her guitar on in front of a microphone, she could make men and women alike fall in love with her. The whole town knew they'd lose her someday—there was no way they could hold her down once she found her wings. Abby, like the twins, seemed to do a lot of dating, but the only guests she invited to Goodacre Sunday Dinner were girls from her close-knit circle of friends.

Up until ten or eleven months ago, Chet had warmed a seat next to Hope every Sunday, too. Now, even though there was no empty chair the way there'd been beside Charity long after Theo's death, Hope still felt Chet's absence acutely. Ironically, it wasn't because she missed him, but because it hadn't escaped her how much more enjoyable dinner was without him hovering at her elbow. And it wasn't just her. The rest of the family seemed much more at ease without him around, too. She knew her father and siblings had never quite understood what she saw in him, and no one had ever seemed inclined to make him feel like family, either. Not the way they did with Levi and Yvette, or Theo, and now Cord. They were perfectly polite to Chet, but they treated him like a guest, like company. It had bothered Hope in the beginning, but when she'd apologized to her husband after one particularly reserved meal, he'd brushed her words away. "I married you, not your father or your sisters. It doesn't bother me if they don't like me; I'm not that fond of any of them, either. To me, they're family in name only, and I don't really want it any other way."

Red flags. They'd been there all along.

"Hope, I haven't had any midnight calls from you lately," Jed spoke from the head of the table. "You been getting a little reprieve, or did you find yourself some help after all?"

Hope explained her arrangement with Doug Hayward, then went on to regale them with the story of the twin calves they'd delivered earlier in the week. "The Fords were so pleased," she said, glad to have something pleasant to focus on. "And Doug is great. I really hope I can recruit someone just like him when the time comes."

"I know this isn't the time or place to do business, but I've been meaning to call you all week. I have a few cows I'd like you to take a look at sometime next week, Hope. Storm Chaser—my randy bull—"

"Oh, we know all about Storm Chaser," Justice interjected, waving her fork at Cord. "He paid Faith's cows a visit last Mother's Day, remember?"

Cord smiled apologetically. "I do, indeed, and we now have a fine mini Storm Chaser to show for it, thanks to Dr. Hope, here." He nodded across the table at Hope.

"That baby should be mine," Jasmine piped up. "We kind of share the same story—we came about because the neighbor couldn't keep his randy self on his side of the fence." She wiggled her eyebrows at Faith, who frantically covered the girl's mouth. Cord burst out laughing, then stifled it quick when Faith shot him a stern look.

"Jasmine Caroline! Where do you get such notions?" she asked in a shocked tone.

Jasmine said nothing, but the glint in her eyes spoke volumes when she shot a capricious look at her youngest aunt.

Everyone already suspected its origins, though, and they all turned eyes on Abby, whose head was bowed in acute concentration over her mashed potatoes, as though she'd not heard a word Jasmine had said. Her quivering shoulders gave her away, though.

But Jed chuckled and said, "Out of the mouth of babes, Faith. She pretty much summed it up." At which point, Abby burst out laughing, and pretty soon, the others joined in.

"I think you might have a point there, pumpkin," Cord said, tugging on one of Jasmine's curls. "We'll talk about what to do with the calf later, the three of us, okay?" Turning back to Hope, he said, "Anyway, Storm Chaser got in with some of our girls back in January, and I'm pretty sure I've got at least three pregnant mamas who look like they're going to drop winter calves, thanks to his unplanned visit. Think you could swing by, maybe the end of the week, and give me a count?"

Hope actually liked confirming pregnancies. The whole burying-her-arm-inside-a-cow's-backside thing wasn't so great, but when she slid her hand over the pelvic rim and discovered the swelling uterus, especially when she was able to feel the growing fetus inside, it never ceased to make her smile. She had a portable ultrasound unit, but for basic pregnancy checks, she preferred the tried and true method of feeling things for herself, no question. "Sure," she said. "I can stop by your place next Saturday morning if that will work for you."

"Works for me," Cord said with a nod. "Thanks."

"No problem." Besides, she might see Levi if she got there early enough.

She'd been looking forward to seeing him in church that morning, having toyed with the idea of inviting the Valientes to Sunday Dinner with her family, but they'd only had the chance for a brief hello. Nona and Yvette were both home sick with matching head colds, and Levi had been in a bit of a hurry to get going. She reminded him to bring the kitten by so she could do lab work and vaccinate the animal, and Levi had promised her he would.

One way or another, she was determined to see him this week.

CHAPTER EIGHT

LEVI HAD GOOD REASON FOR NOT TAKING THE CAT in to see Hope —
Coco, so named because of the black markings that looked like
painted-on rings around the kitten's eyes, reminding the girls of one of
their favorite Disney movies. He'd foolishly believed that spending time
with the woman would make the waiting easier, only to discover that
the opposite was true. Walking her to her door, keeping their brief hug
platonic, and saying good night a week ago last Friday had been a whole
lot harder than he could have imagined.

To his relief, the girls had behaved like angels while he was gone,
and were snuggled together on the sofa, the purring kitten between
them, watching the movie that inspired the animal's name. He agreed
to let them finish the film if they got completely ready for bed first.
They both looked tired, so he suggested they bring their sleeping bags
and pillows out to the living room, expecting them both to be sound
asleep before too long. Once he had them settled, he warmed himself a
cup of the leftover hot chocolate Nona had made for the girls earlier and
headed out to sit in a chair on the front porch.

It wasn't terribly cold this early April night, so he drew the chair a
little closer to the edge of the porch, pulled his quilted flannel little

tighter around him, then he sat down and propped his feet up on the railing. The sweet cinnamon flavor in Nona's hot chocolate always made Levi smile. It was a staple of his childhood in New Mexico, and he was glad that it would also be a staple in his own children's lives.

At least, he hoped there'd be plural children one day. He pictured the two little girls sprawled sleepily on his living room floor, conjuring up a child who shared features from both of them. Sure, he was jumping the gun, but he loved being a father, and he wanted more children almost as much as he wanted a wife. Fortunately, Levi had come to his senses about the order of things, and after that one year of behaving like a selfish idiot, he'd determined that he would, indeed, be married again before he took any chances with having children. The second time around, he wanted it to be forever.

He'd wanted the first time around to be forever, too. He'd done everything he knew to do to please Veronica, provided for her in every way he could. In the four years they were married, he gutted the kitchen and updated everything to her liking, he'd replaced every piece of furniture in the living room, one by one, as finances would allow, all but eliminating evidence of his life before her, and he'd repainted their bedroom six times. That, alone, should have been enough to tell him he would never be able to make her happy. But ever hopeful, and a believer in the notion that commitment and hard work reaped rewards, he had doggedly pursued their happily ever after, pulling Veronica along with him every step of the way.

It hadn't always been that way between them. When they were newly married, Veronica had been as passionately in love with him as he had been with her. That first year, especially, when he carried her over the threshold of the little home he'd restored with his own sweat equity, her eyes had sparkled with such anticipation for their future. She'd complimented him on every little thing he'd done around the house, from the refinished wood floors and muted paint on the walls to the restored antiques that had been left behind in the old farmhouse. But it wasn't long before she began to grow restless, and then dissatisfied, as though the source of her unhappiness was due to the people and possessions she surrounded herself with rather than the condition of her heart.

The day he came home to find her sitting curled in the corner of the sofa, her arms wrapped around her knees, he believed something terrible had happened, a death in the family, or a dire diagnosis. He remembered she had a doctor appointment that morning. Terrified, he crouched on the floor in front of her and cupped her face in his hands, tilting her chin up so he could look at her. "What's happened, my love?" He'd been so worried, his voice had come out just barely a whisper. She had told him that she was pregnant, and for a few brief, euphoric moments, Levi had felt transcendent happiness consume him. She must have seen it for what it was, and when she pulled away from him, it dawned on him that she wasn't sharing happy news with him. His wife, it seemed, was indeed in mourning.

By the time she was six months along, Veronica had spent more nights on the sofa than she did in their bed, and things were never the same again. Yvette's conception marked the beginning of the end for their marriage.

After Veronica left, Levi didn't stop with getting rid of his truck. Over the next several months, he brought back his old furniture from storage — much of it had been pieces he'd grown up with, and hadn't had the heart to get rid of — and out of a secret hope that maybe, just maybe Veronica would change her mind and come home, he'd put her things in storage, instead. If nothing else, Veronica, or even Yvette, might one day want them back.

These days, he rotely paid the storage bill, knowing the items were safer there than in an attic or basement in his little farmhouse. He knew he needed to go through it and get rid of her things; after ten years, it was clear that Veronica had no interest in what she'd left behind. But he never gave it a thought until the bill rolled around, and the longer he let things go, the less he wanted to go back.

In fact, he knew it was something he needed to deal with before he got serious about anyone else. He didn't want to have to explain that bill to Hope Goodacre, that was for sure. Of all people, he supposed, she would understand. There was no easy way to take apart a marriage, and when there was shared property between them, things just got complicated. He'd had it far easier than most, Levi was well aware, simply because Veronica had wanted no part of him, not even the child they shared.

That night, sitting there on his porch, watching the stars twinkle in the night sky, Levi imagined what his home would be like if Hope lived inside these walls. He wanted to see her face first thing each morning, to see her soul shining out from those big eyes of hers when she looked at him across their pillows. He wanted her robe hanging on the hook behind the bathroom door, her fragrance lingering in the air behind her as she moved from room to room. He imagined the sound of her voice, her laughter, as she talked about her day. He wanted to be the one she nudged awake in the middle of the night, whether it was to go tend a wounded animal, or to lose themselves inside each other.

No, spending time with Hope right now, knowing he couldn't act on his feelings for her, was proving to be more difficult than he'd ever imagined. "Help me, Lord." Levi bowed his head and poured out his heart to God. "I can't do this on my own. I'm going to need some serious self-control and patience. I want to do right by her, Father. I don't want anything to stain or twist up the start of something between us." After a few moments of silence, he said again, "Help me, Lord."

Two days later at church, the moment the service was over, he'd been cornered by Edith Jurgen and her pretty young niece, Bethany, who was visiting for a couple of weeks. In his distracted state, Levi realized too late that he'd allowed Edith to orchestrate him taking Bethany out the following Friday night. And by the time he freed himself from the conversation, the Goodacre crew was already rallying at their vehicles and leaving the parking lot, one by one. Faith and Cord were still outside talking to Pastor Treadwell, and Jasmine and Yvette played on a swing set nearby. He found Nona sitting on a bench in the shade, keeping an eye on the girls, and he dropped down beside her. When she saw his face, she gave his knee a consoling pat. He hadn't told her what was going through his mind, but his mother was as intuitive as they came, and he had no doubt she knew exactly how he felt about Hope.

He'd taken a long ride that afternoon; time spent on horseback always helped him sort through things. Maybe it was better that he stayed away from her after all, he'd decided by the time he returned home. The moment he'd seen her in church, his mind had begun figuring out ways to get around the fact that she was still a married woman. He wouldn't do that to her, and if he had to keep his distance to keep his promise to her, then that's what he would do.

So he'd stayed away from the clinic all week. Coco seemed fine, anyway. She ate heartily, slept well, played hard, and thrived under the attention she received in the Valiente home. Eventually, maybe when he got some perspective on things with Hope, he'd take the kitten in to get her vaccinated and fixed.

He'd dutifully taken Bethany out to The Smokehouse Grill on Friday night, not because he was in the mood for dancing, but because the music was so loud he wouldn't have to worry about carrying on a meaningful conversation with someone he really didn't want to spend time with. Bethany hadn't seemed to mind, or even notice his distraction. As far as he could tell, she enjoyed herself thoroughly. He'd danced with her twice, then handed her off to Julian Bay, one of the local boys whose family came from coal mining in the Appalachians and had the clogging moves to show for it. He'd given Bethany a few basic lessons, and when the live band recognized what was going on, they changed up their music to accommodate the two of them, and anyone else game to try the toe-tapping, foot-stomping dance. Bethany went on to circle the floor with several more guys Levi knew from around the hollow, and a cowboy or two he didn't recognize, but every time she was escorted back to the table where he sat nursing his drink, she gushed over how much fun she was having, never once complaining about his minimal participation.

It wasn't a bad time, and he was well-bred enough to be courteous and friendly to Bethany. He didn't want her to get any ideas about future dates, but there was no reason for her to feel like she was an obligation, either. He complimented her on her pretty green dress, paid for her food and drinks, kept the conversation pleasant and upbeat when there was a lull in the dancing or music, and when she was ready to call it a night, he smiled as he listened to her talk about all the people she'd met. When they pulled up in front of her aunt's home, she'd stopped her rambling and momentarily laid a hand on his arm.

"Levi, I know Aunt Edith left you with little choice about taking me out tonight. I wasn't sure what to expect—you could have been awful to me, and I wouldn't have blamed you. But you were the perfect gentleman, and I had the best time tonight." She turned toward the house as a movement in the transom window beside the front door caught their attention. "She just worries about me, that's all. My mom was her twin sister, but she passed away last year, and Aunt Edith, who as you know has no kids of her own, has taken it upon herself to do what she can to fill Mama's shoes. I only hope she didn't offend you."

Levi laughed softly. "Your aunt is a fine lady, Bethany. She may be a little bit over-zealous at times, but her heart is in the right place."

"Over-zealous?" Bethany asked, a cute little smirk on her face. "That's a kind way of saying she's a busybody, Levi, and we both know it." She reached up to sweep her shoulder-length hair back from her face. "I'd have to agree with you on both counts. My aunt is a busybody with a heart of gold. I can't stay mad at her, even though she does embarrass the snot out of me on a regular basis."

Levi chuckled again and nodded, and then because he didn't want the evening to turn awkward, he reached for his door handle. "Sit tight. I'll come around and let you out so I can walk you to your door." He circled the hood and offered her his hand to help her out, then the two of them made their way up the walk to the front stoop.

Doffing his hat, Levi thanked Bethany for going out with him and told her to tell her aunt hello from him.

"You're a nice man, Levi Valiente," Bethany said, surprising him by standing up on tiptoe to plant a quick kiss on his cheek. But it didn't take a genius to recognize that she wasn't expecting more from him. Right before she pushed the front door open, she said softly, "I hope that whoever has your heart will treat it well, Levi. You deserve the best. Good night." Then she disappeared inside, and from where he stood, he could hear Edith's voice asking if she'd enjoyed herself, followed by the rush of words as Bethany regaled her aunt with the night's activities.

Levi felt about ten feet tall as he walked back to his truck...until the moment he closed himself into the quiet of his SUV, and his eyes landed on the empty passenger seat. He imagined Hope sitting there in her jeans and flannel shirt, her hair pulled back in that long ponytail she always wore, nuzzling Coco up against her cheek as she told him about her day. How he longed for every night to end with her beside him.

He'd returned home to a quiet house, Nona and Yvette having already gone to bed, and by Saturday evening, they both coughed and sneezed and sniffled through dinner.

He'd gone to church on Sunday just so he could get a glimpse of Hope—surely, he wouldn't be tempted beyond what he could endure with everyone around them—then hurried home to check on his girls. Just exchanging a few words with Hope had set his heart to racing. How was he going to survive until things got sorted between her and her soon to be ex-husband?

CHAPTER NINE

BY CLOSING TIME THE FOLLOWING THURSDAY, Levi still hadn't brought the kitten in. It had been two weeks since their Friday night meal together, and Hope was pretty sure she'd done something to put him off. He'd acknowledged her when she'd driven by his shop earlier in the week, but only because he'd been out front talking to a customer, and Hope had waved first.

That was before she'd overheard Patty Lynn on the phone during her break that afternoon, talking in the hushed tones that characterized gossip in any language. According to the receptionist, last Friday, Levi had taken Edith Jurgen's niece, Bethany, out dancing a The Smokehouse Grill. From what she'd seen, though, Levi had spent most of the night warming his seat at their table while Bethany indulged in Plumwood Hollow's nightlife. "She's a pretty girl," Patty Lynn told the person on the other end of the line. "But our cowboy butcher clearly wasn't interested in her."

Hope had rolled her eyes at the possessive pronoun. But then, Levi kind of did belong to the folks in the hollow, didn't he? They'd taken him under their wings when he'd moved to town right out of high school, having accepted a job working on a local ranch. During a routine task, a cow had been gravely injured and needed to be put down. Unable to find a source where the bovine could be slaughtered and salvaged on such short notice, so Levi had offered to do it on the spot. With few options left, the rancher let him do his thing, and to everyone's astonishment, the eighteen-year-old kid had pulled a case of ancient, but well-kept butchering tools from his truck, and proceeded to do the job with remarkably little mess and waste.

He'd grown up on a ranch near the panhandle, and Levi came from a long line of vaqueros who worked the cattle on the wide open plains. He'd learned to use the blades from his father, who'd learned from his father, and so on. In fact, Levi's knives had been his father's before him.

Word of his skill spread quickly, and folks all over the hollow started hiring him to do their personal on-site slaughtering. In the beginning, he didn't turn down anything. Within a year, he'd outfitted himself with a gas-powered generator for a power supply, a crank lift he'd fabricated from scrap metal, a water tank, hanging racks with hooks on a pulley system, and the various implements and tools of his trade, such as knives, bone saws, meat hooks, and more.

It didn't last. Someone turned Levi in for not having proper certification, and he almost loaded up his horse and left town. But some of the local farmers and ranchers who had benefited from his services got together and offered to help him get set up the right way in Plumwood Hollow. It had taken more than a year before he officially opened his doors, and a lot longer than that before he started to see a solid profit, but he'd made a promise to the folks who'd believed in him, and he was going to make it work, or die trying.

As a vet specializing in stock animals, Hope was all for craft butchers like Levi. His method was so much better for the animals in every way, and in turn, that meant a much healthier meat product on the other end of the process. For instance, rather than cows being herded into a massive cattle truck and convoyed across miles of road to

WHERE THERE IS HOPE

an over-crowded feedlot for the last weeks of their lives, with Levi's operation, a cow's final days were much different. The animal could peacefully graze in the comfort of its own pasture right up until an hour or two before being loaded up into a trailer with a few of its buddies. They'd be taken straight to the shop for an appointment with a gentle and humane death at the hands of a man who had nothing but compassion and gratitude toward every animal that passed through his shop.

Butchers like Levi would never be a threat to the big meat business. But he filled a niche market for people who raised their own meat, ranchers and farmers with smaller herds who struggled to afford the long hauls to feedlots, and individuals, restaurants, and chefs who wanted to know exactly where their meat came from and how it was raised. Levi could answer those questions with firsthand knowledge.

So yes, in a big way, Levi Valiente was an essential thread in the fabric of Plumwood Hollow, and like it or not, the close-knit community looked out for their own.

Hope knew that to be true from firsthand experience. She was often surprised at how kind folks were toward her since Chet left. She didn't know what they said about her behind her back, but she'd only ever heard words of encouragement and support expressed to her face. No one seemed to hold her responsible for his decision to leave, and even though that was a guilt trip on which she sent herself on too many occasions, it helped her to know that because she was "theirs," she would be taken care of.

Which meant Chet Willis better mind his manners. No one would let him take her clinic without a fight. And as her days and nights got busier with the slew of new babies being born all over the county, Hope made up her mind that she wasn't going to let Chet's selfishness keep her from doing the best she could for her patients. That meant not waiting to hire new staff. Levi had been right about one thing; if she collapsed from sheer exhaustion, there'd be no one to take her place.

Hope had reopened her files and reached out to three veterinarians who'd responded to her ad. She'd be happy with someone fresh out of college, partly because she could pay them less to start, and partly because she'd learned so much of what she knew and the way she practiced from Doc Harper, not from school. She wanted whoever she hired to bring their up-to-date education to the table, but to learn how to implement that knowledge by firsthand experience using Hope—and Doc Harper's—methods. As far as assistants went, she was looking for muscles and stamina, a willingness to learn, and someone who didn't mind getting their hands dirty on a farm call. If she could find a licensed Vet Tech who wanted to come to Plumwood Hollow to work for her, that would be great, but she'd be just as happy with a hard-working farm kid who wanted a job. Someone like Doug would be an answer to prayer.

Tomorrow, she would be interviewing all three of the vet candidates. She'd meet with Carl Jorgenson on video chat and Josie Silverton at the clinic in the morning, both of whom had a couple years of farm and ranch experience under their belts, and then Hunter Morgan was driving in to meet with her an hour before closing. Hunter was her top choice, which was why she wanted to interview the other two first, just to make sure she didn't make a rash decision. He had little hands-on experience outside of the program and internships, but he'd grown up in a farming community, had ridden horses his whole life, and had been a rodeo junkie from the time he was old enough to remember his first mutton ride. After seeing an animal injured in one of the competitions, Hunter had made the decision to be a veterinarian with an equine specialty, which is what brought them into the same circles on campus, as Hope, too, had an equine specialty. Hunter wanted to practice in a rural setting, preferably where rodeo was alive and well, and because he had no hard and fast ties to any one place, he was willing to go anywhere the right job was. Best of all, the guy was a good six feet tall and built like a cage fighter. It didn't hurt that he had a rather pretty smile—the crooked kind that hitched up on one side and made his eyes crinkle at the corners—and he had the innate ability to put people at ease, which was an excellent quality to have when dealing with worried pet owners and concerned farmers. He was genuinely friendly and courteous—a great guy who happened to be very nicely put together.

Patty Lynn wouldn't know what to do with herself if they did, indeed, hire on Hunter Morgan.

Hope prayed that it would be a quiet night on the home front so she could look over the candidates' files again, make some phone calls to referrals she hadn't gotten around to, and to come up with a few more questions to ask each of them. The last thing she wanted to do was come across as unprepared; she wanted to make sure the order of the hierarchy was established up front without having to spell it out in words.

The phone did ring around nine o'clock, right as she was closing the last of the three files she'd gone through with a fine-toothed comb, but it wasn't a farm call, even though it came through from the clinic line.

It was Chet Willis.

"Hello, Hope," He began, almost formally. But Hope didn't miss that undercurrent of seduction he'd plied her with so easily in the past. Like a good salesman, Chet knew when to let the silence linger, and when to fill it in. In fact, he used silence like bait on the end of the line. She could almost sense him waiting, listening, pausing just long enough for her to bite, to say something that would be his cue to set the hook and reel her in.

Today, however, she wasn't interested in what he had to offer. She had no compulsion, whatsoever, to take the bait. So she waited for him to speak first.

And Chet set the hook too soon. "I'm glad I caught you at home. I was worried you might be out on another one of your farm calls. Must be fate."

Really? Really? Did he think it would be that easy? Gah! She wanted to reach through the phone and spit in his eye. But at that moment, Hope decided she didn't want him to know that he got to her in any way at all. No, she had to remain utterly calm, and completely unaffected. He wanted to act like they were just two normal people having a normal conversation? Well, two could play this game. "Hi, Chet. Your call was directed through the clinic line. Are you calling about an animal?"

A soft chuckle emanated from the phone, sending a tiny shiver down her spine. She hadn't heard that sound in a very long time, long before Chet left, in fact. Tonight, it didn't stir her blood the way it had in the past. In fact, now that she'd ripped off her rose-colored glasses, she heard it for what it was. An act. A ploy. A tool — or perhaps a weapon — that Chet wielded with the precision of an artist.

A con artist.

"I'm calling about you, Sugar." Pause. "I'm calling about me." Pause. "I'm calling about us."

She kept her voice carefully modulated, ignoring the pet name, and said, "You know better than to call me on the office line for personal stuff, Chet. Why didn't you call me directly?"

There was that chuckle again. "I wasn't sure you'd pick up if you saw my number."

"You're probably right," she replied. "But now that you have me on the phone, what is it you need? I am on call, remember? So I need to keep this line open for emergencies."

"I remember." Chet's voice dropped another notch. "I remember lying in bed next to you every night, wondering if you were going to be dragged from my arms by someone or something you thought needed you more than I did."

Hope could hardly believe her ears. What was the guy pulling now? She wasn't the kind of person to play games or to toy with other people's hearts. She'd taken Chet at face value before, not once imagining that his feelings for her weren't exactly what he said they were. Because she was a transparent person, in her naivety, she expected the same of other people, especially those she cared about. So to discover Chet's duplicitous nature, to see him change before her eyes after they were married, well, it had been a brutal wake-up call. She wasn't sleeping now.

"I wish you could hear my heart beat right now, Sugar. It's racing at the sound of your voice." If it were possible for a human being to actually purr, the rumble behind the words he was speaking would certainly qualify. "It's been too long since we talked."

"You should probably get that checked," Hope said, as casually as she could muster. "I don't work on people, but tachycardia is a serious symptom." She stood up and stretched her back. She'd been sitting hunched over her table for too long. "Look, Chet. Before you continue, let me just say this. If you are calling to ask how I'm doing, I assure you that I am doing quite well. If you are calling to tell me how you are doing, that's not necessary. Your well-being is no longer my concern. If you are calling to find out if there is a possibility of an 'us' ever happening again, then I suggest you take a look at your copy of the divorce papers that you filled out and sent to me. Irreconcilable differences, they say. Your choice of words, not mine."

"Does that mean you think our differences are reconcilable?"

She wanted to slam the phone down, but cell phones made that really difficult to do. "Not a chance," she ground out, hoping she'd answered his question the right way. He was so good at phrasing things in a way that made a person doubt themselves.

And...there was that chuckle again. "You're awfully cute when you get angry," Chet said, speaking like he would to a child. It turned Hope's stomach.

"Actually, I'm not angry. I am tired, and I need to get some sleep, because it's quite likely that I will, indeed, get a farm call at some point tonight." She wandered into her little kitchen, filled her teakettle, and put it on the stove top to boil. One of Prudence's calming sleepy time blends would be just the thing, especially after this ridiculous conversation. "That said, if you want to re-evaluate the demands you're making about my clinic and my home, then I'm at least willing to hear you out, but not tonight. Like I said, I am tired, and I know that I don't make good decisions when I haven't had enough sleep." Which is probably why he called her so late on a work night. If nothing else, Chet knew his prey. He made it a point to do so.

"How about tomorrow night? I'll come by with dinner," he said, as casually as though it was something he did on a regular basis. It used to be, but Hope wasn't going there ever again. "I haven't had Toscano's spaghetti and meatballs in forever, and I know that's one of your favorites. Will six work for you?"

"No, Chet. Let me reiterate." Now, she was getting angry. How presumptuous of him. " If you'd like to withdraw your demands for half of my clinic and my house, then I'll gladly talk through the details with you over the phone. And yes, I will record the conversation."

"Come on, Sugar. Don't be like this. You and me, we were good together once." His voice all but dripped honey.

"Are you calling tonight to see if I will take you back?" They might as well get straight to the point.

"Would you like me to ask you to take me back?" And there was another one of his favorite tactics: he answered her question with a question.

How had she gotten herself looped into this conversation? She'd sworn she wouldn't play his games, and even when she drew solid lines in the sand, he found a way to slither around them, or over them, or under them to get to her. "When — if — you're interested in settling this thing out of court, you know what to do. Until then, please don't call me. And certainly do not use my call service to get to me."

The silence on the other end of the line made Hope wonder if he'd hung up on her. But then she heard his sigh. "I miss you, Sugar. I miss the way you feel cradled against me. I miss the smell of —"

"Goodbye, Chet." Hope pushed the 'end' button on her phone.

First thing in the morning, she was calling her lawyer. Chet Willis was definitely up to something, and Hope would bet her practice on it not being something good.

CHAPTER TEN

BY NOON ON FRIDAY, LEVI KNEW he could put off the visit no longer. He'd promised to bring Coco in to see Hope this week, and although she was open on Saturday, he knew it was her busiest day. So after the lunch rush of folks buying steaks, ribs, and chicken parts for weekend barbecues and Sunday dinners, Levi called the clinic. Patty Lynn assured him that he could bring Coco in anytime that afternoon, that Hope had told her to expect him this week. So an hour earlier than usual, he flipped the sign on his door to closed and headed for home to pick up the cat. He and Yvette had spent quite a bit of time online last week purchasing all kinds of paraphernalia for the little feline, and the pet crate had arrived a few days ago. He felt a little silly carrying the pink cage with its colorful decals from the Coco movie and the streamer of rainbow ribbons tied to the door handle, but he loaded up the animal, said a quick prayer for courage, and headed back to town.

The waiting room wasn't terribly crowded, much to his relief. Hope was known for getting patients in and out in a timely manner, a tradition she'd carried over from Doc Harper's time, but not today, she wasn't. The door through which she and her staff took patients back to the exam rooms remained closed, and as far as he could tell, there was no evidence of the usual chaotic activity back there—barking dogs, squawking birds, talking customers. After a while, Levi opened the cage and picked up the cat, tucking her up under his jaw so her front paws rested on his shoulder and her furry head pressed against the column of his neck. For some reason, the cat loved to be held that way and would perch there indefinitely, purring like a Harley Davidson.

Truth be told, Levi found it rather cathartic himself. It reminded him of those bittersweet months when he'd held Yvette the same way, cradled high against his chest, her downy little head nestled into the curve of his neck. He absentmindedly stroked the cat's back, eliciting that predictable purr that was so loud, a woman sitting across the room looked up at him and smiled.

"That's one happy kitty," she said, and Levi nodded gently, not wanting to disturb Coco.

After another fifteen minutes had passed, Levi was beginning to think that maybe it would be better if he came back another time. He should have made an appointment rather than pulling a walk-in. Making up his mind to do just that, he approached the reception desk slowly, not wanting to hover while Patty Lynn finished the phone call she was in the middle of. He could tell it was a personal call just by the way she kept her voice lowered, and her face turned away.

"It's the sweetest thing," she said in a voice just above a whisper. "He's so gentle with her. A big guy like that with a —" She suddenly looked up to see him standing there, and blushed furiously. "Oh! He's — a patient is waiting to speak to me," she mumbled into the phone. "I'll call you later, okay?"

So she'd been talking about him. Not that he was surprised. He was accustomed to being the topic of conversation, especially among women with eligible daughters and single ladies like Patty Lynn. He didn't like it, and truth be told, he sometimes felt like more of a commodity than a human being, but he refused to be offended by it or to take it personally. Plumwood Hollow was a community of fewer than a couple thousand residents, and even though it was primarily a farming and ranching community, the latest census taken a few years ago indicated that the women outnumbered men almost two to one in their neck of the woods. Granted, the numbers were partly due to women merely living longer than their male counterparts, but the fact remained that in Plumwood Hollow, there were more single women under the age of forty than there were single men, and as long as Levi remained a bachelor in this town, folks like Patty Lynn would talk about him.

He knew what he looked like, too, but that was only because he came from good genes. Tall, broad-shouldered, with the well-defined muscular arms of a hard-working man, he carried very little extra weight on him, partly because of the manual labor he did, but partly because he was built like his father, and his father before him. The Valiente men where the embodiment of the proud vaqueros who'd been rounding up and herding cattle across the wide-open plains between New Mexico and Texas since the late 1500s. Levi had grown up on the back of a horse, riding alongside his father, Luis, and his grandfather, Sandro, and the other men in their extended family. From them, he learned how to sit tall in a saddle, how to listen to the woman he loved, how to provide for the children under his care, and how to respect the land he worked.

It was from those same men that Levi learned to butcher the animals he worked with. Standing beside his father, wielding the knives with bone handles that had worn down to the shape of a man's hand, he realized he'd found his calling. To be sure, there was nothing like the rush of the wind whipping past his ears under the wide brim of his hat, or the fluid movement of a muscular horse beneath him. No engine-powered machine could compare to the maneuverability of a horse who stopped and started, veered right or left, backed up or turned in a circle at the slightest tap of the heel or twitch of a rein. There would always be a place for the Spanish-Mexican cowboy in the Southwest, but a man who knew how to efficiently process an animal from stockyard to table would have a place anywhere there were people who ate meat.

Luis Valiente's untimely death during a longhorn roundup had young Levi questioning his future in ranching. With his mother's blessing, he set out to find his own way, not to get away from New Mexico, or the life he was living, but to experience something new. He loaded up his horse and followed the rodeo circuit across the United States and into the Midwest until he ran out of money. Young, unfazed, and as spirited as the palomino mustang mare he'd wrangled and trained himself, he took a temporary job branding cattle at a ranch near Louisville, Kentucky. From connections made there, he wound up at a cow-calf operation just outside of Plumwood Hollow, where he'd met a need in the local community as a whole animal butcher. The ranches and farms were tiny compared to what he was accustomed to back home, but folks in these parts paid extravagant prices to truck their stock to feedlots and stockyards miles away. Levi gave them another option, and within a few short years, he'd put down roots and started a life in the hollow. It took some time for folks to stop seeing his different colored skin, for them to no longer have to repeat themselves so he could understand some of the heavier accents, but by the time he'd met and married Veronica Lipton, a waitress at one of the restaurants he supplied, Plumwood Hollow had become his home. His business thrived, he began selectively breeding Fiebre de Oro— Gold Fever — and selling her colts for good money, and the day he found out he was going to be a father felt like the pinnacle of success to him.

When Veronica left him and their tiny baby, the community surrounded him in ways that reminded him of the tight-knit family he'd been raised in back in New Mexico. Folks in the hollow were his new family; they treated him like one of their own. And when Nona came to live with them, they took her in, too.

So it was no surprise that folks in the hollow paid attention to his comings and goings, to the people he spent time with, and to how he operated his business. They'd made room for him and his little family in their hearts, and they'd stood by him through thick and thin. They wanted to know if he'd find happiness and love again. They wanted to know who he'd find those things with. They wanted to know how he was going about finding those things.

Because the truth of the matter was, the tragic ending of his first marriage hadn't soured him against the institution itself. He did want to marry again, and he had no qualms about telling people that, much to their delight. But it had certainly made him step cautiously when it came to choosing a woman he wanted to spend the rest of his life with.

So when he looked up from the comfort zone he'd settled into, and discovered that woman in Hope Goodacre, only to lose her to a man who would never be worthy of her, Levi turned his attention back to his daughter and mother, to his beloved Fiebre de Oro and her remarkable offspring, and to his butchering business. All three aspects of his life flourished under his renewed dedication.

Life, however, had a funny way of circling around on itself. Because here he was, a stray kitten perched on his shoulder, waiting for Hope to grant him some of her time.

Waiting for Hope.

Was it a curse? Was he doomed to always wait for Hope to notice him?

"Your little kitty is so cute," Patty Lynn cooed, standing up at her desk so she could reach across the high counter and scratch the animal's soft head.

"Thanks, Patty Lynn. We're kind of smitten with our kitten, as Yvette likes to say." He chuckled softly when the cat batted at the receptionist's fingers. "Hey, I should have made an appointment instead of just showing up like this."

"Oh, it's no problem. We've been expecting you all week. Dr. Hope will out shortly, so just stay. I know she'll want to see you." She returned to her chair but continued smiling warmly up at him. "There's fresh coffee over there if you'd like some," she offered, pointing at a table near the back of the room. On it was a large-capacity coffee dispenser, a stack of disposable cups, and a basket of sugar and powdered creamer packets and red stir sticks. "I just made it about half an hour ago; Dr. Hope loves her coffee at the end of the day, and she doesn't mind sharing. Help yourself."

Levi hesitated for a moment, then nodded. "I think I will. Thank you."

As he crossed the room toward the coffee station, a door somewhere down the hall beyond the receptionist's desk opened, and laughter echoed through the corridor of exam rooms. A deep male voice spoke with confidence and charisma, then Levi heard Hope say, "Oh, Hunter, it's so good to see you again. Give me a half an hour or so to close up shop, then I'll be free, okay? You're welcome to grab another cup of coffee and hang out here, or if you'd rather, I can give you my keys and you can go put your feet up at my place."

Levi's blood ran cold. Hope was gushing. Gushing. Like a teenager over a crush. Come on, man. She's offering her house keys to the guy. Like a woman reuniting with a past love, he amended.

He angled his head, trying to see around the open window at Patty Lynn's desk, but couldn't see beyond her cubicle. As he watched, Patty Lynn beamed up at someone on the other side of the hall door, then told him she was looking forward to seeing him again. "I hope she chooses you," she said. "You're perfect for her." It was a rather bold statement, even for Patty Lynn.

"I'm perfect for her," he muttered under his breath so that only

Coco could hear. Then the door opened, and the man who walked out of the inner sanctum of the clinic made Levi's eyes widen and his jaw clench. Who was he? Levi had never seen him before; he definitely wasn't from around Plumwood Hollow. A guy didn't look like that without folks remembering him.

Who was he kidding? Even Levi had to admit that the Adonis who'd just made Hope laugh out loud appeared to be perfect in every way. If this was the guy Hope had been in love with before Chet showed up, then there was no hope—and no Hope—for a cowboy butcher like him.

"We're outta here," he growled, then started back toward the pink crate he'd left on his seat. But he pulled up short, opting to wait until the guy left the building; he wasn't about to let Mr. Perfect Macho Man see him shove a cuddly kitten into a hot pink crate with rainbow streamers tied to the handle.

The moment the clinic door closed behind the guy, Levi strode across the room to snatch up the crate. He just wanted to get out of there, and he'd wait until he was in the car to put the cat away. But he wasn't fast enough to miss overhearing the conversation between the doctor and her receptionist. "Oh my goodness, Patty Lynn," Hope gushed. Yep, she was still gushing. Quietly, for sure, but she sounded absolutely smitten. "He's perfect in every way, right? I want him so bad."

Patty Lynn clapped her hands together in shared delight and nodded, her huge hair lagging slightly, making it look to Levi like she wore a wig. "This is the guy you're always talking about, isn't it?" she asked Hope. "I think he'll be back in the hollow as soon as he can pack his toothbrush. Mark my words; he's yours for the taking."

Levi kept his head down and slipped out of the waiting room, the obnoxious pink crate bumping awkwardly against the side of his knee as he pushed through the door.

CHAPTER ELEVEN

THROUGH THE WINDOW OVER THE RECEPTIONIST'S DESK, Hope saw Levi Valiente leave the clinic. "Hey, is Levi here to see me? Did he bring his new cat?" And where was he going?

"Yes, and yes," Patty Lynn said, her eyes bright with speculation. "He's been here a while, so maybe he's taking the kitty outside to go potty." Then she pressed a hand to her chest. "Oh my goodness, Dr. Hope. That man is simply divine. I don't know how you can stand it."

Hope laughed. "Which one? Levi or Hunter?" She kept an eye on the door, watching for Levi's return. He had seemed in a bit of a hurry.

"Well, both of them, now that I've met Dr. Morgan." Patty Lynn flapped her hand in front of her face as though trying to get more air. "Be still my beating heart. Please tell me you're hiring him. I mean, I liked Dr. Silverton well enough, but she seemed a little opinionated to me, if you know what I mean. Like she had something to prove." The receptionist's brow furrowed. "People pick up on that stuff pretty quickly, you know. It doesn't go over well, at least not in these parts."

Hope nodded. She'd gotten the same vibe from Dr. Silverton, and although the young veterinarian came with solid credentials, Hope got the feeling she'd be hiring competition rather than a comrade. One of the things that made Plumwood Hollow Animal Hospital so successful was the way the whole staff worked together as a team. They needed another team player, not a team leader, and Hope had already made up her mind about the woman, even before Patty Lynn threw her two cents in.

Carl Jorgenson, on the other hand, had been a delight to talk to. He was a little older than she was, but he came from sturdy Norwegian stock, and he loved his farm animals. He laughed readily, had answered every question without reservation, and had somehow managed to give her some suggestions that she was anxious to implement in her own practice, all without making her feel like he was talking down to her. She really liked him, and now she wished she'd included some of her other staff in on the online interview.

"But no," Patty Lynn said. "I wasn't talking about Dr. Morgan."

Hope frowned at her, forgetting for a moment what her receptionist was referring to. "I'm sorry?" she prompted.

"Levi Valiente, Dr. Hope." Patty Lynn fanned her face again. "I get weak at the knees over the way he looks at you. Even when he says your name, his eyes go all soft and gooey, like melted chocolate."

Hope straightened and pushed away from the counter she'd been leaning on, her brows raised disbelievingly. "Whoa. Whoa, Patty Lynn. No." She said the word emphatically, shaking her head and crisscrossing her hands in front of her. "And hush," she added, dropping her voice to just above a whisper. "There are people in the waiting room."

"Oh, my goodness gracious sakes alive!" Patty Lynn exclaimed, pressing her palms to her cheeks. "Hope Goodacre — I mean Hope Willis. You have got to be kidding me," she said. "You really don't know? That man is head over heels in love with you!"

Hope brought a finger to her lips. "Shh! Be quiet, Patty Lynn. What if he comes back in and hears you?" She crossed her arms over her chest, her receptionist words hitting her like a mule kick to the ribs.

"You do not know what you're talking about," she muttered, but her voice shook with agitation.

"Lord, have mercy," Patty Lynn declared. "I have never met anyone so blind in all my life. I mean, for someone as smart as you are, Dr. Hope, you can sure be stupid when it comes to matters of the heart." Then her eyes grew wide, and she covered her mouth with one hand.

Hope could feel her blood drain from her face, so she was sure her receptionist could see it, too.

"Oh, Dr. Hope," Patty Lynn said in a small, apologetic voice. "I am so sorry. That was totally out of line. Me and my big mouth." She shook her head, clearly wishing she could take it back.

Hope closed her eyes, just for a moment, fighting back the sudden spring of tears that welled up behind her lids. When she opened them again, Patty Lynn was offering her a tissue, her own eyes glistening in sympathy. Hope took the proffered Kleenex, but she knew if she headed back to her office the way she wanted to, her friend would feel like crawling under her desk in misery.

"Please don't cry, Dr. Hope," Patty Lynn begged, reaching up to lay a hand on Hope's where it rested on the counter. "Then I'll cry, and my mascara will smear, and your patients will set to barking and howling and squealing in terror. And we can't have that, now, can we?"

Hope swallowed hard and shook her head. "No, we can't have that. And it's okay, Patty Lynn," she told her. "It's not like I haven't said the same thing to myself a hundred thousand times." She glanced over at the door again, just in time to see Levi's silver SUV driving across the parking lot. "He's leaving," she said, and shot her receptionist a bemused look. "He didn't say where he was going?"

"Who? Dr. Morgan?" Patty Lynn frowned. "He took your keys, remember? You told him he could wait at your place."

"No. Not him. Lee—Levi." For a moment, she'd been afraid she wouldn't be able to get his name out. She dabbed at her eyes quickly, then hurried out into the waiting room and toward the door. She made it outside just as Levi turned out of the parking lot. She waved frantically, trying to get his attention, but the man didn't stop.

Behind her, Patty Lynn stood on the top step, her arms wrapped around herself against the chill in the late afternoon air. "That's so strange," she mused. "He asked about coming back next week, but when I told him you were almost done, and that you really did want to see him today, he said he'd wait. He was going to get some coffee —" she broke off mid-sentence, then frowned as Hope approached. "Maybe he tried my coffee and didn't like it, and decided to go get a cup somewhere else." The look on her face told Hope that Patty Lynn wasn't keen on the notion of Levi not liking her coffee.

But that didn't sound like Levi, either. The man wasn't a snob of any kind, and she highly doubted he would be so rude as to turn his nose up at Patty Lynn's offer. Besides, the woman knew how to brew the black magic drink. "I highly doubt that, Patty Lynn. Your coffee is bomb." She shook her head, then turned to gaze down the now empty road. "Maybe Yvette called him and needed him for something," Hope said contemplatively.

For a moment, she considered calling him, but then decided against it, especially since he'd made no attempt, other than this aborted visit, to reach out to her in the last two weeks. "Why don't you give him a call. See if he wants to set up an appointment for next week. I'll take care of Mrs. Norman and her dog, then we can call it a day." She nodded toward her cottage on the far side of the clinic. "I'm taking Hunter out to dinner so we can catch up on old times," she said. "Got any suggestions for a place that isn't too loud to hear each other speak?"

Patty Lynn giggled. "Are you sure you want to talk? The Smokehouse Grill's house band plays every Friday night, and they know how to get folks out of their seats." She winked at Hope. "If that man

WHERE THERE IS HOPE

were my date, I wouldn't care what he had to say. I'd be hauling Mr. Perfect out on the dance floor and letting our bodies do the tal —"

Hope raised both her hands frantically, but had to bite back a laugh. "Stop it, Patty Lynn. You may be working with that man soon, and what you just said could be misconstrued as sexual harassment."

The receptionist rolled her Kohl-rimmed eyes. The mascara on the left side was, indeed, smeared just the tiniest bit. "I can't stand all this sexual harassment stuff. What happened to the good old days when we could just compliment someone on how sexy they were without being afraid of getting a pair of handcuffs slapped on your wrists and getting your backside hauled off to jail?" She shook her head, her hair frantically trying to keep up with the motion. "I have never had a man say something so offensive to me that I wanted to have him arrested. Sure, there were times when a comment was inappropriate or totally out of line, but people do stupid stuff, you know? I mean, take what I said to you! Are you going to have me arrested for harassing you about your love life? Because you know I didn't say what I said to hurt you." She paused in her tirade and reached out to rest her hand on Hope's shoulder. "You do know that, right? I was only saying what I thought you already knew. About Levi, I mean. That other stuff, well, that was completely out of line. Totally inappropriate, and I know it. But I did not intend to hurt you or offend you or harass you. It was just a poor choice of words on my part, something I'm prone to do."

Hope and Patty Lynn had had this conversation many times before. Hope understood where her receptionist was coming from, but it didn't change the rules. The workplace had to be safe for everyone, and not everyone was as receptive as Patty Lynn toward flirtatious compliments and cliché come-ons, the giving or receiving of them. "You did not offend me, my friend. And no, I am not going to have you arrested for harassment." She put an arm around the woman and gave her a quick squeeze. "I don't know what I'd do without you. You are the finest receptionist I could ever hope for, and you treat everyone like they were your best friend, even cantankerous patients like old Mr. Filbert and his mean, mangy cat."

"Oh, Mr. Filbert isn't such a bad nut." She snickered and winked at Hope. "See what I did there? Filbert? Nut?"

Hope chuckled, too, and rolled her eyes at her friend's silliness.

"He's just sad because his wife left him to fend for himself on this earth. That's hard on a man, especially an old one who's been married to the same woman for a thousand years. They get used to having someone looking out for them, feeding them, loving on them even when they don't deserve it, right? And then when that gets ripped away, they're stuck with the hard cold truth that the best part of them is gone." Patty Lynn squeezed Hope back. "Sometimes I think he comes in just so he can talk to somebody about his wife and her cat. Jan Filbert loved the god-awful creature."

Hope reached for the door and opened it for her receptionist to walk through ahead of her. "That's exactly what I'm talking about, Patty Lynn. You see right through people, even when the rest of us can't." She stepped up beside her as they crossed the waiting room, and bumped her with a hip. "Especially those of us who are, you know, blind." Then she turned to Mrs. Norman who'd been waiting so patiently. "Give me just a minute to grab your chart and get your room ready, and I'll be right with you," she said to the smiling woman.

Once they'd closed the door separating them from the waiting room, Patty Lynn paused, her face growing serious. "Dr. Hope, I am sorry for hurting you." When Hope started to wave her apology aside, Patty Lynn held up a hand to stop her. "Let me finish, please. I love my job, and I love you, so I hope that what you just said was true, because what I'm about to say could be taken the wrong way."

Hope stepped back to lean against the corridor wall, sliding her hands into the pockets on her pale blue scrub top. "I meant every word.

Go ahead."

"That man you were married to, he did you wrong. From the very beginning. At first, I couldn't figure out what you saw in him. But then I realized that you're the kind of person to take everyone at face value. You focus on the best in folks. You trust people. That's one of the things I love about you."

Hope nodded, not sure what to say, and not certain her voice would work even if she did.

Patty Lynn continued, not waiting for a response. "He told you what you needed to hear, and you trusted him."

"You're right about that," Hope said with a slow nod. "He knew how to play me, and I believed every word he said to me. He had me figured out from the very beginning."

Patty stepped forward and wrapped her hands around Hope's upper arms, squeezing gently. "What he did—what he's doing—is wrong. Pure evil. And the fact that you missed it, well, that doesn't mean you're stupid. And it doesn't mean you're blind, either. I was wrong about that part. Completely wrong."

Hope wanted to pull away. She wanted to tell her receptionist to get back to work and not talk about this anymore. "I know I can be pretty oblivious," she said instead.

But the woman wasn't finished. "You are not oblivious; don't say that. It means you are good, Dr. Hope. It means you're brave. You're not afraid to trust people, and that's the scariest dang thing in the world, trusting people. Because it's people who tear our hearts out, who throw them on the ground and stomp on them. It's people who hurt us, who embarrassed us, who mistreat us. And yet, you expect the best from everyone, including people who don't have a whole lot of good in them. That's what Doc Harper saw in you. That's why he chose you to take over his practice. Not because of how great you are with animals — and believe me, you're awesome. You're like the animal whisperer. But that's not it. He chose you because you look at the world with…well, with hope." She smiled sweetly. "Your parents named you well."

Hope pulled her hands from her pockets and wrapped her arms around her friend. "I love you, Patty Lynn. Thank you." She gave her an extra squeeze that made the woman grunt with surprise, making them both laugh. Then she pulled back and added, "I needed to hear that today."

"And I'm not wrong about Levi, either," Patty Lynn added as she circled the end of the counter and dropped into her chair. "Trust me on that." Then she winked at Hope and reached for her phone. "I think I'm going to give that boy a call right now. He needs to get his butcher butt back in here, yes, indeed. Now there is a real man for you; a guy who isn't afraid to be seen in public carrying a hot pink pet crate all tied up with ribbons, and cuddling a tiny fluffy kitten."

Hope just shook her head and headed down the hall to prepare an exam room for Mrs. Norman and her dog. She still had no clue where she would take Hunter Morgan to dinner that night.

CHAPTER TWELVE

WATCHING THAT MAN CROSS THE PARKING LOT TO HIS CAR, pull out an overnight bag, and head for Hope's cottage had been almost more than Levi could bear. But he'd sat in his vehicle until her cobalt blue front door closed behind him. Closed him inside.

Closed Levi out once again.

In the rearview mirror, he caught a glimpse of Hope just before he pulled out onto the street. She hurried out the clinic door and waved both hands in the air in his direction, but he didn't stop.

Part of him knew that it wasn't fair to jump to conclusions about the guy in her cottage at that very moment. Maybe he was just a friend from college. A family member from out of town. Surely there was some reasonable explanation for her familiarity with him. And wasn't this precisely how people let their assumptions turn them into idiots? He should at least give her the benefit of the doubt, right? Why not just ask her who the guy was? In fact, he should be upfront about his own feelings for her. He knew there was a connection between them. He knew it in his gut, in the marrow of his bones. He'd seen her eyes darken in response to him; he wasn't imagining it. What if she was waiting for him to make the first move?

But he couldn't get the conversation he'd overheard between Hope and Patty Lynn to stop playing over and over in his mind. I hope she chooses you. He's perfect in every way. I want him so bad. He's yours for the taking.

To make matters worse, he couldn't stop thinking about what Hope had said to him two weeks ago after he'd asked her to go with him to the Overman's barn dance. "I'm still married. Can we call it something besides a date? I'm just kind of old-fashioned that way."

Apparently, she was only old-fashioned that way with Levi, because Mr. Perfect and his duffel bag had looked like he was ready for an all-nighter with Dr. Hope.

Levi knew a brush-off when he heard one.

What was he supposed to do about the dance next month? Should he back out?

"No!" he exclaimed out loud, slamming his hand down on the steering wheel. "No. I have waited for years—years!—to take Hope Goodacre out, and no one—no one!—is going to keep it from happening this time." If Hope didn't want to go with him, she'd have to work up the courage to tell him so herself.

Levi somehow managed to be courteous through the evening meal with Nona and Yvette, but when his daughter asked what movie they should watch, he pulled her into a big bear hug and told her he wasn't really in the mood for a movie. "I'd like to go riding, instead, and I won't be able to ride Fiebre after the end of this month, not with her baby coming in a few months. Do you want to come with me?" he asked.

Yvette hesitated just long enough for him to notice, and his heart plummeted. Was he going to be rejected by yet another girl he loved?

"It's okay if you'd rather stay in with Nona, *pepita*. I can ride alone."

"It's not that I don't want to ride," she said, cupping his face in her little hands and gazing into his eyes with a concerned expression on her face. "It's that I think you're sad and it makes me sad. Are you sad, Daddy?"

He almost denied it, but then decided against it. He didn't want his daughter to ever feel like he was shutting her out. "I am a little sad today," he said with a nod. "And I think if I sit here, I'll just feel worse. I don't want to feel worse. I want to feel better, and riding Fiebre always makes me feel better."

Yvette frowned, her dark eyebrows drawing together as she considered his words. "I wish we could bring Coco," she murmured. "I want to ride, but I feel bad about leaving my kitty alone."

"I'll watch out for Coco," Nona said. "You two get out of here for a little ride."

Levi had picked up Yvette's horse in a trade for his services, and it had been one of the best deals he'd ever made. The gelding didn't stand much more than ten hands, it was patient and attentive to whatever rider was on his back, and especially responsive to Yvette's voice. He seemed to know that she was his human. On top of that, Fiebre actually liked Charlie; Levi's wild mustang mare was as alpha a horse as they got, and she was picky about who she spent time with. Her attitude made her a joy and thrill to work with, but Levi had learned the hard way that she didn't play well with other horses. Even breeding her could sometimes be a bit of a circus, but it was that same spirit that made her a champion.

They saddled up and headed out the back gate to the wooded area behind his house. He owned just under five acres, two of which he kept in pasture for the horses, the rest he left wooded for trail riding. With the time change a couple weeks ago, the sun wouldn't go down for another hour, so he led them across the near pasture to the woods.

Levi liked these evening rides with his daughter. They talked of mundane and seemingly trivial things, but it was a sweet time of connecting with Yvette with no one else around. She did most of the talking, relating to him about school and friends and some of the other activities she was involved in. This evening, her mind was consumed with the upcoming barn dance, and the new dress Nona was making for her. "I'm so glad you're taking Miss Hope, Daddy. She's a really nice lady and her hair is so long." As though the two traits had anything to do with each other. "I think she's sad, too, so maybe when you guys go to the dance together, you can figure out how to make each other happy again."

If only life were that simple. Levi let her ramble, knowing she'd eventually move on to another subject. He made agreeable noises at appropriate times, listening with one ear, so he didn't miss anything, but he couldn't seem to stop his mind from wandering back to Hope again and again. He was like Charlie that way; given his head, the gelding would instinctively veer toward home, and Levi's thoughts, when left untethered, instinctively veered back to Hope.

By the time they returned to the stable, Levi had made up his mind. He was finished waiting for Hope Goodacre. He would take her to the dance, treat her like the magnificent woman God created her to be, and at the end of the night, he would deliver her to her blue door and say goodnight...and goodbye.

That would be the end of things.

He had a few short weeks to get his heart to agree with his decision.

CHAPTER THIRTEEN

SATURDAY MORNING DAWNED COLD AND MISTY, and Hope bundled up against the chill before hurrying out to her Jeep. She had promised Faith she'd head out to Seven Virtues to check on her pregnant cows—she had several first-time heifers calving this season, and she wanted to make sure she knew what to expect. Hope had also promised to stop by Whispering Hills on her way to verify a few new pregnancies...and to try to catch Levi there with his mobile butchering unit.

But when she pulled up the long drive, she was met near the big ranch house by Cord on his black Morgan. He directed her to follow him up a dirt lane toward a far pasture. "I rounded the three up and closed them in one of the calving barns early this morning," Cord explained. "Thought it would be easier than trying to bring them down here to the chute or taking the portable unit out there for only three of them."

It would be easier on everyone, Hope agreed. Her and the cows. But it meant she probably wouldn't stumble upon Levi that morning.

Two of the three were, indeed, pregnant, and after a few minutes of comfortable conversation, Hope left the way she'd come, Cord staying behind to escort the cows back to their herd. Just as she rounded the last bend in the dirt lane where it joined up with the paved drive that circled the main group of buildings, she saw him. Or at least she saw his Durango. He was pulling onto the driveway some distance ahead of her. She had missed him entirely.

Cord had told her that Faith was already over at Seven Virtues getting ready for her, so Hope didn't dally, but headed down the drive from Whispering Hills, turned onto Carpenter Road, then took the next driveway—the Goodacre's was gravel, not paved—up toward the ranch house and the barns. Sure enough, Faith had about a dozen cows corralled in a holding pen, and between the two of them, they had the whole lot of them checked and given a clean bill of health. "Number 318B is carrying a pretty big baby, so she'll probably need help, and 572B is presenting breech, but there's still time for it to turn." It was likely they'd be pulling that one, too, especially if there was a twin in there. A case could be made for the sonogram, but Hope had every confidence that Faith would keep a close watch on her girls, and would be ready to assist if needed.

They headed to the house together to eat breakfast with Charity, Courage, Justice, Prudence, and Jasmine. Jed was at Carla's Cafe where several of the older generation met for Carla's strong coffee and all-you-can-eat pancake breakfast every Saturday morning, and Abby simply refused to get up before noon on Saturdays.

Back at the clinic, the waiting room bustled with the chaos of pets and owners needing attention of one kind or another, and Hope stayed busy right up until the first farm call came in right before noon; a calf that needed pulling. She was getting about one calving call a day as they were in the throes of spring calving season, and all things considered, it was one of her favorite tasks, helping a mama deliver her baby, but with only her making the farm runs, she was beginning to dread the phone ringing. But ring it did, and she had to move quickly.

Every exam room was filled, but the call was an emergency, and the farm was a good half an hour drive away. She could have used another vet at that moment, and for a few desperate moments, she seriously considered calling Hunter to see if he wanted to do some freelance work for her while he was in town. She apologized to her staff who would have to cover for her while she was out. Her licensed techs could do quite a lot without direct supervision, and she trusted Sarah more than she would most of the classmates she graduated with, but she still hated leaving them on their own. But she loaded up her supplies and headed out quickly, praying she'd make it there on time.

The drive gave her time to go over the evening she'd spent with Hunter. He was polite, chivalrous, and friendly to everyone, and he took the time to learn the name of their server—Laura—and to thank her for her hospitality. He'd refused to let Hope foot the bill for the evening, but she'd paid close attention to the kind of tip he left. Hope had a special place in her heart for wait staff; the twins were servers over at Schooners, and some of the stories they told made her greatly appreciate everyone in food service. She always made a point to tip extravagantly, and it pleased her to no end to see that Hunter had left far more than the suggested gratuity on the check.

Hope had driven him out to Seven Virtues after dinner to show him where she'd grown up. The sun was just setting as they pulled into the driveway, and Hunter had been deeply moved by the beauty laid out before him. His response had made Hope look at the place from a fresh perspective, and she, too, had experienced a sense of wonder in the old place.

Her dad and sisters were warm and welcoming to him, and when Charity invited them to stay for a slice of her mud puddle cake, Hope knew Hunter had won the family over. Justice, always a little too forthright for her own good, did corner Hope in the hallway outside the bathroom long enough to ask if Hope had any designs on the guy, but other than that, the evening had been comfortable and without pressure. The mud-puddle cake was even better than usual, and Charity beamed at the compliments, but refused to give away her secret ingredients.

Hunter turned down Jed's offer to spend the night at the ranch—Hope couldn't help wondering if her daddy thought Hunter planned to sleep at her little place, and she ducked her head to hide her smile at the thought. Hunter explained that he'd already paid for a room at the Plum Blossom Inn on the other side of town, and planned to be up early to spend some time wandering around town before he got on the road and headed back across the state line to Evansville, Indiana, where he was from. "I don't want to have to worry about waking anyone in the morning; I'm an early riser and a morning person, and I know that combination can be a little much to some people." He'd laughed good-naturedly at himself, then thanked Jed and the girls profusely for their kindness to him.

As they headed back to town shortly before ten o'clock, Hope had been confident she would make an offer to Hunter before the next weekend. The guy really was perfect in every way.

But the next morning, the person that kept coming to her mind was Carl Jorgenson, and it donned on her who he reminded her of: Doc Harper, but a younger version. He carried himself the same way, he had the same silly, but dry sense of humor, and he had a warm and friendly way with everyone who showed up on his doorstep.

The girls had talked exuberantly about Hunter around the breakfast table, but when Hope described Dr. Jorgenson to them and explained some of the reasons she thought he might be the better choice, they all agreed she had a dilemma on her hands. They'd really liked her handsome classmate—what was there not to like?—but they could see where Dr. Jorgenson might have the upper hand, especially because he had farm and ranch experience already.

But right at the end of the evening, Hope had gotten her first sign of a red flag with Hunter. Dr. Jorgenson requested at least a two-week lead time in order to give appropriate notice to the hospital where he worked. Hunter, on the other hand, initially told her he needed two weeks, but that his preference was thirty days. On the drive back to town, he'd amended that and said he really liked what he'd seen of her operation, and he could be available immediately if that's what she needed. "My contract states I'll give my clinic thirty days' notice, but if you need me now, I'll be here tomorrow." It was the one flaw she'd found. If he was willing to bail on his contract to get the job at Plumwood Hollow Animal Hospital, then why wouldn't he do the same to her if a better offer came along?

Sunday arrived, and other than shooting off an email to Josie Silverton thanking her for her time, and wishing her all the best in her future endeavors, Hope wasn't any closer to a decision about whom to hire. She had a pressing desire to ask Levi what he thought, but she didn't get a moment to even speak with him. Word had gotten around that she was seen out on a date on Friday night, and every time she tried to make her way to him, she was stopped by someone else wondering who the handsome guy was. She explained multiple times that she hadn't been on a date, that it was a business meeting only, and she had to repeatedly insist that she wasn't in the market for a new husband, a new boyfriend, or even a casual date. She considered asking Trudy to post something on the marquee, just to make things abundantly clear, but protesting too much would only give people more fodder for talk.

And she ended up missing Levi altogether; by the time she'd extricated herself from folks wanting to hear about her not-a-date, Levi was ushering his mother and daughter toward his SUV as though someone was in hot pursuit of them. She hoped he wasn't hurrying away from her; the thought completely deflated her.

Halfway through dinner, she got another emergency call, and Jed refused to let her go alone. It was nice having her father in the car with her, and she unloaded on him about the situation with the two vets. He didn't even hesitate when she asked him what he thought. "Sounds like this Dr. Jorgenson is your man. Invite him for a visit before you make him an offer, but I believe you're right to worry about young Hunter's commitment. He may be an exceptional animal doctor, and he is certainly the most gregarious young man I've met in some time, but he's the one who said he has no roots and is willing to go anywhere the job is. What's to keep him from telling the next person that?" They pulled off the main road and onto the long drive that led to the farm where a worried farmer awaited them. Right before they climbed out of the Jeep, Jed turned to her and said, "Trust your gut, Hope. You know what you want."

CHAPTER FOURTEEN

"DR. HOPE! WHO WAS YOUR HANDSOME date Friday night?" How many variations of that question had he heard after church on Sunday? Levi had finally ducked out of the building just to get away from the chatter centered around Hope. She hadn't looked thrilled to be talking about it, not like she'd been in the clinic on Friday afternoon, but that didn't really mean anything, did it?

Levi had been dreading the service, wondering the whole time he was getting ready if the guy would be sitting in the Goodacre pew beside Hope. When there was no sign of him, Levi had relaxed a little and had done his best to listen to Pastor Treadwell preach the gospel. He spoke on a chapter out of the New Testament letter to the Philippians, reminding folks of how the apostle Paul had encouraged his fellow believers to rejoice in the Lord, to not be anxious when things feel out of control because God is still on his throne, and to focus on the good and noble, the just and virtuous things in life because that's how peace is found. Levi needed to hear the words that morning. He needed to give the situation with Hope over to God and let the king on the throne figure out how to sort it all out. He'd actually started to feel a whole lot more at peace about things...until Pastor Treadwell prayed the benediction and folks practically launched themselves across pews and aisles to be the first to ask Hope for her news.

He didn't want to hear her answer, so he let Yvette lead him forcefully out the back door and over to the playground where they found Jasmine already on one swing and holding tight to another one by the chains. "Finally," she said. "I've been saving this one for you for hours. Will you push us, Mr. Mostacho?"

"Yes, Papa, push us super high!" Yvette begged as she settled into her own swing.

He gallantly did as they commanded, and before long, the girls were shrieking with delight. "Higher, please!" Jasmine cried out. "Higher!"

Levi laughed in spite of himself, glad the girls were enjoying themselves that morning, even if he was struggling to find good in the day. His daughter was indeed his greatest blessing. "Your mother will have my head if she sees how high I'm pushing you," he said, glancing over at the churchyard to see if Faith was around. Knowing her, though, she'd give him the go-ahead. Fearless Faith, folks called her, and she was raising her daughter to face life the same way.

"Off with your head!" Jasmine shouted as she pumped her legs to go even higher, her long hair swirling madly around her face every time she changed direction.

"Off with your head, Papa!" Yvette joined in, her braids flipping back and forth, too.

A few minutes later, Nona moved across the lawn toward them, and Levi stopped pushing. "Time to go, pepita," he told her. "Nona looks like she's ready."

"I am, *mija*," Nona said to her granddaughter. "I have a delicious chicken in the oven, and I don't want it to get dried out." She waved brusquely at them. "*¡Ándale.* Hurry up, you two. Let's go now."

All that week, Levi found himself warring with his own thoughts.

He was desperate for peace and anxious for answers, but the pastor had talked about how futile it was to spin in head trip circles the way Levi was doing. "Give your worries over to God, then don't take them back again. He knows what to do with your anxious thoughts. He knows how to bring order into chaos, and He offers peace even when things feel like they're out of control. Trust him," he kept saying. "Trust that he not only knows what's best for you, but he also doesn't want you to suffer needlessly with worry and anxiety and frustration."

"Yes, but—" Levi broke off without completing the sentence, even though he was just talking to himself. Yvette said those two words all the time, and he constantly asked her to rethink what she was going to say, because ultimately, she was initiating an argument with those words. And right now, so was he. Because really, he was talking to God.

Saturday afternoon, a trio of women swept into the butcher shop and spent a few minutes browsing his meat selection. Sonya Boulder was hosting a dinner party at her place on Sunday evening and wanted the biggest and best crown roast Levi had on hand. While he prepared the cut of meat, she and the women with her spoke in hushed tones not quite low enough that he couldn't hear what they were saying. It often amused him how people seemed to forget he was there, just on the other side of the counter. He'd grimaced through some terrible arguments, witnessed some borderline child abuse, and had heard variations of rumors about him being discussed by customers practically right in front of him. He'd learned to shut out all but the worst of it, but when the woman mentioned Dr. Hope, his ears perked up.

"That husband of hers is out of his league—or should I say in over his head this time around," Sonya was saying. "Not only is he dating another woman while he is still legally married to Dr. Hope, but it's Clyde Whitaker's daughter, Shelby, and her daddy isn't taking too kindly to her new beau being a married man. To make matters even more complicated, I just heard a rumor that she might be pregnant, and Clyde is insisting that Chet wrap up this divorce and marry his little girl before everyone finds out about the baby."

One of Sonya's friends let out a nasal giggle. "Too late for that." Her hair was as black as Levi's, but anyone could tell she wasn't born that way. "We all know already. What I want to know, and what Chet Willis should be asking, is if the little bun in the oven is actually his."

Levi glanced over at the women, but they were too caught up in their gossip to pay him any mind.

"No kidding," said the third woman, Linda Goodnight, another regular customer in his shop. "That girl has been on the arm of quite a few good-looking men over the last few years."

"At the same time, no less," Sonya said with a roll of her eyes. "And from what I've garnered, this isn't the first time she's had a pregnancy scare." She lifted her fingers to mime quotation marks as she said the last two words.

"So instead of wondering if the baby is his, he should be wondering if there is a baby at all," the black-haired woman stated.

Sonya nodded emphatically, then lowered her voice a little more so that Levi had to strain to hear what she said. "I've heard Shelby is the one who starts the pregnancy rumors."

Levi wanted to stop listening, but he was morbidly fascinated by the unfolding story.

"I've heard the same thing," Linda agreed, pressing a palm to her sternum in feigned shock. "One of my daughter's friends dated a Whitaker. From what I gather, Clyde has Shelby on a strict allowance while she's still his responsibility. She doesn't get access to her trust fund until she ties the knot, then Clyde will hand her over, along with a nice, fat bank account."

Black Hair let out another humorless snicker. "Daddy has to buy his baby a husband, it seems. Is she really that awful?"

"So I've heard," Linda said. "I mean, when a woman has to use a fake pregnancy to get a marriage proposal?" She left the thought unfinished.

"And the fact that she's set her sights on Chet Willis, him not being from around these parts—"

"Right. He doesn't know about her track record with men."

"Or false alarms," Black Hair chortled.

"Well, I hope she snags that awful man," Sonya said, straightening her shoulders and glancing over at the meat counter. Fortunately, Levi had his gaze averted, and she continued. "They deserve each other. I don't know what Dr. Hope saw in him, but she's a good girl who got taken by a bad apple, and I think turnaround is fair play where he's concerned."

"I don't know what we'd do without our sweet veterinarian," Linda said, nodding emphatically in agreement. "I never believed anyone could fill Doc Harper's shoes, but that girl is practically an angel, and Chet Willis doesn't deserve to kiss the ground she walks on."

"Amen, sister," Black Hair murmured. And with those words, all three of the gossips basically redeemed themselves in Levi's opinion.

They fell silent, and Levi thought they were finished. He wrapped the roast carefully, placed it in a cardboard box, then taped to the top of the box a little pamphlet with instructions and suggestions for preparing and serving the roast.

"Speaking of Dr. Hope," Black Hair said, tapping a finger against her chin, a sly look in her eye. "Did you hear she's hired a new veterinarian? He starts next month."

Levi kept his head down, feeling just the slightest bit sick to his stomach for eavesdropping so blatantly. This was news to him. The last he'd heard was that the divorce was keeping her from hiring. Well, good for her. Maybe she'd acted on his advice.

"I did," Sonya said with a hint of elevated self-worth in her voice.

"I actually met the fellow she's hiring. He's a lovely man," she added. "He came to town to interview with Hope and her staff, to check the place out, and get a feel for things. Hope introduced us at Schooners the other night; Jim and I were having dinner, and they came in and sat at the table next to us."

Levi stiffened, his breath catching as all the puzzle pieces fell into place to form an entirely different picture of what he'd seen in her clinic last week. I hope she chooses you. He's perfect in every way. I want him so bad. Hope and Patty Lynn weren't gushing over a new man—or an old heartthrob—in Hope's life.

They were gushing over much-needed and long overdue help. A new vet.

"I'll be right back, ladies," Levi managed to say before he pushed through the swinging steel door into the workroom where he did the majority of his butchering. He dropped to a stool, shaking his head at what an idiot he'd made of himself. Storming out of the clinic like an angry little boy. Assuming the worst of Hope, jumping to conclusions about a romantic relationship between her and the man who'd been there to 'check the place out' as Sonya put it, and avoiding her at every turn because one, he didn't want her to know his true feelings for her, and two, he was hurt because she disregarded his feelings for her.

Feelings she didn't know existed because he hadn't dared to tell her about them.

And now, he was giving up on her based on his completely unfounded assumptions.

Giving up on her.

Giving up.

Levi Valiente giving up? He let his gaze roam around the large workroom, the place he hadn't given up on, even when the odds were stacked against him. He wouldn't give up on this shop, but he'd give up on Hope? The woman he claimed to love?

What a fool. "You're a fool, Levi Valiente." He let out a dry, humorless laugh. "Levi Cobarde," he muttered. He was not valiant, as his name claimed he was. He was nothing but a coward, waiting, and waiting, and waiting still more for just the perfect time. For years! He'd been afraid of being hurt. He'd been afraid of hurting her. He'd been afraid to act too quickly, and fearful of scaring her off. He'd been afraid of starting rumors, and he'd been afraid of nameless, faceless ghosts from Hope's past. And most recently, he'd been afraid of a guy he'd jealously dubbed Mr. Perfect, based on an unfounded assumption he'd conjured out of thin air.

"Enough," he snarled. "No more fear. Claim your birthright, *mijo*. *Se Valiente*," he commanded himself. Be brave. "*Soy valiente*." I am brave. He grinned when Jennifer Lopez's song "Brave" started playing in his head. Yvette loved the gorgeous Latino performer, and Levi had heard the song enough times to know that it really did apply today.

Because things were about to change. How did that line go? Thanks to the power of love, right?

Granted, the new vet was a rather handsome and confident new vet, he grudgingly conceded, but then, Levi wasn't Plumwood Hollow's most eligible bachelor for no reason. Sure, his thick mustache hid a nasty scar—a memento he'd given himself when he'd carelessly wielded one of his father's blades without realizing how dangerously sharp they were—but he wasn't that hard to look at. He had his own successful business, a home of his own with a little bit of property, one fantastic daughter, and a mother who didn't meddle too much. He could sit a fine horse, he had a fine horse to sit on, and the folks in these parts loved him almost as much as they loved their Dr. Hope. If anyone had a chance with her, Levi decided, it was him. What had she called him?

Levi Valiente. The Cowboy Butcher of Plumwood Hollow. Champion of True Love, Father of the Year, Defender of Lost Baby

Animals, and Rescuer of Hungry, Weary Vets.

"That's me," he said, a cocky grin lifting the corners of his mouth. "Levi Valiente, the Brave."

He pushed up from the stool and practically marched back into the front of the shop. All three women looked up as he scooped up the box and set it on the counter. "I'm sorry to keep you ladies waiting."

The moment the women left Levi's shop, he picked up the phone and dialed the number for Trilby's Blossoms and Books.

CHAPTER FIFTEEN

ANOTHER WEEK WHIZZED BY AT BREAKNECK SPEED, but that was how the spring birthing season always went, and Hope was determined to stay positive. Carl Jorgenson had come early in the week and had taken the initiative to stay a few days so he could shadow Hope on the job. He'd spent his downtime getting to know her staff, many of her patients and their owners, and several folks in town. He'd won over everyone, even though Patty Lynn had bemoaned the loss of the delicious Hunter Morgan. But only for a moment or two. Hope got a funny feeling that her receptionist, who was actually closer to Dr. Jorgenson's age than Hunter's, didn't mind the switch one bit.

The moment Hope officially offered Carl the job, she'd been overwhelmed by a sense of relief. Especially when he accepted. He would begin work in Plumwood Hollow the week of the Whispering Hills Barn Dance, which would be perfect timing for him to be publicly introduced to the folks in the hollow.

Dreading the conversation she needed to have with Hunter, Hope had called him the night Carl accepted her offer. But to her surprise and relief, it had turned into even more validation. Hunter had two other offers waiting for him, and he'd been dreading having to call her to bow out after being so enthusiastic during his visit. They'd talked for over an hour, catching up on each others' lives since school. She'd admitted to her failed marriage, but Hunter, ever the gentleman, had offered his sympathies, then moved on to safer subjects. He'd promised to visit again, and she'd told him he'd always be welcome, and they hung up with the silent understanding that it would probably never happen.

Hope had required Doug's assistance on two more farm calls early in the week, after which she'd sent the young family a gift basket with a floppy stuffed animal—a black and white calf, of course—and a family pack of tickets to a water park in Bowling Green to thank him for his timely help. As far as she was concerned, he'd gone above and beyond what he owed her, but he'd insisted she get her full three weeks out of him. She hoped the gift wasn't too extravagant, that the family would have the means and the time to get over to the city and enjoy a day away later that summer.

On Thursday morning, a bouquet of hothouse lilies was left on her doorstep with a note that simply said, "I miss you." Hope threw them in the trash on her way to the clinic.

On Friday, a single red rose tied to a box of chocolate-covered peanuts was dropped off by one of the high school kids at noon. Once again, the little note card read, "I miss you." There was no signature. Hope let her staff share the candy, but the rose and the accompanying card went outside into the dumpster to join the bouquet from the day before.

"I know you don't listen to gossip as much as I do, Dr. Hope," Patty Lynn said, a frown furrowing her kind face as she popped another peanut into her mouth. They were gathered in the tiny kitchenette next door to Hope's office, having closed the clinic for their lunch break.

"That's the understatement of the year," Sarah retorted from where she stood at the sink washing out her mug. She was right. Hope wasn't above listening in on conversations enough to be 'in the know' about things, but she didn't have time to sit around discoursing over who was dating whom and wearing what and coming and going to or from where the way Patty Lynn did. Her receptionist lived for gossip in all shapes and sizes, from local rumors to celebrity tabloids. But because she kept her ear to the ground for all the latest nuggets, the clinic was well-informed about everything important going on in Plumwood Hollow.

Patty Lynn stuck her tongue out at Sarah. "Anyway, I thought you might want to hear the latest from me."

Something about the way she said it made Hope sit up a little straighter. She shot Patty Lynn a questioning look, but said nothing.

Sarah slid into a chair next to Hope and nudged her gently with her shoulder. The supportive gesture made her even more worried.

"Word is that Chet's little trollop is pregnant and that her daddy is pushing him to wrap up this divorce and marry her. Make it legal."

Hope closed her eyes and took a long, slow inhale, then let it out even slower. Finally, she lifted her gaze to the woman across the table from her. "You know," she began quietly. "It's been almost a year since he moved out. You'd think news like this wouldn't bother me, right?"

Sarah leaned in again. "You'd be an ice queen if it didn't bother you, and that's pretty much impossible," she said.

Hope smiled sadly. "Thank you." She picked up a paper napkin and began shredding it into thin strips, piling the pieces up like pasta in front of her. "Chet didn't want kids."

"Not ever?" Patty Lynn asked, her eyes wide. "What about you?"

"Not ever," Hope said with a nod. "Before we were married, I used to talk about how wonderful it was growing up in a big household, and how I was looking forward to having our own children running around our house making too much noise. You know, comments like that." She pressed her lips together as she thought back to all the conversations they'd had about children. "He says I never came right out and asked him if he wanted kids, and I don't ever recall him coming right out and saying he didn't want kids. Not until after we were married."

"Oh, Dr. Hope," Sarah said softly. Her tech was the mother of two darling little boys whom she talked about every chance she got. "What a horrible man."

Hope shrugged. "I should have asked. I should have made the effort to find out how he really felt, and not just assume we were on the same page."

"Stop it," Sarah said with gentle admonishment. "It wasn't like he misunderstood what you wanted. He purposely deceived you, Doc."

Hope snorted softly and shook her head. "I remember one time I told him I wanted at least three or four kids. He laughed and told me he'd buy me my own pet goat, and then I'd have all the kids I wanted."

Sarah and Patty Lynn looked aghast at her. She nodded slowly.

"Not kidding," she said, then smiled wryly at the unintended pun. "He meant it. He told me so in no uncertain terms about six months after the wedding. He said he'd have a goat over a child any day, because you could raise a goat and then sell it, and you wouldn't have to worry about it showing up on your doorstep when it was full grown, asking for handouts."

"Horrible doesn't begin to describe him," Patty Lynn declared in a shaking voice, her expression a combination of disgust, horror, and bewilderment.

"So needless to say, hearing that he's going to father a child with someone else is a little like taking a punch to the gut." Hope snorted derisively. "Actually, I've never been punched in the gut, but I have been kicked in the ribs by an angry Billy goat. This feels a little worse than that, I can honestly say."

Patty Lynn stood, picked up the box of remaining peanuts, and carried them over to the trash can. "These are making me sick," she said, then she circled the table and wrapped her arms around Hope. When she pulled back, her eyes were bright with tears. "You wouldn't want that animal to be the father of your children, Dr. Hope. Anyone can be a sperm donor, but a father, a daddy? It takes a superhero to be a good dad. Chet is more like a super villain, as far as I'm concerned."

"Amen to that," Sarah said, lifting her hand to high-five the other woman. "I should know. I've got a superhero in my house." Sarah was crazy in love with her husband, and even more so since they'd had children. She was always talking about what a fantastic father he was.

Chet, on the other hand, would have been the worst father imaginable, and the sudden wash of relief made the news about him a little easier to bear. Hope wiped her eyes and nodded. "You're right. Thank you. I hadn't thought of it that way."

Patty Lynn returned to her seat, and they sat in silent camaraderie for a few moments. But just when Hope thought her legs might support her enough to get up and go back to work, her receptionist spoke again. "What about Levi?" she asked.

Sarah said nothing, but turned toward Hope, one eyebrow lifted.

"What about him?" Hope replied.

"He's a great father. We've all watched him with his darling daughter. And did you see him with that hot pink cat carrier the other day? Only a manly man could pull that off without any shame."

"Yes, and did you see him not come back for his cat's wellness check? Ever?" Hope asked, this new topic of conversation not any less painful than the first.

"Have you talked to him about that?" Patty Lynn asked her. "You said you were going to when he didn't answer my call."

Hope shook her head. She'd had every intention of it, but in the last few weeks, she and Levi had barely crossed paths, no less had a moment or two to talk. The loss of his friendship—or what felt like it—weighed on her like a bag of rocks around her neck. She'd been so vulnerable that night when she acknowledged to him how badly she'd messed up with Chet when she'd admitted her feelings for Levi. Granted, she had kept his identity vague, not wanting to put him on the spot, but she had believed him when he promised he wouldn't judge her, that he understood what she was going through. Yet he'd started avoiding her immediately after that, going out of his way to be anywhere but where Hope was. It hadn't escaped her attention last Sunday after church the way he'd glared at her, then all but fled the building. She'd seen him over at the swing set pushing Yvette, looking about as antisocial as he could get, until Nona rounded them up and they left without so much as a goodbye.

No, she hadn't spoken with him about the day he walked out of her clinic without letting her see his cat. She hadn't spoken to him about much she'd enjoyed the evening she'd spent at his house. She hadn't spoken to him about the dance they were supposed to be attending together in less than two weeks.

"He asked me to go to my sister's barn dance," she said out loud. "But that was a couple weeks ago. We haven't spoken since. He's kind of been avoiding me, in fact."

"Wait. What?" Patty Lynn sat forward, slapping both hands down on the table hard enough that Hope jumped. "You said yes, didn't you? Please tell me you said yes." She cocked her head and glared at Hope, her eyes narrowed.

Hope actually laughed—the receptionist looked a little like a colorful parrot with her head angled to the side, her black-ringed eyes staring unblinkingly at her. "I said yes, but you missed the part where I said we haven't talked since. I have no idea if he's still up for it. His daughter and my niece practically forced him to ask me," she said.

"Yes, well Jenny Stuben is practically forcing him to ask her, too—believe me, I've seen her in action, and in church, no less—but he didn't invite her. What did I tell you?" Patty Lynn turned to Sarah. "What did I tell her? Levi Valiente has the hots for you."

"He pretty much always has." Sarah let the casual comment fall out of her mouth as though it meant absolutely nothing.

Hope turned in her seat to stare at her tech. "Excuse me?"

"You're excused?" Sarah shot back, mimicking Hope's challenging tone. "You're also not going to find a better man than Levi. My husband thinks the world of him. Says he's the ultimate man's man." Sarah nudged her with her shoulder again. "Superhero material, that's what I think."

"He is, isn't he?" Patty Lynn murmured appreciatively. "I mean, come on, Dr. Hope. A cowboy butcher who loves his baby girl? And have you seen him ride that horse? Of course, you have. And that mustache? He reminds me of the old Louis L'Amour movies with Tom Selleck and Sam Elliott, or that Tombstone movie with all those guys and their epic mustaches." She pressed both hands to her chest and sighed dramatically. "Oh, I loved that movie."

"What's the plot?" Sarah asked, making Hope smile. The two women constantly poked at each other, but somehow, the relationship worked.

"I don't know," Patty Lynn shot right back at her. "Who cares? It's just fun to watch. Oh! And that Magnificent 7 movie!" The woman was on a role. "When Chris Pratt died, I ugly cried."

"Thanks for spoiling the movie for me." Sarah didn't miss a beat. "Guess I don't have to watch it now."

Patty Lynn just clicked her tongue in admonishment. "It's not my fault if you haven't seen it yet. It's not a new movie, girlfriend."

"I've seen it, and just so you know, Chris Pratt didn't die," Sarah said with a chuckle. "His character did. Chris is alive and well on a farm somewhere, raising his own animals for meat like a good old country boy."

"I love him," Patty Lynn said with a dreamy sigh. "You could marry him, Dr. Hope," she suggested.

"I hear he loves God and children and farm life," Sarah added. "Sounds like a match made in heaven."

Hope laughed out loud, feeling much better than she had only a few minutes ago. The antics of her beloved staff never failed to raise her spirits, and today was no different. "And on that note," she said, pushing to her feet. "I think I'll go unlock the door. Surely, there are patients waiting to be seen."

"She can't marry him, Sarah. Our poor cowboy butcher would die of a broken heart, and then where would we be?"

"You guys are too much," Hope said, putting an arm around Sarah when her tech stood up, too. "And I love you both. Thanks for being good friends to me. I've said it before, and I'll say it again; I don't know how I'd survive without you."

"All kidding aside," Sarah said, giving Hope a quick side hug in return before she stepped back and scooted her chair in. "I've been thinking about this situation with Chet and the Whitaker girl. Be careful. If what you say is still true, that he doesn't want children?"

Hope gathered up the pieces of her shredded napkin, not liking the sudden seriousness of her tone. Patty Lynn stilled, too, apparently sensing the gravity in Sarah's tone.

"If he isn't happy about this pregnancy, he may try to get back into your good graces to get out of having to follow through with that girl. He is still married to you, so it's not like he wouldn't have a really good excuse not to marry her if he didn't want to."

"Oh my gosh, Dr. Hope!" Patty Lynn exclaimed in a hushed voice. "That's got to be what this is all about." She waved at the trash can. "Didn't you say he left you flowers yesterday morning, too?"

"He also called late one night last week, telling me he missed me and wanted to get together to talk." If it were anyone but Chet, Sarah's suggestion would have been too far-fetched to believe. "I told him that unless he wanted to drop his claim on this clinic, he wasn't to call me anymore."

"I think he called here asking for you, too," Patty Lynn said, her eyes narrowed. "I thought I recognized his voice, but I couldn't place it. You were out on a call, and he wouldn't leave a message. That was...um...Thursday afternoon, I think." She nodded slowly. "Yeah. Thursday. I remember because it was the same day we had that boxer go crazy in the waiting room. Remember that?" she asked Sarah.

"How could I forget?" the tech said, rolling her eyes. "I had to clean up after him."

"I just thought of something." Hope's mind was spinning a mile a minute. "I found a bottle of black cherry cordial in my car the other day. I never lock my car—who does around here?—and I didn't think anything of it. I just assumed it was from a patient because there was no card or note with it, but now I'm pretty sure it was from him. Someone gifted us a bottle of the stuff for our wedding, and we took it on our honeymoon. He loved it." She grimaced at the memory. Chet had started drinking it as soon as they arrived at their hotel room, and by the time they went to bed, he was sloppy drunk—there was no other term for it—and she'd been scared and unsure of herself already. It had been a less-than-stellar experience for both of them. Chet had apologized in the morning, and he'd been lovely to her the rest of their short time away, but she hadn't thought twice about emptying the bottle from her car down the drain. She'd never drink the stuff again in her life.

"That's breaking and entering," Sarah said. "Doesn't matter if your car was locked or not. If he accessed the inside of your car without your permission, he's breaking the law."

Hope nodded slowly. It was all just the tiniest bit scary, now that she really thought about it. But she made a dismissive sound in the back of her throat. He wasn't dangerous...was he?

"So he's not calling you," Patty Lynn concluded, crossing her arms dramatically. "He's stalking you instead. He's dropping stuff off on your doorstep without your knowledge. He's getting into your car to leave you nasty wine that has a nastier memory attached to it. And he's writing you anonymous and slightly ominous notes, and hand delivering them to your home and your place of work. Those things might be fine and dandy if his attention was something you wanted, but you made it clear that you didn't. This guy is out of line, Dr. Hope. Even I know that, and I don't agree with half of what people call harassment these days. Downright creepy."

"I think you need to let the cops know." Sarah spoke with great solemnity. "This isn't the kind of thing to take lightly. Patty Lynn is right; he's creepy, and I think he sounds a little desperate, and desperate is only a hair away from dangerous."

"At least tell Levi," Patty Lynn suggested. "Maybe he can stand around in front of the clinic sharpening his knives for a couple of days."

"A butcher sharpening his knives in front of an animal hospital?" Sarah said, a droll expression on her face. "That would go over well with all our animal patients and their owners, especially the farmers and ranchers."

Hope giggled at the thought, then Patty Lynn joined in, and finally, Sarah laughed, too, but it was obvious they were all a little unsettled after their conversation.

"I'm going back to work," Sarah said. "I need to leave in an hour if you want me to be on call tomorrow. Is your dad coming in this afternoon?"

"He is."

"Please tell him what's going on." Sarah wasn't going to let this go. "I mean it. I don't like this."

Hope promised she would talk to her father about it, and if he thought she needed to involve the police, she would.

Jed agreed with Sarah whole-heartedly and made Hope file a complaint without delay. Then he suggested she write everything down and have her lawyer contact Chet's lawyer. "You know," Jed said as he was putting on his jacket at the end of the afternoon. He made it sound almost like an afterthought. "I still have his number, and by law, he is still my son-in-law. I think I'll give that boy of mine a call."

Saturday afternoon, just before closing, Hope was at her desk reading over a patient's chart while she waited for Sarah, who had come in to help with an emergency surgery. She was down the hall prepping the dog at that moment. There was a knock on her office door, and Megan, a high school student who worked at Trilby's Blossoms and Books, stepped into the room.

"Hey, Dr. Hope. I have a delivery for you." The girl held out a beautifully gift-wrapped box.

Hope hesitated, her gaze darting from the box to Megan and back again. She wasn't pleased to see it, and the girl caught on quickly. "Who is it from?" Hope asked.

With a worried frown, Megan turned the package around so she could read the card. "I'm not sure," she hedged. "The card is sealed inside an envelope. It just has your name on it."

Hope suddenly realized how oddly she was behaving. "I'm sorry, Megan. I'm a little distracted right now. I have a dog in a bad way down the hall—poor thing swallowed a chicken bone that needs to come out, and my mind is already in surgery." She pulled open a desk drawer where she kept a little mad money, tipped the girl, and took the gift from her. "Thank you."

She would call Trilby if the card wasn't signed.

But it was. And it wasn't from Chet.

In fact, the moment she peeled back the wrapping paper, she knew without a doubt that it wasn't from her soon to be ex-husband. He would never have given her such a thoughtful gift.

CHAPTER SIXTEEN

LEVI HAD SEEN THE BOOK AT TRILBY'S a few weeks earlier and had been fascinated by it. It had taken him several minutes of perusing the pages before he realized what he was looking at. The coffee table book wasn't ostentatious by any means, but it was a sturdy hard-covered tome with a colorful dust jacket. On the front of the book was a photo of a cobalt blue door, and although it wasn't Hope's cottage in the image, the door was identical to hers, right down to the heavily-scrolled brass plate behind the round knob and the brass ring door knocker. It was the oddest thing to see it out of the context he was accustomed to, but there it was. The door must have originated on the building in the picture, and then been purchased somewhere by someone who wanted it for the little house behind the clinic. There had to be a story there, and he was sure Hope would be at least as fascinated by the discovery as he was.

He'd returned the book to the shelf with the intention of bringing her into the bookstore one day so he could surprise her with it in person. Then, if all went well, he'd purchase the book and gift it to her to commemorate the moment.

It was the first thing he thought of when he made the decision to stop waiting, to be brave, and to tell Hope how he felt about her. It was a unique gift, and one she'd really appreciate. She loved her blue door; she'd told him so on several occasions. He didn't want to just send her flowers and chocolates; those things were very romantic and sweet... and completely cliché. Hope, however, was anything but cliché, and he wanted her to know that he knew that. He wanted her to know that he thought about her when she wasn't around, that he saw her everywhere he went, and not just in photos on book covers. He saw Hope in branches laden with the bright redbud blossoms in spring, in the long lashes of newborn calves, and in freshly-mowed fields dotted with huge, round hay bales. He saw her in the way his daughter's eyes lit up as she played with Coco, and in the flickering spark of fireflies at twilight.

He'd handwritten the note himself; he'd called Trilby to make sure she still had the book, then headed to her store as soon as he had the chance. He really needed to hire some help himself, so that short runs like this didn't require him closing up shop while he was gone.

I would recognize the door to your home anywhere. I'm learning to recognize the door to your heart, as well, because one is just as beautiful and true blue as the other.

He signed his name with brave, bold strokes of his pen.

He returned to his shop feeling like the weight of the world was lifted from his shoulders. "Maybe it's the wait that's lifted," he said aloud with a little chuckle at his own pun. Joke or not, he was done waiting, and it felt great. Liberating. Exhilarating.

He spent the rest of the afternoon with a self-satisfied grin on his face that had more than one customer looking at him awry. He didn't care. He had a plan. It wasn't much of one, but he wasn't to wait until his plan was perfect. It started today.

Trilby promised to have his gift delivered at 4:30 in the afternoon. He would make his appearance at 5:30, a half an hour after closing to give Hope time to finish up with any last patients, or wrap up her paperwork before she headed over to her cottage. He wanted to catch her before she had time to make dinner plans, because he already had dinner plans in mind for both of them. For all of them.

She was still married, as she'd pointed out, and he would respect the law of it. But he wasn't going to hide behind it.

His mother was even now putting together a pan of chicken enchiladas with a mild green sauce, and seasoned rice and beans to go with the chicken *posole*—a soup that went with everything—she'd been slow-cooking all day. They would have a feast as a family. Then he would take her out for a moonlit walk and tell her what he should have told her years—years!—ago. That he loved her.

He would lay his heart at her feet, and let her decide what to do with it.

Trilby shot him a text at 4:45 p.m. letting him know the book had been delivered into Hope's hands.

At 5:10 p.m., Levi locked the butcher shop door and slid behind the wheel of his Durango.

At 5:25 p.m., he parked his SUV in front of the clinic, circled around to the back employee entrance, and tried the door. It was locked as he'd suspected it would be.

At 5:30 p.m., he crossed the back lot to the front door of Hope's little cottage and lifted the round brass knocker, once, twice, and then a third time.

At 5:31 p.m., the blue door opened, and Chet Willis greeted him with a look of unfiltered disdain. "What are you doing here, Mr. Butcher?"

"I'm going to ask you the same question, Mr. Willis." Levi had very good reason to believe that the man before him, his shirt unbuttoned to the middle of his chest, his shoes kicked off, and his hair rumpled like he'd been napping on the couch, did not have permission to be standing in the open blue door of Hope Goodacre's home. Levi straightened his shoulders and crossed his arms over his chest, a move that made him look even broader than he already was. "What are you doing here?"

"This is my home," Chet retorted, crossing his own arms and spreading his feet in a defiant stance. He was only a couple inches shorter than Levi, but there was a good fifty-pound weight difference between them. Levi flexed his crossed arms, knowing the tight Henley shirt he wore hid nothing, and he was gratified to see the thinner man's eyes flicker briefly in cautious awareness of Levi's superior size and strength. He didn't need to know that Levi would never hit the man unless seriously provoked, and there wasn't a whole lot Chet could do to Levi that he would consider provocation.

"I'd like to speak to Hope," Levi said, his biceps twitching ominously.

"She's not home yet," Chet began. "And don't come onto my property and start making demands."

Levi almost laughed at Chet's show of false bravado, but instead of acknowledging the smaller man's challenge, he said "Here's what I think. I think you're not supposed to be here. I think you showed up unannounced and without Hope's invitation or permission. And I think—no, I know—that in this part of the world, what you have done by going inside Hope's home without said invitation or permission, is called breaking and entering. If you've eaten any of her food, if you've poured yourself a glass of the tap water that she's paid for? If you've so much as wiped your backside with a piece of her toilet paper, then you, sir, could also be found guilty of robbery." He had no clue if that was true or not, but it sounded good. He reached into his back pocket and pulled out his phone. "Let's call her, shall we?"

Chet slammed the beautiful true-blue door in Levi's face. But not before Levi saw the look of panic in the man's eyes.

Levi didn't call Hope. He hit 9-1-1 and explained the situation to Kelly Thompson, the dispatcher, who connected Levi to Officer Bobby Slater. Bobby informed him that Hope had filed a complaint against Chet only yesterday.

"We're a few minutes away," he told Levi. They were longtime friends and Bobby's daughter, Sharon, was in Yvette's class at school. "Think you can keep him inside long enough for us to get there? If so, we can take him in for actual criminal behavior."

"I'll do my best." If Levi had to camp out on the doorstep to keep the man inside, he would. If Chet got arrested, especially if the courts could be convinced that he was a threat to Hope's safety, then the divorce might get pushed through a lot faster. He got off the phone and made his way to the side of the little house where he could keep both the front and back doors in his line of vision. The clinic was behind him, so he'd be able to intercept Hope on her way over.

Five minutes later, two cop cars pulled into the parking lot, one with lights flashing, but no sirens. Bobby got out of the vehicle and approached Levi, while the other officer circled around the house to the back door. "Hey, Levi," Bobby greeted him with a hearty handshake. "Dr. Hope around?"

"I think she's still next door at the clinic. Her jeep is here, and that's her tech's car," he said, pointing to the row of parking spaces labeled 'Employee Parking.' "The place is locked up, and I knocked, but no one answered. Could be running a vacuum cleaner or performing surgery, for all I know," he added with a grin.

"Why don't you go see if you can rouse the good doctor, and we'll take care of this intruder." Bobby said the word with dry emphasis. "I think it's time the city slicker get a lesson in what we folks in the hollow consider good manners."

"Sounds good to me," Levi said, still grinning. "Give me the word, and I'll bring my blades."

Bobby laughed out loud, but shook his head. "You go on and tend to your woman, Levi. We've got this."

It wasn't until he'd taken a few steps toward the clinic that Levi realized what his friend had said. Your woman. Was he so obvious?

Just as he lifted his hand to knock on the employee door, it opened, and Sarah Rathbone stared out at him, her eyes wide as she took in the scene unfolding in the parking lot. "Wow. What's all this about?" she asked.

"Hope around?' Levi wanted to push her out of the way and go after Hope himself, but he hooked his thumbs over his belt and said, "Chet Willis is hanging out at her place, so I invited a few of my buddies over to have a word with him. Is Dr. Hope in there?" he asked again, dipping his head toward the corridor behind Sarah. "She might want to get in on this."

"Oh, my gosh. Are you serious?" Sarah responded, clearly aghast. "He's in her house right now?" Usually so calm, it surprised Levi to see Sarah this worked up. "I knew something like this was going to happen. That guy is a freak."

"Yeah." Levi nodded. "I need to speak to—"

"Hey, Levi. What's going on?" Hope came bustling down the hall from a room with a placard that read Surgery. She was drying her hands on a towel as she hurried toward him, and she still wore a mask looped around her ears, although she'd pulled it down under her chin.

"Chet is in your house as we speak," Sarah declared before Levi could say a word.

"He's what? He's here? At my house?" Hope said, looking aghast at Levi, then stepping forward to push past him.

"Wait," he commanded, grabbing her gently by the arm and pulling her to a stop. "Hang on, Hope. The police are handling things over there."

Hope swallowed hard, and her eyes grew wider still. "The police?"

"She filed a report against him yesterday," Sarah ground out as she crossed her arms and glared at Hope's cottage. "That man has some nerve."

"I know. That's why they're here."

"Did you call them?" Hope asked him. Her voice was trembling just the slightest bit, and Levi studied her for any signs of full-on panic.

"I did. I came to see you, and when I found the clinic doors locked, I thought you might have made it home on time for once, so I headed over there to check. Chet met me at the front door as though there was nothing out of the ordinary going on."

"How—how did you know?" Hope stammered out. "I mean, how did you know I didn't want him there?"

Levi paused before answering and considered his words carefully. He'd given Hope no reason to trust him. In the last few weeks, in fact, he'd done just opposite. She'd asked him not to judge her and told him how important it was that she didn't lose his friendship, then he'd gone and all but abandoned her. A mouthful of placating words wasn't enough; he had to make each one count. "The other night?" he began. "I listened, Hope. I heard what you said about him, about yourself, and I heard the things you didn't, or couldn't say." He tapped his chest over his heart. "I listened with my heart because I wanted to know what was going on in yours."

Behind her, Sarah let out a whispered, "Wow."

Levi kept talking, his eyes never leaving Hope's. "When he opened your blue door, I didn't doubt what you'd said to me that night. Not even for a moment. I trusted you because you are a good judge of character, even when people fail you."

Suddenly, Sarah gasped and grabbed Hope by the shoulder. "Oh, my gosh. If you'd gone home right after work? If you hadn't had that emergency surgery?"

"I know," Hope murmured. "I was thinking the same thing."

"I wouldn't have come in at all, if not for that surgery," Sarah added.

"I know. I would have been a—alone." Hope's voice broke, and suddenly, there were tears in her eyes.

Levi stepped forward and put his arm around her, drawing her close against his side. When he saw the same look of near panic on Sarah's face, he chuckled softly as he held out his other arm, and she stepped into the safety of his embrace as well.

"Thank you," Hope whispered against his shoulder after a few moments. Her breath was warm on his neck when she added, "I'm going to have to add Superhero to your list of titles, Levi."

He said nothing, but kept his arms looped around both women as the three of them watched the Plumwood Hollow Law Enforcement escort a handcuffed Chet Willis through Hope's true-blue door and into the back of a police car.

Levi kinda felt like a superhero at that moment. "They call me Mr. Mostacho. The Cowboy Butcher of Plumwhood Hollow," he drawled, his Kentucky hollow accent laced with his Mexican Spanish upbringing.

The two women in his keeping burst out laughing, but when Sarah stepped away, Hope remained pressed to his side, her arm curved contentedly around his waist.

CHAPTER SEVENTEEN

IT WAS THE LONGEST NIGHT HOPE could ever remember enduring. No problematic birthing, no intricate surgery, no multiple-farm-calls-in-a-row night could ever compare. Her personal life had been dragged out and poured over in front of her friends and acquaintances down at the police station, with Sarah—who'd come to give her statement, and had stayed for moral support, until Hope insisted she go home to her family. Levi promised Sarah he wouldn't leave Hope alone for even a moment until she was ready, and Sarah had hugged her tightly, and whispered, "He really is your superhero, Dr. Hope. You're going to okay; you've got Mr. Mostacho, The Cowboy Butcher of Plumwood Hollow taking care of you now."

Worst of all, it had all been laid out for Levi, himself, the last man on earth she wanted knowing the ugly details of her marriage and subsequent dissolution of it.

He'd refused to leave her side throughout the ordeal, and even when she insisted he didn't have to stay, she'd clung to his hand in direct opposition to her words.

If he hadn't judged her before, he'd have every reason to now. What a fool she'd been. What a sucker for sweet words and magnanimous gestures. She'd taken Chet's bait, hook, line, and sinker, and he'd reeled her in without a fight.

But Levi's words kept replaying through her mind. I listened with my heart because I wanted to know what was in yours. If she told him how she felt about him, if she opened her heart completely to him, would he still feel the same way?

Under duress, Chet had come clean, not just because of her, but because his arrest had dredged up a whole file of complaints against him, including a couple arrest warrants for breaking and entering, for identity theft, grand theft burglary, as well as one charge of grand theft auto—he'd left his last wife in her pretty little BMW.

Charles "Chuck" Wilton, aka Chet Willis, aka Toby Wilkins, aka Thomas Williams, and quite possibly a few more, was a con man, through and through. Hope wasn't the first woman he'd taken to the cleaners, and if she'd had anything to clean out, she might not have been his last. Before he even filed for divorce, he'd had his next victim, Shelby Whitaker, lined up and waiting. He'd done his research on the Plumwood Hollow Animal Hospital, and he knew what it was worth—a pretty penny by all accounts—and he believed her when she told him it would be hers as soon as Doc Harper retired. Hope didn't lie. Everything she said could be trusted, taken at face value. She wasn't the kind of girl who would intentionally mislead or misdirect a person, and when she told him that the old vet handing the practice over to her, he'd accepted that as God's truth.

So he'd stayed behind in Indiana, but kept tabs on the goings-on of the clinic until he learned that Doc Harper had, indeed, retired, and Hope had taken over as she'd said she would. He didn't wait a moment longer, but picked up and headed for Plumwood Hollow, where he single-mindedly wooed and wedded Hope Goodacre. "I really did love you for a little while," he had the audacity to tell her, as though that would soften her heart toward him. The first couple of months hadn't been so bad; he reaped the benefits of being married to a woman so many people loved and adored, because they transferred that adoration onto him. At first. Soon enough, though, the facade he'd created began to crack and crumble, so that the real Chuck Wilton seeped out into the lifeblood of the hollow. Hope had been the last to see it; he'd made sure of that. As long as he had her believing in him, it didn't matter what everyone thought.

A year into their marriage, he met Shelby Whitaker and set his sights on her. It had taken nearly six more months to hook the wild child of Clyde Whitaker, but he'd done it. When she told him exactly how much she'd get the moment they signed their marriage contract, he knew it was time to move on from the past and move in for the kill. That meant claiming his share of Hope's inheritance and saying goodbye to life as the husband of a country vet.

Knowing how much Hope hated drama, he'd made it abundantly clear to her that his attention was drifting, then accidentally let it slip that he'd been unfaithful, but he was so sorry and would never do it again. Hope cried in his arms and promised to try harder to be there for him. He took her on a weekend getaway—he used a credit card he'd opened in her name—and they came back to the hollow with stars in their eyes. At least in her eyes. He had to go away for business. He was sorry, but he'd gotten drunk and messed up again. Don't cry, baby. I love you. It meant nothing. Throw the baited hook out, let it drift with the current, jerk it back just enough to have the fish coming after it, let it drift, jerk, drift, jerk, drift...and set the hook and reel it in.

Chuck had paid a high schooler to hand Hope the divorce petition while he'd been out of town on yet another business trip just after Mother's Day last year. When Hope begged him to come home, to reconsider, he gently explained over the phone that he no longer loved her, that he'd met the woman of his dreams, and in fact, wasn't on a business trip at all, but on a romantic getaway with Shelby Whitaker.

His hope had been that her aversion to drama and conflict would have expedited the divorce along with his share of the proceeds, but he'd been shocked to discover that his little mouse of a wife had a backbone. When she explained away his terrible misunderstanding, Chuck's world began to crumble. For the next several months, he doggedly clung to the belief that she was lying, that she was holding out on him. When his lawyer confirmed Hope's story and then sent out his first bill for services rendered, Chuck had realized that he was in trouble.

He'd gotten cocky, and that had turned into sloppy.

By then, he'd spent enough time with Shelby to know that a marriage to her would not garner a sweet first few months like he'd experienced with Hope—and they had been sweet, he'd assure her again. She'd felt Levi's biceps bulge where his arm rested around her back, saw his fists clench, but he'd remained steadfast and stalwart at her side.

In fact, the longer Chuck stayed with Shelby, the more he began to loathe her. He just really, really, really loved the money she'd be getting when he put his ring on her finger.

Finally, having no recourse but to admit defeat, Chuck readied himself to cut his losses with Hope, and throw in his hat with the Whitaker lot. But Shelby got the jump on him, and to his utter astonishment, she announced to the world that she was pregnant. And that he was the father.

Marriage to the girl was distasteful at best, but it was a contract that could quickly be dissolved, and he would be free to take his winnings and move on to his next sugar mama. A baby, however, would tie him to the shrew for life. Besides, he had no clue what to do with a child. He hated the little beasts, and wouldn't he be stuck paying child support for the rest of his life?

His best bet was to get back in Hope's good graces long enough to prove to Clyde Whitaker that he wasn't a good choice for the man's youngest daughter, then he'd cut and run and start over again somewhere else. He still had several thousand dollars on a couple credit cards in Hope and his name; it wasn't much, but it would get his feet underneath him, and he'd started out on far less than that a time or two before.

It had all come to an end tonight.

Although Hope should have felt exonerated and free, she was only hollow, cut open and turned inside out. She dreaded returning to her cottage alone, knowing that Chet—Chuck—had been inside, rooting around in her beloved sanctuary. It had been nearly a year since he'd set foot in her home, and she'd pretty much erased any evidence of his existence. It had become her safe haven, her hiding place, and knowing he'd been in there without her permission, left her feeling violated and fearful.

Levi had been so sweet; he'd offered to take her home to his place where she would be coddled and nurtured and fed by him and his family, or to Seven Virtues where she could sleep in her old room with the sounds of her own close around her. But she'd turned down both options. Nona, after Levi called to tell her why they wouldn't be there for dinner, had packaged up enough food to feed an army, and she and Yvette brought it to the station and fed everyone dinner, even Chuck. He and his family had already done so much for her. And her father and sisters? She hadn't let Levi call them—she simply wasn't ready to face their overwhelming love and affection for her. She'd see them in the morning and explain everything then. Of course, it was possible that the gossip had already reached them, but her phone had been silent, except for the text from Rodney around eight, letting her know that the dog's owner had arrived to pick up the groggy pet, and he was locking up the clinic and going home. Sarah had called him before they went to the police station, and he'd graciously agreed to come in. She had good employees, Hope knew; they didn't just work for her, they were her friends, and they cared what happened to her.

No, she wanted to go home to her own place. Afraid, angry, hollow, yes, but she needed to face her fears, and if Levi would accompany her, she could be brave. *You're going to be all right now,* Sarah's voice murmured inside her head.

Hope leaned into Levi's side as he guided her out of the police station into the chilly dark night. She could hardly believe that the man was still beside her, still holding her up. He'd kept her close the whole night, an arm around her, his fingers linked with hers, a comforting palm pressed to her low back. The few times she'd stepped away from him, his eyes had followed her, found her again the moment she returned. And miracle of miracles, what she read on his face and felt in his touch was not disgust or disappointment. Nothing like what she felt churning around in her empty stomach. He looked at her the way she looked at one of the animals she'd just spent hours trying to save. With hope and expectation that the creature would get up and walk, run, live.

She took his hand and let him steady her as she climbed up into the passenger seat of his car. "Thank you," she murmured, the words filled with gratitude for far more than just his gentlemanly assistance. She turned to look at him, the soft glow of the interior lights illuminated his face.

No. She was wrong. He was looking at her the way Cord looked at Faith. The way Theo had once looked at Charity. The way Hope had dreamed of being looked at by the very man who stood in front of her right now. "Oh," she murmured. Then she closed her eyes, lowered her chin, and licked her lips. "Oh." This time, it was only a whisper.

She felt his fingers slide around the back of her neck, felt his slightly rough palm brush against her jaw, felt the pressure of his thumb against the tender spot just in front of her ear. She waited, her breath held.

"Look at me, Hope." It wasn't a command, not when his voice was so tender. A request. A hope.

She opened her eyes and slowly lifted her gaze to his, tipping her head ever so slightly to lean into his hand. He hadn't moved, but with him cupping her face the way he was, they were so intimately connected, she felt it all the way to her soul.

"You made me so proud tonight. You stood tall and unmoved as that man did everything in his power to tear you apart. You are an amazing woman."

Hope started to shake her head, his words a complete contradiction to how she felt. "No, I'm not. I—"

"Yes, you are. Amazing. Brave. Strong. Whole." He acted like he was going to keep going, but his voice caught, and he swallowed hard. "Beautiful."

"But I feel so broken," she murmured, closing her eyes against what she was seeing in his. "So used up and—and empty."

She felt him move closer, felt the heat of his body as he drew near, but he didn't kiss her. His fingers slid into her hair to cradle the back of her head, his other arm slipping around her so he could pull her close enough to press her cheek against his shoulder. Then he turned her head so that her face was tucked into the curve of his neck, and he rested his cheek against her hair. He was so big, and so warm, and relaxed against him. No wonder Coco loved to be held just so.

CHAPTER EIGHTEEN

BY THE TIME THEY REACHED HER HOME, Levi had made up his mind to stay the night with her. He was sure someone would see, and there would be talk, and he was sure she'd argue and try to send him home. But none of that mattered. He'd seen the fear in her eyes. He'd meant it when he told her she didn't have to go through this alone. He'd meant every word he'd said to Sarah; he would not leave Hope until she was ready, and as far as he could tell, she wasn't even close to being okay on her own. He wasn't looking forward to trying to get comfortable on her overly-soft loveseat, but he'd sleep on the floor if he had to. He wasn't leaving her alone in that house. Not tonight. Maybe not even tomorrow night. Gossips be hanged.

He pulled into the clinic parking lot, then circled around to the side of her cottage and pulled in next to her Jeep, his wide tires loud on the loose gravel of her private driveway. He was glad to see that they'd already impounded Chet's—or Chuck, or whoever he was—car, but he wondered if they'd find other things of his still inside the house. He turned off the engine, and they sat in silence for a few moments, their hands clasped on the console between them. "You ready to head inside?"

It took her a moment to respond; when she lifted her gaze to his, he was glad to see that her eyes were dry, and she wore a look of determination on her face. "I think so. Thank you for coming with me, Levi."

"I wouldn't let you face this alone."

She nodded. "I know. You're the reason I'm able to face it at all tonight."

He squeezed her hand, told her to sit tight, then hurried around to her side to let her out. It was cold and clear, and it seemed natural for her to press into his side as they made their way around to her front porch and her blue door.

"Oh!" Hope brought both hands up to cover her mouth, and stopped dead in her tracks, gazing up at him with wide eyes. "Oh, Levi," she said. "The door. The book. Your gift." She lowered her hands slowly. "And all this craziness, I almost forgot. Oh Levi, thank you." She grabbed his hand and tugged him toward the clinic door. "Come with me. I want to go get it, but I left it in my office when we dashed out of here in such a rush."

He chuckled softly as she all but dragged him across the lawn. He was thrilled at her response, and the fact that it was distracting her, even just a little, was icing on the cake.

She fumbled with her keys, and when he saw the tremble in her fingers, he reached over and took them from her. "Which one is it?"

He went in ahead of her, flipping the lights on as they made their way down the corridor toward her office. On her desk was a pile of charts in one corner, a two-tiered in- and out-box in another, a coffee cup on a coaster, and other paraphernalia you'd expect of a busy, caring animal doctor. But right in the middle of it, as though she'd been perusing the pages moments before she'd heard the commotion outside, was the book with the cobalt blue door on the cover. The box it had come in rested on top of the pile of charts, the wrapping paper folded neatly on top. His card, he noted, was sticking out of the top of the book, marking a page about halfway through.

"I haven't had the chance to look at all the pictures," she said, as she circled the desk and gathered up the book. Holding it to her chest, she smiled shyly over at him. "I know it's really late, but would you like to come over and have a cup of tea or coffee, and look at this book with me?"

It was late, well past eleven o'clock, but he knew sleep would come difficult for both of them that night, and he was grateful neither of them had businesses to open first thing in the morning. "I'm not going anywhere tonight, Hope."

"Oh." She lowered her gaze, but her smile stayed on her lips. Then she opened the box, carefully, tenderly placed the book inside, then folded the sheet of wrapping paper on top of it, and closed the box again.

"I'll take that," Levi said, holding a hand out to take it from her. Instead of giving him the book, however, she took his outstretched hand in hers.

When they reached her front porch, she dashed up the steps and stood in front of her door, staring at it and wonder. "It's uncanny," she said. "It has to be the same door. It's not possible that there are two so exactly the same." She turned around to look at him over her shoulder. "And if there are two of these, I want to know where the other one is." She held up the box. "Let's go inside and see if there's any information in here."

Levi could tell she was trying very hard to keep her mind off the events of the last several hours. She was so brave and didn't even realize it. He knew that now wasn't the time to talk about it, but he loved the irony of Chet's — or Chuck's — downfall. It was because Hope was so trusting, and so trustworthy, that the man had gotten caught in his own snare. He still had her keys, and he found the one that fit the blue door without any trouble. It was an old brass key, the bow end heavily scrolled in a pattern that matched the brass plate behind the doorknob.

Inside, the front entry light was on, as well as one over the sink in the kitchen. It was plenty to see by, but the moment they stepped through the front door, she tucked her hand into his arm and clung tightly to him. "I'm kind of freaked out," she whispered. "I didn't think I'd be scared with you here, and I know I have nothing to be afraid of, but my heart is pounding, and my hands are sweaty." She grimaced and looked apologetically at her hand where it rested on his arm. "Sorry."

Levi turned, took both her hands in his, and ducked his head so he could look her in the eye. "Hope. You are safe. I will take care of you. I won't let anything happen to you." He paused, then asked, "Do you trust me?"

Hope nodded without hesitation. "I trust you with my life, Levi."

Would she trust him with her heart?

"I've got you," he said, drawing her against his side, as they began to move slowly through the house. Once again, he turned on lights as they went, and by the time they made it through the whole house, all the way to the mudroom at the back door, every light in the house was on, and Hope was beginning to relax. "All clear."

Levi leaned against the counter in her little kitchen while Hope filled her bright yellow teapot with water and put it on the stove. She pulled two mugs from the cabinet, then offered him a choice of several different teas Prudence had concocted. They both settled on an orange spice blend, then headed into the living with the book.

Hope didn't even hesitate, but settled in next to Levi, their knees and elbows bumping. She laid the book in his lap and poured tea for both of them. "Careful, it's hot." She handed him his cup, and he sipped carefully. It was good, a little spicy, and sweet with the raw honey she stirred into each cup. She settled back into the cushion beside him, jostling him a little as she did. "I'm sorry."

WHERE THERE IS HOPE

Levi just smiled, lifted his arm, and draped it around her shoulders, pulling her close to his side again. "You're making this too easy," he said with a chuckle. "I don't even have to do the yawn-and-stretch maneuver."

"Yawn and stretch maneuver?" Hope sipped her own tea delicately.

"You've never heard of it? It's the oldest move in the book," he said, enjoying the feel of her relaxing into him. "You know, high school date night. The yawn—" He opened his mouth wide in a fake yawn. "And stretch." He raised his arm high above his head, arching his back as he stretched, And gingerly lowered his arm again, draping it in exaggerated moves back around her shoulders.

"Oh," she said with a giggle. "Right out of the movies. Never happened to me in real life, but you're right. I've seen that move a dozen times in movies and on TV." She cocked her head and looked up at him, a sweet smile on her face. "I guess I'm just kind of a face value girl. I'd rather you just skip the pretense and put your arm around me, if that's what you want to do."

"It's exactly what I want to do," Levi said. She was so close that if he wanted to — and oh, how he wanted to — if he let himself, he could lean forward about 6 inches, and his mouth would be on hers. "It's what I've wanted to do for a long time." He took another sip of his tea, and then set it on the coffee table in front of them. He traced the rectangle of the door on the cover of the book in his lap, imagining he was tracing the lines of her face, the column of her neck, the curve of her waist...

He shifted just a little, turning so he could more easily look into her eyes.

Hope did the same, placing her teacup next to his, and easing around in her seat to face him. She lifted her hand and pressed it to his cheek; her fingers were warm from holding the mug. Closing his eyes, he nuzzled his jaw against her palm, relishing in the sandpaper rasp of his day-long growth on her soft skin. The tip of her thumb drifted just below the curve of his bottom lip, and Levi wondered how long he could stay alive without any oxygen, because it suddenly seemed like there was a shortage of it in the room. He opened his eyes to find her watching him, her own bottom lip caught between her teeth, as though she could somehow feel what she was doing to him.

With all the willpower he could muster, he reached up and wrapped his fingers around her wrist, then brought her hand down to press her palm to his chest, directly over his pounding heart. It hadn't stopped after all. A look of uncertainty crossed her face, and she started to pull away, but he wouldn't let her.

"Can you feel it?" His voice came out hoarse, rough with emotion. "Can you feel my heart trying to break out my chest to get to you?"

Hope swallowed visibly, then in a fragile whisper, she asked, "Will you kiss me?"

The thought raced through his mind that in that moment, he could die a happy man. But if he did, he wouldn't know the thrill of her lips against his. He wouldn't know what sounds she made when she kissed him, or how her breathing changed when he kissed her back. Because Levi knew that his answer to her request was no.

He would not let their first kiss, that magical, once-in-a-lifetime event, take place on this night of such misery. He wasn't going to tell her he loved her, either. Tonight, he would show her that he was committed to her, that she could trust him. Tonight, she would discover that she could trust herself, because she was, indeed, a good judge of character. She'd called him a superhero, and although he knew he was nothing close to it, he wanted more than anything to rise to the challenge for her sake.

Instead, he lifted her hand from his chest and turned it so he could press a tender kiss into her palm. With her body still so close to his, he felt her tremble when his lips touched her skin. His mustache must have tickled a little, too, and he smiled at the thought. Was she ticklish anywhere else? He was half out of his mind with the need to find out, but he held back. "I am entrusting this to your safekeeping," he said, his gaze locked with hers. He closed her fingers over the kiss.

She looked at him a little skeptically. "Until when?"

"Do you trust me?" he asked again.

"I do, Levi. I trust you," Hope said, her voice a little stronger now.

"Then trust me when I say that I want to kiss you more than anything in the world right now, Hope. I want to bury my hands in your hair and lift your face so I can have my way with your mouth. I want to wrap my arms around you and crush you to me and kiss you until we both have a hard time remembering our own names."

"Oh," she murmured, her eyes wide, and her cheeks flushed with what he hoped was pleasure over his forthright words. Perhaps the good doctor was even a little scandalized.... And he wasn't finished yet.

"Trust me when I say that I want our first kiss to be about us, and us alone. I don't want to share you with anyone, Hope, and although that man no longer has a place in your life, this night has been about removing him, in every sense of the word." He reached up and cupped her face once more, lifting her chin so he could study her mouth. She self-consciously licked her lips, and a quiet, but slightly desperate sound escaped his throat.

Wait, Levi. Wait for the right time.

He met her eyes again, and said, "Trust me when I say that when I kiss you for the first time, I don't want you to be afraid of anyone or anything. When I kiss you the first time, I want your only thoughts to be about you and me and what our mouths are doing."

"Okay," she whispered, her eyes bright. "I trust you. But Levi?"

"Hm?" He was staring at her mouth again. He had to stop that.

"Trust me when I say that if you don't stop talking about kissing me, I may not be responsible for what happens."

"Oh, really?" He cocked his head and grinned down at her.

"Yeah, really," she shot back. "Because trust me when I say that I want to kiss you more than anything in the world right now, too."

Levi groaned softly, then chastely pressed his lips to her forehead before wrapping both arms around her and pulling her close. She snuggled in, her cheek against his chest, the top of her head tucked into the hollow under his jaw, and he wondered if she could hear his heart trying to beat down his ribs to get to her.

He couldn't believe it, but once again, he was waiting for Hope.

CHAPTER NINETEEN

THE CALL CAME JUST AFTER SEVEN IN THE MORNING, and Hope awoke with a start, unsure for several moments of where she was.

That was it; her living room. And the hard pillow beneath her head wasn't a pillow at all. It was Levi Valiente, her own superhero. He'd been thrilled to discover that her loveseat was, in fact, a combination couch and recliner, and once she came to terms with the fact that he wasn't going to go home, she hauled out blankets and pillows for both of them, then let him pick a movie. They'd watched The Magnificent 7. Patty Lynn would be so proud.

She hadn't intended to fall asleep practically on top of him like she was, but waking up with his arm underneath her, and her head resting on his gently rising and falling chest was awfully nice. She didn't want to move. Her phone had stopped ringing, so she opted not to.

"Morning," Levi said, the husky morning rumble of his voice making her pulse race. "I think that was your phone."

"Mm," she responded, shifting a little so she wasn't pressed so tightly to his side. The longer she was awake, the more awkward she began feeling. "Either the rumor mill is up and running early this morning, or that's a call coming through the clinic." She was so tired. She wondered, for just a moment, what would happen if she simply didn't answer the phone.

When she still didn't get up, Levi slid his arm out from under her and slowly cranked the recliner back into an upright position. "Where is your phone?" he asked, that morning gruffness still doing funny things to her insides. "I'll get it and see who it is."

"In my purse over there on the table," she said, waving vaguely in the direction of the kitchen.

Levi stood, and from the corner of her eye, she watched him stretch, then run his hands through his thick black hair. She could hear the rasp of his stubble as he scratched his jaw. Man, she could get used to the sight of him first thing every morning. It would make those wake up calls almost worth it.

He brought her purse over, then left her to check her phone while he went to the bathroom.

The call was from a farm just outside Plumwood Hollow; a cow was off her feed, had terrible bloat, diarrhea, and wasn't producing milk, so her calf wasn't nursing. Both lives were in jeopardy—the baby was only two days old. Hope had a good idea that it was a displaced abomasum, a twisted fourth stomach, just from the symptoms alone, so she made a quick mental checklist of what was already in her emergency kit, and what she'd need to grab from the hospital before heading out. Her brain was a little fuzzy from lack of sleep, and although her spirits were much better—thanks to the presence of Levi in her home—she needed to have her wits about her, just in case the stomach was twisted to the right instead of the left. The left displaced abomasum required brute force to manhandle a cow—four or five strong people—but if the stomach was twisted to the right, on-the-spot surgery was the only recourse, and that was if it wasn't already too late. With a right side twist, a cow only had about forty-eight hours before she started shutting down.

By the time Levi stepped out of the bathroom, Hope had pulled on a clean pair of scrubs and was brushing her hair back into a neat ponytail. She was alert, but she knew her fatigue would catch up with her if she weren't careful, especially if they had to roll a cow today. "It's an emergency call. I think I can handle it on my own, but if you'd like to come, I wouldn't mind the company."

"I'm ready," he said without hesitation. "What can I do to help?"

"Coffee's brewing—if you can pour us a couple travel mugs, that would be great. There are a few protein bars in my car for mornings like this, but if you need to eat something, you're welcome to anything in my fridge or pantry. I'll be out in a few minutes." She dashed into the bathroom, leaving Levi to figure things out for himself.

They arrived at the farm less than fifteen minutes later. A woman name Janice Hickman met them at the front gate and led the way on her ATV up the lane to a massive barn. "I keep my new mamas inside," she explained. "Gives me peace of mind to be able to check on them easily. I can't imagine what would have happened to poor Daisy if she'd been out in the pasture today. I might not have discovered her in time."

Except that if the cow and her calf had been out in the pasture eating fresh spring grass instead of the large quantities of grain and older baled hay that was readily available in the small stall, the cow might not be having the issues she was. A few taps to her abdomen told Hope it wasn't good news. Definitely a displaced abomasum, but not toward the left, which is always the lesser of two evils. She pulled out her stethoscope and listened on the right side as she flicked the animal's side, then pushed her fist into the hollow in front of the pelvis. Finally, she stepped back and turned to Janice who held the cow's lead rope.

"It is, indeed, a displaced abomasum. The fourth stomach is twisted," Hope said by way of explanation when Janice gave her a strange look. "Happens a lot right after birthing, especially with a big calf or twins. As the calf grows in the uterus, the uterus shoves that particular stomach out of the way, but once the uterus shrinks back to size, the abomasum shifts back into place, and that's when it can happen. Usually, it's a left side displacement, which is something that can be fixed pretty simply, but this is a right side displacement." She stroked the cow's side, grimacing in sympathy at the tightness of the bloated belly. "With a right side displacement, we're working against the clock, so at this point, Janice, as much as I hate to say it, you only have two choices: salvage or surgery." She probably could have explained it in a little gentler words, but from what she could tell, Janice had already waited longer than she should have.

"Aren't you a butcher?" Janice asked, cocking her head at Levi.

Hope raised her brows at him, but said nothing. Was Janice actually contemplating asking Levi to slaughter the animal for her right then and there? Technically, it was a reasonable option, given the cow's condition, but she hadn't brought him along to offer him up as the alternative to her services. Not that she minded—if Janice did opt to salvage the cow, the sooner it happened, the more likely it was that the meat could be saved. But again, that's not why Levi was there.

"Either way, I say goodbye to my cow, right?" Janice asked.

"Right," Hope said, nodded sympathetically.

"What's the surgery?" she asked.

So Hope explained that she would make an incision in the cow's side between the last rib and the pelvis, slide her hand inside the abdominal cavity, locate the twisted stomach, and reposition it. "If we need to drain it, we will," she added, pointing at a 5-gallon bucket and a short piece of garden hose rolled up inside. "As bloated as she is, I'm thinking we'll have to empty her out a little, and I'll warn you, it's not a pleasant barn animal smell. Then we'll put an anchor stitch or two in the cow's side to hold the stomach in place, sew up the incision, and pray for the best. Some cows do great and are pretty much back to normal a day or two later, and some never quite recover; we just have to monitor them and see. She hasn't had an appetite in a while, so we'll probably need to give her a sugar-based supplement to trigger her hunger, to get her eating again, but if we've caught it in time, the treatment is usually quite effective."

"You'll do it right here?" Janice asked, clearly skeptical.

"If you have a head gate, that would be best. We'll have to tie her legs so she doesn't kick—she'll be awake the whole time—but we'll use local anesthesia at the incision site to minimize her discomfort through the process. If you don't have a head gate, we may need to fashion something to keep her head locked down."

"Sounds like that's our best bet," Janice said, nodding contemplatively. "I don't want to lose my cow, and her baby doesn't want to lose his mama. I've got a headgate at the back of the far stall—it's homemade, but sturdy—so we can set you up down there."

The decision made, Hope went to work. With Levi's help, she got the cow's head closed up in the brace, then they strapped the cow's tail down against her hind legs, which they tied together to keep the cow from side-stepping or shuffling back and forth while Hope worked. She explained the surgery in a little more detail to him—as a butcher, he knew exactly what body parts she was referring to, but he'd never seen this particular surgery performed on an awake animal.

Hope enjoyed working with him as much, if not more, than with Doug. The two men really were a lot alike in temperament, and maybe for that reason, she felt a little like she and Levi had been working together for some time already. They fell into a quick and easy rhythm, and by the time she cut through the peritoneum to open up the abdominal cavity, she felt calm and cool as a cucumber, and as steady as a rock with Levi at her side.

CHAPTER TWENTY

LEVI STILL COULD HARDLY BELIEVE what he'd just witnessed, and as they drove back to town, he kept shaking his head at what he considered nothing short of miraculous. "I'm blown away, Hope. What you do is incredible. The way you stuck your hand in there, figuring everything out by feel?" He reached over and ran the backs of his knuckles along her jaw. "That was one of the most fascinating things I've ever seen, and not just because of the surgery, but because of your confidence and your knowledge, and your steady hand in the face of emergency."

Hope laughed softly, but shook her head. "I love what I do, Levi. It's calls like this that remind of why I got into this career. I remember the first time I saw Doc Harper do that surgery. I was floored the same way you are. And by the way, having you there to help me made things so much easier. You can't even imagine. So, again, thank you." She'd already thanked him profusely several times, and so had Janice.

"I doubt you thought of Doc Harper the same way I think of you," Levi said. His tone was light, but there was truth in every word. He couldn't get over how remarkable she was, and seeing her in action today had made him fall even more in love with her. "I'm buzzing inside after seeing you do that."

"Me sticking my arm inside a cow's abdominal cavity and squeezing her distended belly really turned you on, hm?" she teased.

"Um, yes, Hope Goodacre. Call me a freak, but that was hot, okay?"

She looked exhausted, and truth be told, he was, too. They'd only gotten a little over four hours of sleep, and Levi longed to go back to Hope's place and settle into the loveseat recliner with her again, and sleep for another several hours. But he knew that wasn't going to happen. He had to get home to feed Fiebre and put her out to pasture for the day, and he needed to check in with Nona and Yvette, to let them know that everything was okay.

Evidently, they were thinking along the same lines. "I think I'm going to go home, take a shower, and then go to church. I'll join the troops for dinner over to Seven Virtues, and then crash for a couple hours afterward, Lord willing and the creek don't rise. I think I'll be okay for the day since I'll be with my peeps. You've done so much for me already, Levi. I think you should go home and check on your girls. We can touch bases at church, and if you'd like to join us for dinner at the ranch, you'd be more than welcome."

Levi nodded in agreement. She did look much better today, in spite of the sleep shortage, and he needed a shower, too. Granted, he hadn't stuck his hand up to his elbow inside a cow, but the toxic aroma of the stomach's contents and the gas that had been released seemed to be clinging to his clothes, his skin, and his hair. He thought he could even smell it in his mustache. Either that, or it had burned its way into the lining of his nostrils, and he'd be doomed to smell the stench for the rest of his life. How did Hope handle this stuff day in and day out? He was duly impressed all over again. "Anyway, I think I'll pass on dinner, but thank you. I plan on catching a few winks after church, too, but I'll look for you there, okay?"

Hope fed him fried eggs and toast when they got back to her

cottage. "I'm not going to make you work without feeding you something. Coffee doesn't count."

They set the living room to right, and then did a complete circuit of the house in the daylight, looking for any evidence that Chet had been there. Fortunately, other than the dishes he'd dirtied and left in the sink, there was nothing. Levi was greatly relieved; he'd almost expected to find the man had hung his clothes in the closet and lined up his shoes in the mudroom.

Saying goodbye was a little more difficult than he'd expected. He didn't want to leave Hope, not today, not ever, and as he drove away, he watched her in his rearview mirror, a forlorn figure framed against the true-blue background of her front door.

He wanted to let loose a string of unsavory words as he thought of the man who'd caused Hope so much heartache. Instead, he turned his focus to the words Pastor Treadwell had spoken in church a week ago. "God knows how to bring order into chaos, and He offers peace even when things feel like they're out of control. Trust him with your worries, with your fears, and with your heart, because he is trustworthy, and he wants what is best for you." All last week, Levi had struggled with what that meant, what it looked like, but in the end, that's exactly what he'd done. God may not have told those women to gossip about Hope in his shop on Saturday, but he'd used their words to break through to Levi, to convince him to trust his heart, and to be trustworthy in return. And God may not have sent Chet to break into Hope's house, but he'd certainly used the man's actions to give Levi an opportunity to be brave and proactive, to be Hope's superhero. God may not have agreed with Levi's decision to spend the night alone with Hope, but because they'd been together all night, Levi knew she was safe. He knew she wasn't as afraid anymore, and he'd gotten to see her in action during one of the emergency farm calls he'd been desperate to accompany her on since he'd found out about Doug helping her. And holy guacamole, had he seen her in action.

Did she know that when she walked in a room, she made his world stop spinning on its axis, and his heart stand still, whether she wore a short skirt or coveralls?

He had less than two weeks left to come up with a plan to make sure she knew. He wanted Hope to know beyond a shadow of a doubt that she was the moon in his night sky and the sun that lit up his days. He didn't want to steal Cord and Faith's thunder, but after the events of the last twenty-four hours, Levi was going to go all out and make it clear, once and for all, that Hope Goodacre was worthy of being loved just the way she was. And he was going to make that happen at the Overman barn dance.

He wasn't going to do anything as stupid as Chet had done—proposing public—but he was going to make sure Hope and the rest of the world know that he was armed and ready to fight for the woman he loved.

CHAPTER TWENTY-ONE

"COME ON, PAPA!" YVETTE POUNDED on the bathroom door with her little fist. "You're going to be late, and that means I'm going to be late, and if I'm late, then Jazzy will get to dance with Lucas Pithey first, and then he might be her boyfriend before I even have a chance with him!" she wailed.

Levi thought being late might not be such a bad thing after all. "That's the plan, Yvette! You're too young to have a boyfriend," he hollered back, but he grinned at his reflection in the vanity mirror. He was ready. He could think of nothing else he needed to do. His eyebrows were trimmed and even, his nose hairs all but nonexistent, and Nona had buzzed his thick black hair short on the sides over his ears, but left it long on top. He used his usual pomade—Hope had hugged him after church last week and told him she liked the way his hair smelled—but with the sides clipped short and swept back, it reminded him a little bit of Elvis Presley, and when he nodded, a thick strand of hair flopped down over his forehead.

His jaw and neck were shaved smooth as a baby's bottom.

So was his upper lip. He stared at his reflection a few moments longer, knowing there was no going back, but for a brief moment of vulnerability, wishing he could undo the dramatic change.

He hadn't seen his scar in close to fifteen years, not since right after high school when he'd finally been able to grow a thick enough mustache to cover the impetuousness of youth. The thin, pale line that had once seemed so life-altering looked remarkably insignificant now. It angled across his upper lip from the corner of his mouth to the septum of his nose where he still had a small notch in his nostril. No one seemed to notice it when the mustache drew attention away from it, but now with the whole thing bare, he did feel a little exposed.

"But I look like Elvis," he reminded himself, then curled one side of his lip and did Mr. Presley's signature "Jailhouse Rock" hip thrust.

He opened the bathroom door a crack to make certain Yvette wasn't standing just outside in the hall, then crossed to his room where he pulled on a long-sleeved pearl button shirt over his stark white t-shirt. He'd bought a new pack of them from Walmart, along with new socks and underwear, too. He felt like a man reborn in so many ways these days.

He unfastened his black wranglers and tucked the charcoal and cobalt plaid shirt down around his hips, smoothing it over his abdomen so it wouldn't bunch oddly over his belt buckle. The belt had been a gift from one of his high school buddies in New Mexico, Xavier, who'd made it for a class project and found that he really enjoyed working with leather. He'd gone on to make a name for himself in the industry, and Levi wore the belt proudly as one of the first the artist had created. The buckle was a family piece—each of the men in the Valiente had one like it, and several of the women in the younger generations, too. It was simple in its design, a classic rectangle with rounded corners. It sported the skull of a Texas Longhorn, and the words Siempre Valiente in bold letters were pressed into the silver. He always wore it proudly, but tonight, it meant something extra special to him. Tonight, he was claiming his birthright. No more waiting. Superhero brave.

When Yvette saw him, she gasped, and tears sprang to her eyes. "Oh, Papa! What have you done?" she wailed, pressing both hands to her cheeks. "Where is your mustache?" She stepped back when he approached. "Why?"

Levi dropped to one knee and held out a hand to her. Nona stood in the doorway from the kitchen, a tender smile on her face. He'd told his mother what he had planned, so at least he had an ally in her. Yvette stared at him, big, fat tears dribbling from the corners of her eyes. "Come here, *pepita*."

She shook her head. "I am not a little pumpkin seed, Papa. I am a big girl. Why didn't you ask me before you cut it all off?" Her despair was turning to anger. "You don't even look like yourself. Who are you? Are you even my papa?"

Her words bruised his heart, but he'd been prepared for them. His daughter had never seen him without his mustache, and although it was just a small feature on his face, it did change the way he looked rather dramatically.

"Do you like his haircut, Yvette?" Nona asked. "I think he looks very handsome."

"Of course, I like his haircut. But he didn't shave all his hair off, Nona!" Yvette declared, her voice trembling with the need to cry. "But his mustache is completely gone, and I don't like—" Then her eyes grew wide, and she swiped at her cheeks to brush away tears. Taking a step closer to him, she stared at his lip and gasped. "Oh, Papa! What happened?" She brought her fingertips up and traced the line of the scar.

Levi gave her a half smile. "It happened many, many years ago," he began. "I was a teenage boy, and I thought I was big stuff." Levi reached up and touched the scar, remembering the day clearly. He'd been showing off for a couple of friends, and of course, one was a pretty girl—he couldn't even remember her name now. He'd brought out his father's knife set, explaining how they would one day be his. He'd handed one to a friend, Arturo, but the guy started waving it around like he was in a knife fight. Levi knew the blades were seriously sharp—his father always kept his knives ready with clean, razored edges—and he demanded the knife back. When Arturo laughed and pretended like he was going to take off with the blade, Levi lunged at him. "It was such a stupid thing to do, Yvette. I still, to this day, don't know what I was thinking." At the same time, Arturo, who'd only been joking with him, turned to give the knife back, and Levi couldn't stop his forward momentum. "Fortunately, I realized I was going to get cut, so I turned my head. It got me here." He tapped his lip. "It's ugly, but I didn't lose an eye or have my throat cut, right?"

"Oh, Papa, it's not ugly," Yvette said, her eyes warm with sympathy. "Is that why you always wear a mustache? To hide your scar?"

"Yep," he said, nodding slowly. "I was ashamed of it when I was younger. I didn't get it from a bullfight or while trying to save a pretty girl from a bad guy, you know? I got it because I was a stupid boy."

Yvette nodded solemnly. "Boys can be pretty stupid." Then she put a hand on either side of his face and looked him in the eye. "I meant it when I said it's not ugly. It makes you look like a pirate. It's kind of cool. And it was kind of like a knife fight over a pretty lady because you were silly boys trying to show off for her."

Levi chuckled at his daughter's thought process. "When you look at it that way, I guess it kind of is."

"I'm sorry I got mad at you, Papa. I was just surprised. You should have told me you were going to cut it off so I would have time to get used to the idea first."

Levi took a deep breath and let it out. She was right. How would Hope react? Maybe this wasn't such a great way to kick things off after all. Things could backfire horribly if her reaction were anything close to

Yvette's.

"I think Dr. Hope will like it," Yvette said.

"Were you reading my mind?" Levi asked, rising to his feet and shaking his jeans down over his boots. "I was just wondering what her reaction would be."

Yvette nodded dramatically, her dark eyebrows wiggling up and down suggestively. "She will like it, Papa. I think she would like you even if you shaved off your eyebrows and all your hair, too."

"Think so, huh?" He skimmed a palm over the top of his head. "Maybe I should give it a try."

"Don't you dare!" Yvette shrieked, then launched herself at him, wrapping her skinny arms around his waist. "I love you just the way you are."

"No more secrets or surprises, okay?" she said.

Levi frowned, then nodded. "Well, then, I have another secret to tell you. About tonight. About Dr. Hope."

A few minutes later, Nona bustled back into the room. "It's time to go, babies. Are we all ready?"

Levi was going to drop Yvette and Nona off at the barn at Whispering Hills first, then head over to Hope's place to pick her up. He could hardly wait to see her. Over the last two weeks since Chet's downfall, they'd only spent a few short evenings together over supper at his house. Hope was still in the throes of spring calving and would be for another couple of weeks, and the new vet had started just this week. Levi had been pleasantly surprised when Hope introduced him to Dr. Carl Jorgenson, not Dr. Hunter Morgan, and within a few minutes of conversation, he'd understood why she'd chosen the older man over the beefcake Levi had been jealous of. The man had that same calming and transparent quality that Hope did, and it was obvious they were going to make a great team.

On top of that, every spare moment was spent with her sisters helping Faith with last minute decorations and details to pull off the dance. It had consumed the whole town, especially this week, and everyone was excited about it. But between work and play and family, they simply hadn't seen enough of each other, and Levi was hungry for her.

It actually worked out better for his plan. He'd been tempted to kiss her a thousand times since that night she'd asked him to, but he was determined to hold out until the perfect moment. He hadn't practiced waiting for all these years for nothing. No, he was going to do this right.

He wanted her to remember their first kiss for the rest of their lives.

CHAPTER TWENTY-TWO

WHEN THE KNOCK ON THE DOOR SOUNDED, Hope inhaled sharply. She'd been ready fifteen minutes early, and had all but turned herself inside out with anxiety. She let out her breath and shook her hands out at her side, then straightened her shoulders, checked her reflection in the hall mirror one last time, and pulled open her blue door.

"Hello, my beauty." Levi—she assumed it was him because his car was parked in front of her house, and the guy standing on her front porch looked about the right height. He sounded like Levi and even smelled like Levi. But he held a wildflower bouquet so large, she couldn't see his face.

Then he lowered it, slowly, ever so slowly, and as he did, she drank in the sight of him. "Your hair!" she exclaimed in a soft coo. "I love it!" His eyes, that exotic mix of gold and near-black that made her think of coffee, studied her carefully, tenderly, with obvious anticipation, too.

"Oh," Hope murmured when he lowered the bouquet to his chest. "Oh, Levi." His mustache. It was gone. Without thinking, she reached up and touched his smooth lip. "My goodness, look at you." She loved his mustache. There weren't many men who could pull one off the way

Levi did, and as long as she'd known him, he'd worn one. But now he stood in front of her, his hair styled spectacularly, his gray and blue shirt with the pearl snap buttons, the black jeans that accentuated his strong legs, and those black boots. What were they? Alligator? Eel? Her eyes drifted back up to his face and stayed there, then she lifted her fingers to touch the pale slightly jagged scar that ran from the corner of his lip to his nostril. She hadn't noticed it at first. "Wow," she said in a hushed voice. "With or without the mustache, Levi. You are—are—" She broke off, unable to find the right words. She rested her open hand against his jaw and ran the pad of her thumb over his top lip, marveling at it. "I love it."

He smiled, the scar making it just the tiniest bit crooked. "You make me a happy man," he murmured.

Suddenly, a lurid thought crashed through her head. She wanted him to kiss her. She wanted his mouth on hers, now. She wanted to kiss that smooth lip, to run the tip of her tongue over the line of that scar...

"Come in," she said, shaking her head. The words came out breathless and rushed. Her heart was pounding so hard she felt a little lightheaded. She stepped back to let him in. "Are those for me?" she asked, indicating the flowers he still held.

"Oh! Yes," he said, his grin a little self-conscious. "For you."

"Let me put these in a vase," she said, taking them from him.

She turned away, her nose buried in the bouquet, hoping he hadn't seen the flush that had her cheeks burning at the thoughts running through her mind. Before she could take another step, Levi's arm snaked around her waist and drew her ever so gently back against him.

In slow motion—or at least it seemed like it to her—he turned her around in his arms, then he took the flowers back from her and laid them down on the tiny entry table. Every move he made felt deliberate and intentional, and when his hand slid up her back in one long, slow glide, when his fingers threaded through her loose curls as he cupped the back of her head, when he pressed her close and rested his forehead against hers, Hope melted. Her knees went weak, her pulse fluttered erratically, and her skin tingled from head to toe in anticipation.

"You are so beautiful to me, Hope Goodacre. You look amazing tonight in your pretty green dress and your sexy high heels, and with your hair all long and loose down your back." He smiled at her, she could hear it in his voice, but her eyes were closed as she relished being held so close to him. "I like this outfit almost as much as the one you wore when you fixed that cow's stomach."

Hope let out a short laugh. He couldn't get over that, and it thrilled her that he was so impressed by what she did. "Next to my pajamas, it's my favorite outfit," she said.

"Then I can't wait to see you in your pajamas." His voice was a mixture of passion and tenderness, of yearning and certainty.

Hope took no offense in his response; she shared his sentiments exactly. She whispered, "I have something to show you," and started to pull away.

He didn't release her. "Where are you going?"

"I have something to show you," she said again. She leaned her head back so she could meet his eyes. "It's kind of important, especially if you ever want to see me in my pajamas."

His carefully groomed eyebrow rose in a very Elvis Presley like maneuver. "Really?"

"Really. Now let go of me." She put both hands against his chest and pushed. Levi didn't loosen his grip.

"I don't ever want to let go of you," he said, lowering his face to nuzzle her neck.

"Levi!" she gasped when his teeth nipped at her ear, his breath warm against the sensitive skin. She tipped her head to the side instinctively. "Fine, you don't have to let go," she giggled as he pressed soft kisses up the column of her neck. "Walk with me." She pushed harder on his chest, and he groaned and relaxed his hold on her just enough that she could slip away. But she grabbed his hand, scooped up the flowers, and led him into the kitchen.

She set the bouquet in the sink, then picked up an envelope from the counter. It had his name on it. "Here. This is for you."

"Should I open it now?" he asked, propping a hip against the counter.

"Yes. Please." She suddenly felt shy, and a little vulnerable, knowing that what was in that envelope put the ball entirely in his court. She busied herself finding something to put the flowers in and finally had to settle on a gallon-size canning jar because it was the only thing big enough and heavy enough to support the enormous arrangement.

When she finally worked up the courage to look over at him, she was shocked to see his eyes glistening with unshed tears. "Levi?"

"Is this what I think it is?" he asked, holding it up.

"If you think that's my official divorce decree, then yes." She nodded, then began fussing with the bouquet again. "It came in the mail on Thursday, but with the new vet here, I haven't had a chance to bring you the news in person. I didn't want to text or call about it."

"Hope."

Oh, how she loved the sound of his voice. He could make even her single syllable name sound rich and full. She lifted her gaze to his. "Hm?"

"Come here." He set the envelope and the papers down and took a step toward her.

She froze. Her feet wouldn't move. She could not, for the life of her, pick up her feet and make them move.

Levi took another step toward her, his eyes locked on hers. "Hope."

She made a sound, almost a whimper.

He was so close now, she could feel his body heat. "I believe you have something else for me. Something you were saving for me."

She did? She furrowed her brow in confusion. What—

He took her hand, then pressed her palm flat against his chest over his heart. "Can you feel it?"

She could. His whole body seemed to reverberate with it. Not just a heartbeat, but a heart song. A thrumming that made her want to press her ear there so she could hear it more clearly. She nodded slowly.

He lifted her hand, curled her fingers into a fist, then opened them again. "There it is," he said. "I'm claiming it today."

The kiss. The one he'd pressed into her palm and told her to save for him. The kiss.

He was going to kiss her. She licked her bottom lip.

Finally.

He brought both hands up to cup her face, his fingers in her hair, his thumbs brushing gently over her mouth the way she'd done to him at the door, back and forth, ever so tenderly, making her pulse race and her lips part slightly.

"I love you, Hope. I have loved you from the moment you sat down across the table from me at Sunday Dinner four years and ten months ago. I think my heart stopped beating altogether when our eyes met. I couldn't breathe. I couldn't think. There might have been a Mariachi horns playing somewhere, too."

Could it really be true? Was it possible that he'd loved her all this time, too? "What about Faith?" she asked. She had to know.

"Faith?" He frowned, a look of bewilderment on his face. He lowered his hands to her shoulders. "What about her?"

"I don't want to be a runner-up," she whispered. "I love you, too, Levi, and the truth is, I have since high school. I had this massive crush on you; it was right after Veronica left and I came into your shop with my dad one day. You were behind the counter looking all big and strong and sad at the same time, and you had that tiny baby in your arms, like some giant protector, and I just fell head over heels in love with you."

Levi chuckled. "I don't have many memories outside of Yvette from that first year," he said, sliding his hands down her arms until his fingers were laced with hers. "But now I wish I did. I wish I could remember that."

"But then you started dating Faith," she began.

"Faith and I went on one date," he corrected, shaking his head. A chunk of hair fell forward over his forehead and Hope thought it made him look rather rakish. "Two, if you count bringing my mom and my daughter over for a family night supper and a movie at Seven Virtues," he continued. "It was pretty evident we were destined to be friends, and friends only, for life."

Hope clearly remembered the way Levi had looked at her sister that day in his shop. "But you wanted her, I remember."

Levi shook his head. "No. I don't know where you got that idea, but no. We've never been anything but friends."

"But after I graduated," she persisted, "I came into the shop again with Daddy and Faith."

"I remember," he said.

"You do? Well, that day, you hardly even noticed me, but you couldn't take your eyes off of my sister, and the look on your face made it pretty dang clear that you had it bad for her. I mean, I think you might have looked at me twice the whole time I was there." She sighed softly. "I was so disappointed and sad. I'd thought—" She didn't finish her sentence. She'd already told him what she thought.

"Hope, that's not—it wasn't what you thought. You walked in with them, and once again, I thought I was going pass out or something. I wanted to jump over the counter and throw you over my shoulder and carry you off to my cave. You were finally home, and I could tell you how I felt. But I had to pay attention to what Faith was saying, and if I looked at you, my mind would go blank. Whatever you saw on my face? It was about you, not Faith."

Levi suddenly stiffened, his hands tightening their grip on hers. "Wait a minute. It was me?" His eyebrows rose nearly to his hairline. "I'm the one you came back to Plumwood Hollow for? And you thought I was in love with Faith?" He shook his head in disbelief. "It was me. I sent you into Chet's arms."

"No. No!" Hope shook her head, She pulled one hand free and lifted it to his face. "What are you talking about? No, you did not send me into his arms. I did all of that myself, and honestly, if I don't ever have to talk about him or mention his name ever again, that would be lovely."

"But I'm the man you came back for," he repeated. "Me."

"Yes," she whispered, nodding slowly. "Yes. You, Levi. You and that little girl, and your mother. All of you. You're the one I've always wanted."

"And you're the one I've always wanted. You're still the one, Hope." He shook his head and closed his eyes. He let out a low groan. "How did things get so mixed up? So much misunderstanding and confusion."

Hope held up her hand, her fingers curled into a fist. The look on her face was nothing short of fierce. "You listen to me, Levi Valiente. I am done with confusion. I'm done with being in the dark. I don't want to play games, I don't want to guess, and I don't want to miss out on any more of life because I'm afraid, or hurt, or misunderstood. So here it is. I'm going to make this as clear as I possibly can." She shook her fist between them. "I love you. I want you to love me back forever. I want to marry you. Maybe not today, maybe not even this month, but soon. As long as it's not next year. I don't think I could stand to wait that long. That decree is effective as of last week on the date it was signed, so I'm free and available whenever you are. I want to be the mother of your daughter, and hopefully, of a few more crazy kids. I want your mother to be my mother, and I want one of Fiebre's colts for my own, too. It's about time I started riding again."

At first, Levi looked taken aback, but when she said she wanted to marry him, one side of his mouth hitched up, then the other, and by the time she got to the part about wanting a horse, he was grinning ear to ear. "You're awfully demanding," he said.

"Oh, I'm just getting started," she teased him. "I want that first kiss you keep talking about, and I want you to keep talking about kissing me because when you do, it makes me want to kiss you even more." She held her fist up one more time. "So here's the deal. If you want to claim this kiss that you asked me to keep safe, then you're going to have come and get it." With that, she lifted her hand to her mouth and uncurled her fist against her lips. "It's yours for the tak—."

Levi's mouth was on hers before she could finish the sentence, his arms around her, crushing her to him. She arched backward and lifted her face to his, his lips moving over hers tenderly and slowly in a kiss made all the sweeter because of the restrained power behind it. He was so much bigger than she was, so much…more, and she reveled in the knowledge that she could trust him with her heart, soul, and body, that he would protect her and keep her safe. That he would, indeed, love her forever.

Hope stood on tiptoe and wrapped her arms around his neck, kissing him back with all the bottled up unrequited love she'd kept hidden away in her heart. She poured it out as they explored, tested, tasted, their breath mingling, their hearts pounding, the earth trembling just the tiniest bit beneath them.

Levi tightened his arms around her waist, and in one fluid motion, he lifted her like she weighed nothing and settled her on the edge of the counter, bringing her to his height, never taking his mouth from hers.

He stepped into her, cupping her face, his fingers in her hair, turning her head so he could have better access to her lips. She made a soft sound against his mouth, and he finally pulled back ever so slowly, but only a few inches. Just enough for her to see the well of emotions in his.

"I love you, Levi," she whispered, the last drop of that unrequited love evaporating into thin air.

"I love you, Hope." He leaned forward and buried his face in her hair, nuzzling her neck with a trail of kisses that left her breathless.

He lifted his head again and smoothed a few wispy curls from her face. "Forever."

"Forever," she whispered back. She reached up and touched his scar. "Will you tell me about this one day?"

"Knife fight," he said, a cocky grin tugging up one corner of his mouth.

"Oh, really?" She wasn't fooled, but they could save that story for another time. "How about telling me about this?" she asked, rubbing her thumb across his upper lip from one side of his mouth to the other. "Why did you shave it off today?"

"It will grow back, if that's what you want."

"Don't get me wrong, Levi. I love it. I love it either way." She shrugged and shot him a cheeky grin. "It might be nice to know what it's like to kiss you with the mustache, Mr. Mostacho."

The cocky grin turned a little self-conscious in a way that made Hope want to hug him and tell him everything was going to be okay. He leaned forward as though to kiss her again, but instead, he rubbed his face against hers, his mouth brushing over hers, his lips closed, relaxed. "This is why," he whispered against her cheek. "I didn't want to miss anything the first time we kissed. I wanted to feel your mouth moving against my mouth without any barrier." He pulled back to look her in the eyes. "Skin to skin."

Hope sighed at the sheer romance and sensuality of it. She pressed her palm to his cheek and turned his head so she could plant tiny kisses along the curve of his jaw, in one corner of his mouth, then the other. She trailed kisses across his upper lip, then along the line of the scar, before she could bear it no longer, and she pressed her mouth to his, her lips parting in a sigh.

Finally. Home.

Levi lifted her down from the counter as carefully as though she were made of glass, and when she was standing, he took both her hands and waited until she looked him in the eye.

"What?" she asked. "Do I look thoroughly kissed? I suppose I'll have to redo my makeup, hm?"

Levi grinned smugly and nodded. "You do, indeed, look thoroughly kissed. And no, you don't have to redo anything as far as I'm concerned. I wouldn't mind you going looking like you do right now. Let's give folks something to talk about."

"You are incorrigible, Levi."

"As long as you love me, I'll be anything you say I am." Then without preamble, he dropped to one knee and said, "Hope Goodacre, I want to set the record straight, too. No more misunderstandings between us. No more fear, no more doubt. No more stumbling around in the dark. I love you."

Hope could feel the tears welling up behind her eyes, but she didn't care. She kept her gaze fixed on the man who knelt in front of her.

"I will love you forever. I will cherish you, provide for you and protect you. I will stand by your side through whatever life brings our way. I want to be the first person you see in the morning and the last person you see before you close your eyes at night. I want you to be the mother of my children. I want you to be the daughter my mother wishes she had. I want you to ride off into the sunset with me on the back of your very own horse. Or mine, if you're feeling romantic. And I want to kiss you and talk about kissing you, and then kiss you again, all the days of our lives together."

"Oh, Levi. I love you," she told him, moved beyond measure by his words.

Levi licked his lips and said, "I have waited for this moment long enough, and I don't want to let another second go by." With that, Levi let go of her hands, reached inside the front pocket of his shirt and pulled out a long silver chain threaded through what looked like a very old solitaire ring. With great care, he pulled the ring free of the chain, then held it up to her. "Hope Goodacre, will you marry me?"

Hope beamed, not even bothering to wipe the tears that fell. "Yes," she whispered, clasping her hands in front of her. "Yes, Levi, I will. I will marry you."

"This was Nona's engagement ring," he said. "She gave it to me the day after you came for fish tacos. She told me I'd need it soon." He took her hand and slid the ring onto her third finger. It actually fit. "As far as when? My schedule is flexible. Today is fine with me. If Pastor Treadwell is at the dance, he can do the honors. Or tomorrow works, too. I am not waiting until next year, though."

He stood and enfolded her to him. She rested her head against his chest and listened to the steady rhythm of his heart.

She couldn't wait to get to the dance so she could tell everyone that she was in love with the most wonderful man in the whole wide world.

CHAPTER TWENTY-THREE

THE BARN LOOKED SPECTACULAR with the ceiling draped with fairy lights and swathed in sheets of muslin and burlap. Mason jar electric candelabras hung strategically throughout the room, adding to the rustic appeal of the decor, but giving off plenty of light. Tables were piled high with food and drinks. Faith had hired Charity to oversee the main meat dishes—assorted ribs, fried chicken, and barbecue, both pork and beef—and the rest of the food was potluck brought by everyone in attendance.

Hay bales had been stacked in seating arrangements both inside and outside the barn, as boundary lines for dance floors, and as the foundation for a stage where a live band played. Abby would eventually give them a break and perform some of her own music, too.

Out on the lawn, Cord had constructed an enormous sunken fire pit, and folks were gathered around the well-tended flames. Some were roasting hot dogs or ears of corn, some already had s'mores started, and others just lounged comfortably, enjoying the ambiance of the party.

There were more cowboy hats and big belt buckles than anyone could count, but the sea of people was also splashed with pretty dresses, and fancy high heels like Hope wore. It was a party, and everyone was invited to come as they were. No games, no pretenses, just a celebration of life in the hollow.

By the time Hope and Levi arrived at the dance, they were a good half an hour late, and Yvette and Jasmine charged across the dance floor to intercept them. "Where have you been?" Jasmine cried, hands on her hips. "We have been worried sick about you. Vetty told me about your face, Mr. Mostacho," she said, shooting Levi an analytical look. "I'll get used to it, but what am supposed to call you now?"

"I'm still Mr. Mostacho," he assured her. "I can grow a mustache in a week, I assure you."

"Maybe you should get started on that," Jasmine suggested. "In the meantime, I like your knife fight scar." Then she blinked slowly in what she insisted was a wink, and whispered behind her hand, "Vetty told me all about it. Your secret is safe with me."

Turning to Hope, she said, "You guys are late."

Hope chuckled and hugged her niece, then opened her arms to Yvette as well. "I just took a little longer getting ready than I'd planned," she said by way of explanation. It was true; she had not planned to have to redo her hair and makeup after Levi made such a mess of it.

"You look very pretty," Yvette told her. "I like your dress. I like your shoes, too." Then she grabbed her hand. "Hey, you have a ring just like Nona's!"

"She does?" Faith asked from behind Hope. She turned around to find her oldest sister holding hands with her brother-in-law, and looking rather curiously at Hope. She was also looking curiously rosy-cheeked and swollen-lipped. The newlyweds might have stepped outside on the premise of taking a walk, but it wasn't cool enough out there yet to put that kind of color in a girl's face. "Let me see that," Faith said, holding out her hand for Hope's.

"Actually," Levi said, stepping close to Hope and wrapping his arm around her waist. "Yvette, that ring came from Nona. It was hers until tonight. It is now Dr. Hope's." He dropped to his knees in front of his daughter and took her by the shoulders. "Do you remember what I told you I had planned for tonight?"

Yvette frowned, and then her eyes widened and she darted a look back and forth between Hope and her papa. "Did you do it?" she asked him. "Already?"

Levi nodded, that crooked smile lighting up his face.

"Did she say yes?" Yvette whispered. Actually, she tried to whisper, but the group of people who'd started to gather around them all heard her question.

"I did," Hope said, loud and clear. She held up her hand so everyone could see her beautiful ring. "I said yes to Levi Valiente. Sorry ladies. The Cowboy Butcher of Plumwood Hollow is off the market for good."

Faith got to her first, throwing her arms around her and squeezing her so hard Hope thought she might need to be resuscitated. Cord pumped Levi's hand, then gave him a man-hug,

"Welcome to the family, brother," Hope heard him say.

The two girls were hugging each other and jumping up and down like little monkeys. "We're going to be cousins! We're going to cousins!" they shouted with gleeful abandon.

Then Jed was there, pulling his daughter into his arms for a fatherly hug. He nodded at Levi—they'd talked earlier that week, and Jed had given his blessing without reservation.

On stage, the band began a Shania Twain song from days gone by, and Abby leaped up and asked if she could stand in and sing the beautiful song in honor of her sister's new engagement. Faith grabbed Hope's hand and dragged her out onto the dance floor amidst a chorus of hoots and hollers.

"It's my party!" Faith called out. "I can dance with my sister if I want to!" Then she pulled Hope close and said, "I'm so happy for you. Levi is the best guy in the world. I couldn't ask for a better man for my sister."

"He looks at me the way Cord looks at you, Faith," Hope told her with a happy smile. "He's already given me the world in those eyes."

"You deserve it, little sister," Faith said, squeezing her tightly again. "You deserve this, and so does he. I never gave up hoping for both of you, but I had no idea it would turn out like this. I can't tell you how happy I am."

Hope leaned into her sister, pressed her cheek to Faith's, and they swayed to the gentle song.

Someone tapped her on the shoulder at the same time Levi placed a hand on Faith's shoulder. Hope turned around to find Cord behind her. "Mind if we cut in?" her brother-in-law asked. Then he whisked his wife away, leaving Hope to step into the arms of the man she was going to spend the rest of her life with.

THE END

~ ~ ~

Keep reading for an excerpt from
OH SWEET CHARITY
A Seven Virtues Ranch Romance Book 3

A Note from Becky

Dear Reader,

DID YOU ENJOY GETTING TO KNOW HOPE and the seven sisters who call Seven Virtues Ranch home? I have a special place in my heart for sisters, and I love to write about them. You'll find sisters in every one of my books: some by birth, some by adoption, and some in name only—friends who have become sisters.

You'll also find HOPE in every one of my books.

I like to say I write HOPE-fully ever afters. Hopefully ever after because real life isn't always wrapped up in a pretty pink bow, is it? I write fiction about real-life people and real-life situations. Because we love to escape into our fiction, but we want that escape to resonate with us, right?

If you're looking for fiction with relatable characters, relevant situations, and redemptive storylines, I invite you to check out some of my other books and series. You may meet your next BFF (Best Fiction Friend)! Or visit me online: BeckyDoughty.com.

I write heartfelt and wholesome Contemporary Romance, Romantic Suspense, and Women's Fiction. I write fiction, mainly because nonfiction is hard! Yes, I've tried. Let's just say I like to color outside the lines when it comes to facts. But emotions and feelings and the roller coaster ride that comes with all relationships? Oh yeah. That's where you'll find me.

Where hope lives and love wins. Every single time.

Becky Doughty

Books by Becky Doughty

ELDERBERRY CROFT: Seasons of the Heart
ELDERBERRY DAYS: Season of Joy (A sequel novella)

THE GUSTAFSON GIRLS SERIES
~ Juliette and the Monday ManDates
~ Renata and the Fall from Grace
~ Phoebe and the Rock of Ages
~ Gia and the Blast from the Past

THE SEVEN VIRTUES RANCH ROMANCE SERIES
~ Gotta Have Faith
~ Where There is Hope
~ Oh Sweet Charity
~ The Heart of Courage
~ The Soul of Justice
~ My Dear Prudence
~ Something About Abby

THE FALLOUT SERIES
~ All the Way to Heaven
~ A Light in the Dark
~ A Long Way Home

PEMBERTON MANOR
A Short Story Collection

STANDALONE BOOKS
~ Waters Fall: A Novel
~ Life Letters: A Devotional

An excerpt...

OH SWEET CHARITY
A Seven Virtues Ranch Romance Book 3

Chapter 1

IT WAS ALWAYS THE SAME, THE DREAM. And every time it came, Charity awoke with a start, breathless from the exertion expended in her sleep. Theo standing just off to her right, not speaking, not moving, just standing, waiting. Waiting for her.

And smiling in that heartbreakingly tender way he did when he looked at her.

In her dream, she was always trying to get to him, her legs moving in slow motion as she maneuvered the rough terrain between them. If she kept her gaze fixed on Theo, the way seemed easy and short, but the moment she glanced down to see where she might put her next step, boulders and mud pits, sand dunes and brambles would form before her eyes.

She hated those dreams.

But she always lay there in the dark after each one, waiting for her pulse to slow, for the trembling in her limbs to still, holding onto the fleeting images for as long as she could. Because in those dreams, she saw her husband more clearly than she did any other time.

And he saw her.

Right after Theo died, he appeared everywhere. She'd wake up to find him sleeping beside her, the alluring curve of his spine sweeping up to that vulnerable hollow at the base of his skull, his broad shoulders smooth and muscular in the morning light. In that place between sleeping and waking, she'd reach out to trace the border of a scapula with her fingertips, or to slide her hand, ever so gently, around his waist so she could draw from his furnace-like body heat.

She'd head down the hall in their apartment, and he'd be just ahead of her, slipping into the bedroom or the little office.

She'd be cooking his favorite meal, and from the corner of her eye, she'd catch a glimpse of him standing in the doorway, his face lifted like he was sniffing the air.

But her hands always met with the aching emptiness of his side of the bed, she'd inevitably find the rooms of their home unoccupied, and when she turned from the stove top to smile at her man, he wasn't there.

Charity had moved back home to Seven Virtues Ranch less than a year later, half afraid that if she stayed in their hollow, haunted apartment, she might one day wake up and decide she couldn't live without him anymore.

It had taken her a few months to readjust to living with her sisters, her niece, and her father, but she'd eventually found her place in the household. Ironically, it was in the kitchen, a space so densely populated by Goodacres that there wasn't room for Theo's ghost.

But alone in her room at night, when she closed the rest of the world out and burrowed deep into the covers of the bed she and Theo had shared, he came to her, smiling, his eyes shining with love for her, a beacon that even death couldn't snuff out.

She swung her legs over the side of the bed and sat up. "I miss you so much, Theo," she whispered, closing her eyes in the dark of the predawn morning, desperate to capture the memory of him. Guilt seeped into her bloodstream; no matter how hard she tried to hang on, she was slowly losing the ability to conjure up a clear image of his face. Of the way his mouth moved when he talked, how his eyes crinkled at the corners when he laughed. The upright posture, his shoulders straight, his chin lifted, as though never out of uniform. His confident swagger, because yes, Theo did have a delicious swagger.

The last time she'd said goodbye to him, he'd pumped up the swagger as he walked away, just to get a smile out of her. That was right after he'd kissed her so sweetly and told her he'd be back before she knew it.

"Might as well get my day going," she mused aloud, glancing over at the clock on her nightstand. The sun would be up in less than an hour, but she had a full schedule before noon, and getting a jump on things wasn't a bad idea. It was a big day over at Whispering Hills, the expansive ranch next door to Seven Virtues. Skid and Ernie Maddox from Maddox and Sons Construction, along with their crew of more than a dozen men, were putting the finishing touches on a massive pole barn and indoor arena for a new Quarter Horse breeding program. The program, in fact, wasn't new; Cord Overman, the new owner of Whispering Hills Ranch—and husband to Charity's oldest sister, Faith—had purchased much of the best stock from a well-established breeder outside Louisville who was closing his doors. The horse breeders, Dennis and Nancy Bastion, were ready to retire, but had no children to take over the business. They also happened to be long-time friends of the Overman family, and when the Bastions learned that Cord was interested in their operation, they'd been only too happy to work with him. Dennis and Nancy planned to deliver the horses themselves the following week.

Accompanying them was one of their most sought-after trainers, Terrell Jackson, but Terrell would be staying on at Whispering Hills.

He'd accepted a position to take over running the breeding and training program at Whispering Hills, and he'd been out to the site multiple times throughout construction, giving his stamp of approval all along.

Today, they were celebrating a job well done. The stables were ready, tack rooms stocked, the surrounding pastures cleared and newly fenced, corrals and paddocks cordoned off, round pens and wash stations, even a brand new two-bedroom foreman cabin that Terrell would soon call home. The whole crew would gather at noon for Charity's famous smoked ribs, bacon mac and cheese casserole, oven fries, and dilly bean potato salad, along with a few other assorted side dishes. She'd been cooking meals for Cord and his work crews and ranch hands for over a year now, and these were some of their favorites.

Yesterday, Charity had coated the racks of ribs in her own special dry rub and had sealed them in plastic wrap to rest overnight, letting the salts, herbs, and spices go to work tenderizing the meat. She needed to get back over to Whispering Hills first thing so she could pack the ribs into the two huge smokers by six o'clock that morning. They needed as many hours as she could give them before noon; the lower heat and long grill time made the meat practically fall off the bone. Her mouth watered just thinking about the scent of the mesquite and apple wood chips she always used, and between the rub, her secret mop sauce, and the homemade barbecue sauce she slathered on generously at the end, she knew she'd be fending off hungry men all morning.

She made her bed, kissed her fingertips and pressed them to Theo's pillow, then hurried to dress in the quiet of the still sleeping house. Daddy would be up any time now, and as much as she loved sitting with him in the early hours, sharing a cup of coffee and some quiet conversation, today, she wanted to slip away. Dreams of Theo always left her feeling introspective and withdrawn.

Carrying her boots, she tiptoed down the hall to the kitchen. On the counter where she wouldn't forget it was the gallon jar of dilly beans she'd canned last summer. They'd had a bumper crop of beans, and this was her contribution to the meal today. Her dilly bean potato salad was practically legendary with the guys.

She shoved two huge muffins from the breadbox into a brown paper lunch bag; she'd make a fresh pot of coffee next door. Knowing Binks, he was probably already up and prowling around for the day, and if he saw her truck, he'd stop in to say good morning. He always took pleasure in whatever homemade breakfast treat she shared with him.

She snatched her keys from the hook by the back door, then ducked out, making sure not to let the screen slam closed behind her. On the top step of the porch, she shoved her feet into her boots, climbed into her little pickup, then headed down the gravel drive toward Carpenter Road.

Whispering Hills was the next driveway, less than a mile up the road, so it wasn't long before she was wending her way up the pristine blacktop lanes that led through pastoral fields to the beautiful ranch house at the top of the knoll.

Cord and Faith and their daughter, Jasmine, didn't live in the big house, but in a darling two-story home Cord had built for them. It nestled right up against the property line between Whispering Hills and Seven Virtues and had been his wedding gift to Faith and Jasmine. Their future plans for the big house were still a little ambiguous, but they'd made its renovation a top priority job as Cord wanted to make sure there was a place to stay for visiting family, friends, and guests—like the Bastions—who came and went. He'd turned the large, somewhat dated farmhouse into a gorgeous ranch house that managed to retain the old school feel, but with all updated amenities.

Especially the kitchen. It was practically state of the art, with stainless steel appliances, granite counter tops, beautiful hardwood cabinets, a massive butcher block island, and a pantry large enough to operate a small grocery store out of. He'd hired Charity early on to cook for his work crews, so he'd made certain she had everything she could possibly need or want at her fingertips, and all the room she needed to cook for the masses.

For Charity, the last year had been like the sweetest dream working in that gorgeous kitchen, mostly alone and uninhibited by the presence of anyone else around. She loved the homey feel of Seven Virtues, but she felt so professional and legitimate in the Whispering Hills kitchen. She was queen of her domain there.

Binks, the old foreman, sometimes poked his gray, fuzzy head in the door. More often than not, he just stopped in to greet her, or to catch a whiff of whatever she was whipping up that day, but he always asked if she needed help with anything. She rarely did, although she wasn't above coming up with small tasks he could do for her. Binks had married young, had lost his wife early on, and had never remarried, and Charity liked having him around; she felt a kindred spirit with him.

Other times, if he'd catch her singing some old Elvis or Patsy Cline song, he'd join in. "You've got great taste in music, Mr. Binks," she'd tell him. He'd nod and return the compliment before heading back outside to tend to whatever business he had on hand.

Charity pulled around the house and parked near the back porch with it's door that led into the kitchen just like at Seven Virtues. The black sky was just beginning to soften to a murky violet, darkness reluctantly giving way to the light, as she climbed out of her truck. With the jar of beans in one arm, her bag of muffins tucked gingerly into the crook of the other so she wouldn't smash them, she fumbled with her keys to find the back door key.

She nearly dropped the beans when a voice reached her from out of the shadows on the back porch. "You look like you could use another hand."

Chapter 2

IT WAS NEVER THE SAME, THE NIGHTMARE THAT HAUNTED HIM. Oh, it always *ended* the same, but the circumstances changed again and again. Every horror story he'd ever heard came to life in his dreams. The buried IED detonating underfoot, the insurgents hiding in the ruins, ready to ambush the convoy as they drove through what was supposed to be a deserted village, the suicide bomber charging into camp, screaming the name of his god in zealous triumph—or terror—before tripping the wire that would end his life...along with all his intended victims.

Victims Frank couldn't save. Victims he couldn't reach in time. Victims who called for him, begging for his help. Victims who belonged to him, men and women under his care and leadership.

"Help me, Sarge."

"Mama. I wanna go home."

"Oh, God. I'm hurt real bad, Top." It was the ones who'd earned the right to call him Top that really ate him up.

Their voices echoed in his mind long after the dream faded. Especially Stanley's. "I'll be okay, Top. Go help someone else."

They both knew Stanley wasn't going to be okay.

Stanley was just a kid from New Jersey. No one special, not according to his paperwork, his rank, are even his stature. But in some ways, Stanley had been the lifeblood of their unit. His voice rose above the others during drills, he sang like an angel during their small Sunday church service, and his laughter could be heard throughout camp at all hours. That laugh. It was irritatingly contagious. Something in that cockeyed grin, the missing eye tooth, and the way he talked about home made the other guys hold on to hope. The kid had been in his unit for almost a year before Frank learned that Stanley had no home to go back to. His fiancée sent him off to war with a Dear John letter, and the only family the guy had was an elderly grandfather who'd raised him, but who'd been left behind in a nursing home. Stanley's paycheck covered his grandfather's expenses over and above what his meager Social Security and retirement didn't.

By the time Frank had recovered enough to hunt him down, Stanley's grandfather was dead. Knowing the old man had spent his last days utterly alone tore Frank's guts out every time he thought about it. And when Stanley showed up in his dreams, Frank woke up in tears.

It was the only time he cried. And he hated it every time.

Tonight Stanley had been there, running alongside him, just out of reach. When the first bullet ripped through the underbrush, Frank had lunged for Stanley, but the kid had laughed and kept running, straight into the fray. Had gone down in slow motion, his body twitching and jerking as he was hit time and time again, his laughter turning to mournful song, before those final, whispered words. "I'll be okay, Top. Go help someone else."

There was no way Frank could go back to sleep. Beyond weary, he began his midnight pacing around the small set of rooms that made up his apartment, his crutches squeaking and clicking irritatingly with each jarring step. But tonight, nothing soothed him. Not the Scripture he repeated like a mantra in his head about keeping his eyes on the goal, about running the race, about staying the course. Not the hitched cadence as he hobbled around and around the room. Not the pain that spiraled up his tibia like a serpentine branding iron, or the ache in his left ankle where they'd fixed the joint with titanium pins. Not the ice cold water splashed on his heated features, not Harry Connick, Jr. crooning on the stereo.

Not the pain pills calling out to him from behind the bathroom mirror. He wanted to be done with them. He *needed* to be done with them.

"I gotta go," he muttered, the words coming out a low growl of frustration. His skin crawled with his mounting anxiety, his forehead and upper lip beaded with perspiration, and sweat trickled in an irritating rivulet down the middle of his back. "I gotta get out of here."

He didn't care where he went, not really. But by the time he'd put fifty miles under his wheels, he knew exactly where the road was taking him.

Home.

Whispering Hills didn't belong to him anymore, but he had no doubt that Cord Overman would welcome him back, even showing up unannounced the way he was. He hadn't told anyone he was stateside. Not even his own mother. He'd had no intention of staying stateside so long, but his recovery had been hindered by one infection after another, by flesh that had been damaged beyond repair. They'd released him from the hospital last month to continue therapy as an outpatient, but his physician warned him that as long as he opted to keep his leg, he'd be living with debilitating pain the rest of his life.

Frank raged against the choices he'd been given; keep the leg, endure months, maybe years of therapy and surgeries, and, of course, the never-ending pain—and still, there would be no guarantee he'd be able to go back—or let them take the leg, as well as the pain that went with it. An amputation would definitely speed up his recovery time, and with advancements in prosthetics these days, there was a good chance he could remain on active duty...at some level. The thought of sitting behind a desk while his men were out there running missions without him just about crushed his soul.

He'd seen too many men and women leave the Armed Forces with fewer limbs, though, and he didn't want to be one of them. Not because he thought any less of them, but because he was reasonably sure losing his leg meant losing his career.

And yet, there was no way he could pass any of the physical tests they'd require of him with his leg intact, at least not in the foreseeable future.

Neither option sounded favorable to Frank, period.

Maybe he was going about this wrong. Perhaps enduring therapy on the parallel bars at the rehab center while waiting for the next surgery wasn't the way for him to regain his strength and endurance, his balance and health.

Home. He knew what Cord had going on back at the ranch. He knew there were a dozen or more projects that Frank could jump in on at Whispering Hills. His crazy horse, Hidalgo, was still in the stables, and there were miles of ranch land Frank could lose himself on if that's what he needed. Surely, he could figure out how to get on a horse and just ride, if nothing else.

He drove all night, arriving just before dawn. He motored slowly up the long paved driveway, taking in what changes he could make out in the long beam of his headlights, marveling at how different things looked, and yet how much it still felt like coming home. He eased the car as quietly as he could manage into what appeared to be a small parking lot at the top of the drive, turned off the engine, and peered out the front window at the house he'd grown up in. Everything was dark, except for a low-wattage porch light at the front door, and a soft glow inside the entry. He already knew there wasn't anyone living in the house. It was a shame; Cord had done wonders with the place. It looked like a classy old broad with a really good facelift and some new duds. Frank wondered what the inside looked like. He was especially curious about what had become of his old room. He suddenly wanted to crawl into his childhood bed and bury his head beneath the covers.

He shook the thought away as he sat in the driver's seat of the Challenger he'd bought on impulse three weeks ago. A muscle car to pump him up, for sure, but he'd chosen that particular model because it came with a beastly automatic transmission. He wasn't in any condition to work a clutch.

Frank's leg ached from sitting in one position for so long, and for a moment, he was grateful for the pain. He was beginning to have second thoughts about his impulsive decision to fly the coop—he didn't do impulsive—but without the Percodan he'd left behind, there was no way he could endure another two and a half hours back the way he'd come without taking a break first. He pushed open the door but had to shove a hand under his thigh and manually lift his leg out from under the dashboard. Why had he tossed his crutches in the trunk with his duffel bag? He wore only the strap-on gel brace he slept in, and although he'd packed the other one with all the bells and whistles, it was in the trunk, too. Without the security of The Beast, as he'd not-so-affectionately named his brace, he wasn't supposed to put any weight on his left leg. When he'd set out a couple hours earlier, he'd had no trouble hopping around the car, but now, he wasn't so sure that was a good idea.

He stood slowly, lowering his left leg to rest on the ground. Maybe, just maybe...but when the pain lanced all the way into his low back, making his breath hiss out between his teeth, he knew he'd overdone it.

No pills, no crutches, no plan.

Glad for the dark, he leaned heavily against the car as he made his way on one foot to the trunk. Perching on the back bumper, he switched out the braces, but when he stood again, it was all he could do to bite back the groan that formed a tight ball in his chest. "Walk it off, man. Walk it off," he muttered under his breath. But walking it off wouldn't help; he knew that. He needed to lie down. He needed to elevate and ice his ankle.

He needed his pills.

I need my mama. The thought came unbidden and he snorted self-deprecatingly. His mother had been gone for more than a decade.

He jerked the crutches out of the trunk and hobbled across the driveway toward the house, eyeing the steps that led up to the front door. He shook his head; he only wanted to do steps once if he could help it. He circled around back; if the kitchen door was locked, surely Binks would be awake soon. Frank could wait for him on the back porch.

To his relief, he found a new set of patio furniture that included matching, remarkably comfortable chaise lounges. Easing his leg up onto the seat, he lay back and focused on his meditative breathing, willing the fire in his bones to subside.

The sound of wheels on gravel warned him of company, and he opened his eyes and turned his head to watch as a small truck rounded the side of the house and parked in the gravel strip nearby. A woman practically fell out of the driver's side, her arms loaded. She seemed oblivious to his presence.

Frank sighed. He didn't want to startle her, but he knew there would be nothing graceful or subtle about his attempt to get up out of the lounge chair. His pain was easing off a little, but ever the gentleman, he wasn't going to sit by and watch the lady struggle with her load. He took a deep breath, clenched his jaws together against the surge of pain as he maneuvered his leg off the cushion. "You look like you could use another hand."

He lumbered to his feet, making the chair scoot noisily backward, knocking one of his crutches to the ground with a loud clunk. He swore under his breath when she let out a blood-curdling scream that was sure to wake every armed man and woman in a ten-mile radius.

Chapter 3

THE MOMENT THE SCREAM LET LOOSE, she wanted to suck it back in. She sounded like a high school girl at a Band Perry concert. The man on the porch didn't look like he was poised for assault, and besides, she had her pepper spray.

"Not that it's going to be of any help," she mused to herself. Her spray was in her purse on the floorboard of the passenger side of her truck, and by the time she got the door opened and started digging around in her floppy hobo bag, the guy could have her tossed over his shoulder and—

"Hey." He waved both hands in the air in a show of truce. "I won't hurt you, ma'am. I used to live here. Frank Flanner. Frankie to folks around here." He slowly made his way along the porch railing toward her.

Frankie Flanner? Judge Flanner's son? Charity squared her shoulders and peered up at him. The porch light was fixed to the wall behind him, back-lighting him so she couldn't quite make out his features, but there was definitely something familiar about him. She hadn't seen Frankie—did he go by Frank now?—in ages, so it wasn't a surprise she didn't immediately recognize him. "Not to mention you rose up out of the dark night like some phantom freak," she grumbled, then grimaced when she realized she'd said it out loud.

"Like a what?" He'd reached the top of the porch steps and stopped.

Charity didn't miss the fact that he held tightly to the handrail, nor did she miss the brace that ran from ankle to mid-thigh on his left leg. "Sorry," she said, hoisting the beans up a little higher. Her palms had gone slick with adrenaline sweat, and the last thing she wanted to do was drop her lovely dilly beans. "Just talking to myself." Should she get back in her truck and return later? Or did she dare brave walking up those steps past him and going in? He seemed harmless enough, especially with the way he was babying that leg…but then again, wasn't that how Ted Bundy got his victims? Hobbling around on a pair of crutches, playing on the tender mercies of unsuspecting young women…alone in the dark…no one around to hear— "Whoa. Get a grip, girl."

"You always talk to yourself?" he asked.

She could hear the hint of mockery in his tone, and she frowned. Could she ask him to please leave and come back when normal people were awake? Then again, if he really was Frank, who was she to tell him he couldn't be there? "I wasn't expecting anyone to loom up out of the dark like that."

"No kidding." He chuckled, a sound so pleasant, it grated against her nerves. "That was some scream."

He was laughing at her. What a jerk. "You know what? Never mind." She'd didn't need this. Not this morning. She'd escaped her own busy household for the peace and solitude of the Whispering Hills kitchen. She'd just come back after the guy was gone, and the crew would have to wait for their ribs if need be—she'd blame any delay on Frank Flanner, impostor or not. "I'm not sorry. I don't care who you are; that wasn't a cool thing to do." She reached for the handle of her truck door, nearly dropping the bag of muffins.

"Wait," he called out. "I'm the one who should be apologizing. I really didn't mean to startle you. I wasn't expecting anyone to show up here at this hour, either." He started down the steps, but when she turned around and glared at him, he stopped, almost as though suddenly self-conscious with her watching him. That wasn't like Frank Flanner at all. The guy she remembered had been a self-assured, cocky cowboy who wouldn't hesitate to take on the fiercest bull, no less some dilly-bean-and-muffin-toting widow.

"What exactly are you doing here?" Charity asked. The question came out surly and rude, but her heart was still pounding against her ribcage in fight or flight mode, and he was still grinning at her.

"What exactly are *you* doing here?" he shot back, crossing his arms over his chest and leaning his hip against a support beam.

"I asked you first," she said, regretting her childish response the moment it was out. "I mean, how do I know you're Frankie Flanner?" she amended.

"How do I know you're not some strange, crazy lady breaking into my childhood home?" Oh, he was enjoying this far too much. He shifted a little, and the light shone more directly on his face. Yeah, it was Frankie, all right. And still cocky after all. Maybe not a cowboy anymore, but in spite of the leg, he looked pretty self-assured. The moment of vulnerability seemed to have passed; perhaps she'd just imagined it.

"I work here. That's what I'm doing here." Charity squeezed the jar of beans against her side, fighting the urge to hurl them at his head. She might not be a very big package at five-foot-three, but she had an arm on her that could make a grown man weep. Especially if whatever she threw his way actually hit him.

"How did you get here?" she asked. "Did someone drop you off?" She waved the bag of muffins at his brace. "I doubt you walked." When he shifted his weight self-consciously, she inwardly groaned. She hadn't meant to be unkind.

"I parked around front," he said, his grin still there, but no longer quite so playful. "And I *walked* around the house." His emphasis on the word only made her feel worse. "I was waiting for Binks; I figured he'd be the first one up. He usually is."

"Sorry," she mumbled. "That was rude of me." Binks would probably be thrilled to see the guy.

"It was," he returned. "What did you say your name was?"

He really was a jerk, she decided. Apologizing for her outspokenness wasn't usually difficult for her—she had a bad habit of blurting out whatever thought passed through her mind, and it had gotten her into trouble more than once. But then, people were usually a little more receptive to her apologies, too. Granted, she wasn't usually so unkind... "I didn't say."

He nodded slowly, then waved a hand toward the kitchen door. "Well, then, be my guest, Mystery Lady. Apparently, my house is your house."

She squared her shoulders again and started forward, then paused at the sound of hurrying footsteps on the gravel drive.

"What's going on out here?" It was Binks, hurrying from the direction of his cabin. "I heard you scream, Miss Charity. You all right?"

"I'm fine, Binks. You have a visitor." She thrust her chin toward Frank again. "He scared the living daylights out of me, creeping around in the dark—"

"I wasn't creeping around in the dark," Frank said with another laugh. "Hey, Binks." He pushed away from the post to stand upright, still not putting much weight on the braced leg. "Good to see you, man."

"Frankie?" The old man moved past Charity and up the steps. "What are you doing here, boy?" Binks stuck out a hand, but Frank pulled him into a man hug instead. "Why didn't you tell us you were coming?" Binks asked when he stepped back.

Frank made an odd face. "I didn't know myself until I was halfway here," he said by way of explanation. "I didn't want to wake anyone, so

I came around back here to wait for you. No creeping around, I promise. I don't do much of that these days, not with this thing." He patted the side of his brace in an affectionate manner. "In fact, I was resting peacefully before I was interrupted by that little tiny thing with a great big voice."

"Miss Charity?" Binks asked with a chuckle of his own. He turned back to look at her, noticed her hands were full, and came back down the steps to take the jar from her. "Let me help you, young lady."

"Wait. Charity?" Frank cocked his head and sized her up. "Charity Goodacre from next door?"

"No," she snapped. "Charity Banner."

"From next door, though, am I right? I recognize you." He nodded as she followed Binks up the steps. "You're married?" he asked as she passed just close enough that she could smell the cologne he used.

"Yes, and yes," she said. Then she decided not to breathe because the smell of him nearly knocked her off her feet. It wasn't cologne after all, but the clean, old-fashioned aroma of Barbasol shaving cream. Theo swore by it, and catching a whiff of it on Frank Flanner made her senses reel uncomfortably. She quickly located the key to the door, pushed it open, and headed inside ahead of Binks. Frank appeared in the doorway a few moments later, a pair of crutches tucked under his arms. Seeing them, she felt even worse for her unkind comment.

She flipped on the overhead lighting, and glanced behind her at Frank when she heard his sharp intake of breath.

"Whoa," he said, surprise and pleasure coloring his tone.

Charity watched him from under lowered lashes, not to be coy, but because she couldn't help staring, and she didn't want to be super obvious. In the artificial light of the kitchen, she saw the telltale signs of fatigue on his face, half-moon shadows under his eyes, the way the corners of his mouth dragged down, the day or two's worth of growth covering his jaw. In spite of it all, something about Frank Flanner had her feeling a little stirred up; her pulse fluttered erratically just under her jaw. He wasn't exactly handsome, but he had the chiseled features and squared-off look that made a uniform look good. Granted, he wasn't wearing one at the moment, but she could totally picture him in one, and the fact that she could completely unnerved her. Even with his messed up leg, he carried himself the way Theo had, shoulders squared, chin up, and his eyes—she couldn't tell from across the room if they were green or maybe hazel—took in every little detail of his surroundings. Including her. She blinked rapidly and glanced away when he quirked a questioning brow at her.

"My cousin has been busy," he finally stated.

"He sure has," Binks agreed. He slid the jar of beans onto the big butcher block table in the middle of the room. "This whole place got renovated, but he handled things with care, son, so don't you worry."

Frank nodded. He pointed at an ornate wall clock mounted above the pantry door. "Mom's Bulova clock. It looks good up there."

"Sure does," Binks said, peering up at the timepiece. "Cord kept the things that belonged."

Charity bit back a smile when she noticed what the old man was wearing—a pair of jeans, a threadbare tank top under a denim jacket, and a pair of cowboy boots, the cuffs of his pants bunched haphazardly at the top of them as though he'd pulled everything on in haste. She set the bag of muffins next to the coffee maker, then crossed the short distance to put an arm around the foreman's waist. "Thank you for coming to my rescue, Binks."

Binks gave her a quick, self-conscious hug, and shook his head. "Nothing to rescue you from, Miss Charity. Frankie here wouldn't let anything happen to you."

"Thanks for the vote of confidence," Frank said from where he stood just inside the kitchen door. The grin was back. "But I think she was referring to you rescuing her from me."

"You know what?" Charity said with a frown. He may be hot stuff in or out of a uniform, and sure, he was sorta family by marriage, being her brother-in-law's cousin, but that didn't mean she had to like him. She moved around Binks to the massive refrigerator. "I have a lot of work to do this morning, so why don't you boys get on out of here and leave me to it."

"You work here," Frank said. It wasn't a question, but an opening to a conversation. The guy couldn't take a hint.

"I do," was all she'd give him. She pulled the first stack of ribs out of the fridge and turned to place them on the butcher block table.

The two men just stood in their respective spots, both of them watching her.

"What?" she asked, placing a hand on her hip. "Is there something you need from me?" She narrowed her eyes at Frank who still wore that stupid grin, then turned her attention fully on Binks.

"You planning on making any coffee this morning?" the old man asked, his brow furrowed as he looked back and forth between Charity and Frank.

"Coffee sounds good to me," Frank interjected in a winsome tone as he moved further into the room. He leaned his crutches against the counter and turned to plant both hands on the table so he was facing her.

Charity pressed her lips together and frowned at him. "You know how to use that machine?" she asked, waving in the general direction of the coffee maker.

"I do. Would you like me to brew a pot?" He straightened, as though preparing to do just that, his pie-eating grin softening his angled features, making him look much more like the boy next door she remembered.

"No, I do not," she shot back. The idea of Frank lingering in her space any longer than was absolutely necessary was more than she wanted to deal with right now. "Why don't you go... I don't know. Check on your room, or something, while I make coffee. Does Cord know you're here? Or Faith?" Surely, Faith would have mentioned it if she knew he was coming.

"Nope. Like I said earlier, I didn't even know I was on my way here until about an hour or so out. Figured I'd surprise everyone."

"Well, you can check that off your list." She rolled her eyes and turned back to start pulling the rest of the racks of ribs out of the fridge. "I'll have coffee ready in fifteen minutes. You can come back then." She'd be ready to take the load of ribs out to the smokers by that time, and hopefully, he'd take his coffee somewhere else and be gone when she got back to start on her side dishes.

"Actually, I think I'll pass on coffee for now," Frank said, a hint of regret in his voice. "I've been up all night, and I think an hour or two of sleep might do me some good. Mind if I take a rain check?"

"Take whatever you want. It's your house." She hated the way she sounded. Besides, technically, it wasn't his house anymore, not since he'd sold the place to Cord. What was it about him that set her off so badly? Sure, the guy was easy to look at, and he wasn't exactly the most sensitive man in the world, but she spent every working day around a crew of guys just like him. Skid and Ernie Maddox were both good-looking local boys who had the world by the tail, but neither one of them affected her the way Frank was now. It couldn't be just because he'd startled her and hadn't really bothered to apologize, could it?

Her stupid pride, maybe? Although, that didn't seem to make a whole lot of sense, either. She'd been embarrassed by her ridiculous reaction, but it was the kind of thing that usually set her laughing at herself.

That was something else she was known for—her contagious laugh. Well, she'd been known for it before Theo died. She didn't laugh very often these days.

From the corner of her eye, she saw Frank nod. "Will do. Thank you. And Binks?" Leaning heavily on the table, he moved toward Binks, and thrust out his hand toward the old man. "It's good to be home. I'll look for you in a few hours, okay? If you see Cord before I do, let him know I'm here."

"I will, son. It sure is good to see your face around here again. You planning on staying for a bit?"

"You know, I wasn't planning on coming here at all, so..." Frank shrugged one shoulder, a wry expression on his face. "Not exactly sure how to answer that."

"Well, even so," Binks said, reaching up to pat Frank on the shoulder. "You being here is all right by me."

Charity leaned into the open door of the fridge to pull out a flat of eggs that needed hard-boiling. "No one bothered to ask if it was all right by me," she muttered under her breath. Did this mean he'd be staying in his old room upstairs? That she'd have to start sharing her sanctuary with Frankie Flanner?

Chapter 4

"THERE YOU GO AGAIN, TALKING TO YOURSELF," Frank said as she straightened, letting the fridge door close behind her. She jumped, nearly dropping the tray of eggs, and he reached for them, his reflexes as sharp as ever. One unfortunate egg flipped out and fell to the floor with a wet crack. "Oops. Sorry."

"Seriously?" she gasped, grabbing the tray back and glaring up at him. She snatched up a handful of paper towels from a holder on the counter and made quick work of the mess. "Why do you keep sneaking up on me like that? What is wrong with you?"

Frank tried not to laugh, but Charity's expression of petulant rage made it impossible to hold it in. He hadn't meant to scare her again—surely, she'd heard him approaching, his ungainly stride not subtle at all. "What's wrong with me? Let me see. Where do you want me to start? I have a bum leg, I'm getting old and have no one to call my own, and my childhood home belongs to someone else now. Someone who apparently has a penchant for hot-headed chefs."

Charity made a sound that might have been a squawk if she was a chicken. A little mad hen, that's what she reminded him of, huffing and clucking and ruffling her feathers.

A very cute little mad hen with all that blonde hair and those flashing blue eyes. Eyes that were zeroed in on him.

Binks guffawed, then pushed open the back door. "I'm heading home to get dressed properly. You two try not to kill each other before I get back. And Frankie?"

"Yes, sir?" Frank turned to salute the foreman.

"A word of advice. Try not to rile up the cook. Especially not on rib day."

"Too late for that, Binks," Charity called after him. She brushed past Frank, purposely nudging him out of the way as she did so, making him stumble slightly. For such a little thing, she sure knew how to throw her weight around.

Frank could still hear Binks' chuckle even after the screen door slapped shut. "Come on, Charity. How about we start over? Let's be friends."

"Why?" she asked from where she stood at the sink, filling a large stock pot with water. "We never were before, and believe me, you haven't really endeared yourself to me since I got here."

"What do you mean, we never were before?" Frank said, his tone now cajoling. He leaned back against the counter, bracing his hands on either side of him, and took the weight off his throbbing leg. Bed still sounded really good right now, but sparring with Charity Goodacre—Charity Banner—was helping to take his mind off his pain quite nicely. "I was friends with everyone in the hollow."

"No, you weren't," she contradicted him. "You were a hotshot teenager when you lived here, and coming home to visit your folks for a day or two every couple of years doesn't make you exactly friendly to the rest of the folks in the hollow. Just because everyone knows who you are—I mean, you are practically royalty around here, you know—doesn't mean everyone is your friend." She didn't even bother looking at him while she spoke, so he took advantage of the opportunity to take a gander at her. She wore a western style navy blue plaid shirt tucked into jeans that followed her curves like they'd been specially tailored for her, a pair of simple cowhide boots, and the biggest hoop earrings he'd ever seen on a woman. Her blonde curls spilled down her back, but they were clipped up and away from her face with what looked like glass butterfly wings. His eyes traced her profile with her slightly upturned nose, arched brows, and that jaw thrust forward obstinately. Was it all a show, or was she really as tough as she made herself out to be?

He lifted one hand in surrender. "Did I somehow wrong you in the past? I mean, is this aversion to me all because I was creeping around and rising up out of the dark like some... What was it you called me?" He winked at her when she tossed a dark look at him over her shoulder. "A phantom freak? Was that it?"

"Why are you still here?" she asked, making him laugh out loud.

"Because I'm curious about whatever this is between us, Ms. Charity." He was goading her, he knew, but he couldn't decide whether he should be offended by her blatant animosity or flattered by it.

She spun on her heel and threw her hands in the air in frustration. A drop of water hit him on the cheek, and he reached up to wipe it away, his eyes locked with hers. "What are you talking about?" She asked, her voice tight. "There is nothing between us, Frank Flanner. You are an egotistical, rude man who scared the snot out of me and then mocked me. You haven't quit mocking me since. You're like a school yard bully, it seems. Is this the way you treat your men, soldier boy?"

"That's First Sergeant Soldier Boy to you," he said dryly, his gut clenching at the thought of the troop he'd left behind. What was left of them, anyway. "I'm a decorated war hero, I'll have you know." He made a sweeping motion with his hand, lifting his leg for her to see.

"Wow. Big whoop-dee-do. Did you get a boo-boo?" She practically snarled at him, her eyes flashing angrily. "At least you're still here to complain about it." She shook her head and gave him one last scathing look. "You're in my territory now, Frankie. Which means unless you're a decorated *cake*, you need to leave."

"Wow," he echoed her, but not in the same sarcastic tone she used. Mad hen, indeed. What had he done to set her off so badly? And why on earth was he contemplating sticking around to find out?

Before he could come up with a good response, she let out a heavy sigh and dropped her head to her chest. "Thank you," she murmured.

Frank reached up to run a hand over his hair. He was a couple weeks overdue for his bi-monthly buzz cut, and the longer hair felt as foreign to him as standing in this kitchen across from Charity and her all-over-the-map emotions. "You lost me," he said.

"Thank you for your service." She fluttered a hand at his leg, then lifted her gaze to his just long enough for him to see the stark pain in her eyes. "Thank you for your sacrifice." The statement seemed to almost strangle her, but without another word, she turned back to the tray of eggs and began loading them into the stock pot, leaving Frank at a total loss for words.

When Charity lifted the heavy load out of the sink to carry it to the stove top, Frank started forward, wanting to help, but his knee buckled at the sudden weight, and he grabbed at the counter to steady himself. How he hated the limitations this leg put on him. He couldn't even be the gentleman his father had raised him to be.

Charity turned glistening eyes on him—had he made her cry?—then she said in a much kinder voice, "You should go lie down. Rest that leg. None of the rooms upstairs are being used if you can manage."

He hesitated, not liking the way this encounter was ending, but his all-nighter was catching up to him, and he was suddenly beyond fatigued. "Will you still be here in a couple of hours?" he asked.

She nodded, switching on the burner under the pot, then turned to face him. She spoke flatly. "I'll be in and out of the kitchen most of the morning, but I won't have time to play hostess, if that's what you're asking. I'm cooking for a big barbecue out on the deck behind the barn.

You're welcome to join us if you'd like. There will be plenty of food."
She'd gone from startled, to wary, to angry, to…was she sad?

"Thank you," he said, his voice a little gravelly. He wasn't sure if it was from lack of sleep or because he was so bothered by her roller-coaster emotions. "I'd like that." He eyed the stacks of ribs on the butcher block. "You need any help before I go?"

She shook her head, glancing tellingly at his leg. "No thank you. I've got this."

Frank nodded. She was right. Charity didn't need the help he could offer her. His leg hurt too much to even attempt walking without his crutches right now, and even then, he'd be lucky to be able to carry half of what she could without tripping over his own foot, or having his knee buckle and end up dropping something important. "Right. Sure. Okay, well, I'll see you later today then. Looking forward to the ribs." He squared his shoulders and reached for his crutches, then started toward the arched opening with the swinging doors that led from the kitchen to the rest of the house.

As they swung closed behind him, he heard her say, "Welcome home, Frankie."

He lifted a hand in acknowledgment but said nothing. For years, home was on the front lines. Home was sleeping back-to-back with a comrade, one eye open, ears tuned to any suspicious sound. Home was where men and women looked up to him, followed his commands at the risk of life and limb… a risk that had become a reality for him, and now he wasn't sure where home was.

The bed in his old room had no sheets on it, but the navy and gray comforter was soft, and he'd showered before he climbed into his car several hours ago. He slipped out of his sneakers, removed the leg brace with a groan of relief, and lay back, his head on the bare pillow. He wrapped the blanket around him like a sleeping bag, then he closed his eyes as morning light began seeping its way through the wooden blinds on his window. Surely, now that the dark was gone, he'd sleep like a baby.

His last thought was of the pretty woman bustling around in the kitchen downstairs. What was her story?

Continued in…

OH SWEET CHARITY
A Seven Virtues Ranch Romance Book 3

9 781798 984642